Bodies in Motion

A MATTHEW PRIOR MYSTERY

by

Anthony Quogan

Bodies in Motion

A MATTHEW PRIOR MYSTERY

by

Anthony Quogan

LITTLE, BROWN AND COMPANY (CANADA) LIMITED

FIRST PRINTING

Canadian Cataloguing in Publication Data

Quogan, Anthony
    Bodies in motion

"A Matthew Prior mystery."
ISBN 0-316-72921-3

I. Title.

PS8583.U63B6 1996   C813'.54   C95-933153-0
PR9199.3.Q64B6 1996

Cover design: Tania Craan
Interior design and typesetting: Pixel Graphics Inc.
Printed and bound in Canada by Webcom

Little, Brown and Company (Canada) Limited
148 Yorkville Avenue, Toronto, Ontario, Canada

Author's Note

Amtrak has three special trains that make the trip between Chicago and Los Angeles: the Texas Eagle, the Southwest Chief, and the Desert Wind. For the sake of this novel I have invented a fourth — the Flying Angel. It takes a route somewhere between the one taken by the Southwest Chief (via Albuquerque) and the more northerly route taken by the Desert Wind (via Salt Lake City). My train follows the Southwest Chief's track as far as Kansas City, but after that heads off non-stop for Caliente, Nevada, right through the territory between the Grand Canyon and Arches National Park in Utah. The U.S. Department of the Environment will I'm sure be horrified that I've constructed this new line with so little regard for the ecology of the area, but it's all in the interests of plot — and what could be more important than that?

In most respects the train is modelled on the Southwest Chief, on which I had a pleasant and comfortable journey in the summer of 1994. I was subject to none of the problems that Matthew Prior encounters on the Flying Angel, but then my fellow passengers, with one exception, were nowhere near as interesting as his.

The usual disclaimers apply with regard to all the char-

Dedication

This book is for the late Bill Burgess of the Central Office of Information in London, England. A great friend, much loved and much missed. He would have been a wonderful fellow passenger on this journey.

Prologue on an Island

Signor Maschietto watched the young couple leave through the revolving doors of the hotel. They were holding hands and laughing, he a dark-haired man of perhaps twenty-seven and she an almost-ivory blonde a few years younger. They had registered the day before as Signor and Signora Hentzen and it didn't take someone of Signor Maschietto's forty-year experience in the hotel business to realize that they were honeymooners. What was also clear was that though the man was an Eastern European of some kind (Romanian? Hungarian?), the girl was indisputably American. Her accent, her confidence, and her energy all told him that.

Something familiar about her had escaped him until he saw her leaving the hotel. Then he realized she looked uncannily like the celebrated Glamora, whose recordings and videos had established her as the queen of S and M rock. But Maschietto dismissed the idea that he might be entertaining an international superstar incognito. After all, it was well known that Glamora stood an impressive 6'1" without her stiletto heels, and this young woman was no more than 5'9" with her shoes on. Shrugging, he turned back to his computerized hotel register. A visit from Glamora would have been good for business, but on the other hand the swarming paparazzi would have caused problems all over the hotel. He sighed and shifted his attention to the next week's reservations, which fortunately promised nothing but the normal flow of ordinary tourists — like the Hentzens.

By that time the young couple had reached the lake shore and were waiting for the ferry to Isola Bella. "The guidebook says the palace looks like a big wedding-cake," the girl laughed. "It'll make up for the one we didn't have."

The young man put his arm around her shoulders and hugged her to him.

"Anna, if I pull this off, you'll have as many wedding-cakes as you can eat. When I get the money back from that fascist scum —"

"Not now, Fedor," the girl answered with a momentary frown. "No politics on our honeymoon. Let's leave all that till later."

His obstinate face darkened for a moment, but then he looked into her eyes and smiled.

"You're right. I spend too much time brooding about it. Today we'll do what they say in the brochure — go to the Beautiful Island, visit the wedding-cake where Napoleon slept, tease the white peacocks — and think only about each other."

She squeezed his arm in response, and the next moment they were boarding the ferry.

It was a misty day on Lake Maggiore and the Borromean Islands seemed to hang in the air like Gulliver's flying land of Laputa. The song of unseen birds drifted faintly through the haze and the voices of the people on the ferry were muffled, as if they were speaking through layers of gauze. Figures came and went along the deck, appearing suddenly a few yards away and then receding again into invisibility. Fedor, standing by the rail with his new wife, felt a tremor pass through her body.

"What is it?" he said.

"Oh, I'm all right. It's nothing. Just that this suddenly reminded me of a painting I saw once — of the spirits of the dead being ferried across the Styx."

"Ah, probably one of those nineteenth-century daubs you were gazing at in the National Gallery when I met you. Something by Gustave Moreau, perhaps?"

She smiled and shook her head, but he had succeeded in turning her mind from the bleak image she had called up, and evoking instead the earliest days of their relationship when he had been a mysterious political refugee and she an earnest student on an exchange semester in London. Almost everything she had been told about the city was true, from the delights of the excursion boats on the Thames and the book shops in Charing Cross Road to the empty grandeur of Canary Wharf, but nothing had prepared her for how completely it could become a city for lovers. She and Fedor had savoured espresso in their favourite coffee bar in Soho, window shopped on Bond Street and in the covered arcades along Piccadilly, explored the maze in the grounds of Hampton Court, and made love under the trees in Richmond Park. It had seemed that her thirst for this dark-browed man and his controlled, skillful body would never be quenched. Only recently had she begun to see the occasional flare of fanaticism in his eyes.

"Anna?"

His voice startled her back into the present, and she realized that the ferry was beginning to dock.

"Sorry, darling," she said. "I was day-dreaming."

"Let's move towards the gangway. We don't want to be last off the boat."

Ten minutes later, they were touring the Borromeo Palazzo, wandering through the airy interior, exploring the artificial grottos in the basement, admiring the collection of eighteenth-century puppets, and exclaiming with mock horror at the tapestries, with their outlandishly brutal scenes of animal carnage. Impatient to get away from the crowd of fellow sightseers, they made their way out onto the grounds, which were almost empty because of the damp mistiness of the day. At first, as they wandered down from terrace to terrace, they thought that every one of the island's famous white peacocks had disappeared, but then they were amused to see them roosting in the lower branches of the trees with their long tail-feathers dejected and drooping. The weather was clearly not to their taste.

"Fedor, we must get some pictures of them," Anna said, laughing. "They look so hopeless."

Fedor took a camera out of the bag that hung at his side, raised it, and focussed on the birds.

Just as he pressed the shutter release, a woman wearing a yellow oilskin slicker and leaning on a metal crutch stepped out from among the trees. She quickly turned her back on them and seemed about to walk away when Anna said: "Fedor, why don't we ask her to take a picture of both of us with the peacocks?"

The woman stood quite still about twenty feet away with her head cocked to one side, as if listening for something. Fedor began to approach her.

"Scusi, Signora," he faltered in his phrasebook Italian.

"Per cortesia, vuole fotografare..."

The woman turned towards him, revealing a face that was as expressionless as a stone.

Fedor gasped, "Oh, my God!," wheeled around, and began to run back towards Anna, but as he did, the woman raised the metal crutch to her shoulder, levelled it, and fired. The blast caught Fedor in the back and toppled him, sprawling, at Anna's feet. Anna had just opened her mouth to scream when the second shot tore her throat out and she collapsed across Fedor's body, her blood spurting onto his face and shirt. The white peacocks, flurried and furious, did her screaming for her.

The woman in the yellow slicker moved quickly towards them, bent over Fedor, and snatched the camera. Without a flicker of emotion she focussed it and took three shots: one of the dead girl, one of her lover, and one of the two bodies lying together. She dropped the camera into a pocket of her slicker, straightened, and walked away from the scene, swiftly but composedly, through the mist-swathed trees. By the time the first horrified tourist came upon the bodies, she had completely vanished.

One
The Passengers Assemble

1

There were terrorist bombings in the mid-West. Earthquakes, floods, mud-slides, and riots were afflicting Los Angeles. Half the American people were running around with assault weapons and the other half were forming militias to overthrow the government. The economy was going through a difficult restructuring and Republicans and Democrats were locked in their usual death struggle. Was this really the time, Matthew wondered, to be visiting the U.S.A.?

The mid-Western businessman sitting next to him on the flight from London to Chicago assured him that the European press had it all wrong as usual and that America was still the greatest country in the world, especially if you had lots of transferable capital. Matthew said, paraphrasing Oscar Wilde, that all he had to declare was a transferable talent. After that, the businessman buried himself in *Forbes* magazine, leaving Matthew to sip thoughtfully on his Kahlua and Coca-Cola.

It had all started with a telephone call from Matthew's friend, Hank Parr, who lived in Bel Air, California, and was an intermittently successful independent film producer. He had become interested in Matthew when, one idle evening in Greenwich Village about ten years earlier, he happened to catch a performance of an early Prior play called *Drummer Toole*. On the strength of his reaction to it, Hank had invited Matthew to stay with him in Los Angeles while they collaborated on its screen adaptation. Though nothing came of that particular project, Matthew made some useful Hollywood contacts, as well as a healthy bundle of dollars by rewriting other people's screenplays. One of them, a drama about fetal alcohol syndrome, was nominated for an Academy Award. Hank's initial offer had coincided with the foundering of Matthew's marriage, so he had been glad to be far away from all the familiar things that sharpened his sense of loss. Then, after a year, satiated with California cuisine (all those sun-dried things and cilantro), California decor (all those beiges and pastels), and California mores (all that working out and coking up), he had given up and gone home to England.

He looked up as the flight attendant came down the aisle asking if there were any more drink orders. Another Kahlua and Coca-Cola would be asking for trouble, but he ordered it anyway. After all, it was either drink or read the in-flight magazine one more time. While he waited for the cocktail, he looked at his watch and realised that they would be almost an hour late landing in Chicago, which meant a mad dash from O'Hare Airport to Union Station where he was to board the Flying Angel. And it was very important that he catch that train.

Hank had called to offer Matthew another job, but this time with a firm commitment. The backers had been lined up and there was a co-production agreement involving

Britain, Canada, and the U.S. One of the most powerful backers was the head of MCN Entertainment, Sir Mortimer March, who had insisted that Matthew be employed to write the screenplay, at least partly in gratitude for the role Matthew had played in saving his life on the Caribbean island of Cabeça de Cabra. Hank had added his urging to Sir Mortimer's and the other partners had fallen into line. Of course, if it had been a project that Matthew didn't like, he might have refused the offer, but instead it was something that immediately appealed to him: a remake of Alfred Hitchcock's classic, *The Lady Vanishes*. True, it had been remade once before — in 1979 with Elliott Gould and Cybill Shepherd, not to mention Angela Lansbury and Herbert Lom — but after a lapse of two decades there seemed to be no good reason why it shouldn't be recycled. Besides, the Gould-Shepherd version hadn't exactly made an indelible impression on the minds of moviegoers.

What the producers wanted Matthew to do was to update the original script and change the setting from a train crossing Europe to an Amtrak express travelling between Chicago and Los Angeles. When Matthew pointed out quite reasonably that he had never taken that particular trip, the producers booked him first-class accommodation on one of Amtrak's star transcontinental trains, the Flying Angel. Hence his anxiety about the delayed landing in Chicago.

Twenty minutes before touchdown, one of the flight attendants announced the various gates at which connections could be made for particular destinations, and asked that passengers who weren't making an immediate connection allow those who were to leave first. She might as well have made the announcement in Urdu because even before the seat-belt sign blinked off, people were jamming the aisle, tugging carry-on bags and portable computers out of the overhead compartments, standing on one another's toes, sticking elbows in one another's eyes, and generally behaving like a herd of stampeding warthogs. Matthew began to ask the mid-Western businessman to let him pass as he had a train to catch, but gave up when he realized that it would have put him mere inches nearer the exit. The solid pack of humanity ahead of him was not about to part like the Red Sea to let him out.

Feeling cranky and dishevelled, he finally reached the arrivals area after a surrealist progress via moving walkways and escalators under a firmament of multi-coloured neon tubes. There he was confronted by a confusion of car-rental outlets, gift shops, bars, cafeterias, and newsstands. Fortunately, not having checked his baggage, he avoided the aggravation of waiting for it in the baggage-claim area. That was very little comfort when the airport clocks were reminding him every second that time was in fast-forward mode. He remembered with a groan that someone had told him that O'Hare was the largest and busiest airport in the Western hemisphere. It was certainly the most congested. After following several false trails, he somehow found his way to the cab-rank outside the terminal. He waited there, a tall, bony figure in a summer-weight suit from Gieves and Hawkes, twitching like a racehorse as the few people ahead of him were loaded up and dispatched at a glacial pace.

At last his turn came. He sat in the roomy back of a cab, listening to the driver say: "Where to, man?" The driver's appearance would have made a Hell's Angel blanch — long, greasy black hair, an untamed beard, tattoos up and down his arms, a gold hoop in one ear, and a sweat-saturated T-shirt with the Harley Davidson insignia on the front.

"Union Station and hurry, please!" Matthew said.

The driver gave him a long, slow look, snorted sardonically, and pulled away with great care and deliberation from the curb.

In a few minutes Matthew understood that snort. The freeway into the city was jammed with traffic, and hurrying was not an option. As they sat in the honking, pollution-belching traffic, the driver's cassette player pounded out a rap song whose lyrics were principally aimed at urging black teenagers to shoot policemen.

"You from the U.K.?" the driver asked suddenly.

Matthew admitted that he was.

"Yeah, you got that snotty way of talkin'. Hey, what's the deal with the Royal Family? They nuts or what?"

Matthew disclaimed any knowledge of the mental state of the Royal Family.

"That Di's gotta be nuts. And that Fergy. I mean they'd haveta be nuts to marry those bozos in the first place. Yeah, I know, prestige — and money."

The driver laughed bitterly.

"Guys like me don't stand a chance. I mean take that Larry Fortensky — marrying Liz Taylor. Do I get a shot at Liz? No way, man. I bust my butt fifteen hours a day drivin' this pile of junk. When do I get to meet any Liz Taylors?"

It was clear that the driver was going to keep up a steady flow of complaint and rancour all the way to Union Station, so Matthew did his best to switch him off mentally. He began instead to think of his upcoming project. Even before Hank's offer, Matthew had been a great fan of the

Hitchcock film, and since beginning to sketch out a treatment, he had also read the Ethel Lina White novel on which the film was based. It was the story of Iris, a British girl on holiday in the Alps (played in the movie by Margaret Lockwood, one of Matthew's favourite actresses) who is just about to take the train home when she is bopped on the head by a falling window-box. The intended target, however, is a tweedy middle-aged woman called Miss Froy, who later befriends Iris on the train. In her semi-concussed state, Iris falls asleep and when she wakes up Miss Froy has disappeared. Worse, no-one on the train will admit to ever having seen her. Iris begins to question her own sanity until a young Englishman, Max Hare, decides to come to her assistance. Even his confidence in her is shaken when a middle-aged European woman, dressed in the same manner as Miss Froy, claims to be the person who befriended Iris.

They persist with their investigation and soon it becomes clear that their stubbornness is being viewed as a threat, to the point where various passengers on the train make attempts on their lives. Eventually, they locate Miss Froy, who has been drugged and disguised as a bandage-swathed patient, attended by a sinister nurse. At the climax of the film, the carriage in which they are riding is deliberately uncoupled from the rest of the train, and they are stuck in enemy territory with a battalion of soldiers firing at them. They create a diversion so Miss Froy can escape and finally are able to maneouvre the uncoupled carriage across the border. At the end, they are reunited in London with Miss Froy, who turns out to be an Allied spy who has been conveying some important information about enemy strategy to the War Office.

The original novel was a competent enough thriller, but the Hitchcock touch had turned it into a dazzling piece of cinema, full of masterly character cameos. Matthew's problem was that it had been set in Europe in the precarious period leading up to the Second World War, a factor that gave the story a special urgency. Could that urgency be recaptured on a train trip across the States? Was he going to be able to come up with a comparable high-stakes, high-risk plot? He sighed and looked at his watch.

"And what about the goddam Arabs?" the driver was saying. "What the fuck those guys gonna blow up next? I tell you, man, this is a crazy goddam world we're living in."

Looking out of the window, Matthew saw that they had finally left the freeway and were passing through an area of graffiti-sprayed public housing projects, where groups of listless young black males hung about on street corners. He noted that the driver instinctively checked to make sure the cab doors were locked. Among the graffiti was a recurring symbol that aroused Matthew's curiosity. It was like the pitchfork that, in popular myth, is carried by the devil.

The driver glanced at it indifferently when Matthew drew his attention to it on the wall of a high-rise.

"That? That's what the Gangsta Disciples put up to warn people off of their turf. The goddam gang practically runs this city, and they're spreadin' out across the country, linkin' up with the Crips and the Bloods in L.A., startin' drug-dealin' operations all up and down the interstates."

He lapsed into a brooding silence for some minutes and Matthew began to hope that the flow of invective had dried up. But no, it was merely a temporary blockage.

"Aaah, what the hell," he resumed. "I guess I should be

glad I'm livin' in the best goddam country in the world. You can stick all them foreign places right up your ass is what I say."

"Are we nearly there?" asked Matthew desperately, feeling like a whining child on a long car trip with its parents.

"Chill out, man. We're gonna make it."

In fact, it was ten more gruelling minutes before they pulled up in front of Union Station. Matthew leapt out of the cab, grabbed up his luggage, flung money at the driver (who was still in full flood) and began to sprint on his long, spindly legs across the sidewalk. There was a rushing sound from his left, a cry of "Look out!" — and suddenly another body collided with his. Though he didn't know it, he had been struck by one of the newer hazards of American city life — an in-line skater.

There he was, flat on his back with a Generation X Chicagoan, in a tangle of limbs, luggage, and spinning wheels. He was slightly dazed, having struck his head as he fell, but he gamely got back on his feet, exchanged apologies with his assailant, grabbed up his luggage again, and ran on. The faux marble halls of Chicago's mainline rail terminal blurred around him as he ran, his suitcase in one hand, his computer tote in the other, and his carry-on slung over his shoulder. If he hadn't been casting his eyes around anxiously for a station clock, he might have seen the Louis Vuitton overnight bag in his path, but he was, and he didn't, and down he came again — this time headlong with such force that he knocked himself out.

2

The headquarters of MCN Television, one of the many enterprises of March Communications Network, occupied a post-modern skyscraper on Michigan Avenue, Chicago — partly because Sir Mortimer March wanted to show his independence of both the Eastern broadcasting establishment and the West Coast entertainment moguls, and partly because Chicago was strategically well-placed in relation to his overall web of interests. The television network was relatively new — launched later than Fox and at about the same time as Warner's and Paramount. It was off to a roaring start with two outstanding successes — a drama series called "Studs and Sirens," and an investigative "reality" show called "Hot Flashes." The investigative show had already exposed a federal judge as a former member of the Hitler Youth, a well-known advice columnist as a child abuser, and a top-ranking rock singer as an erstwhile performer in porn flicks. The most popular member of the investigative team was a lean Bacall-ish blonde with a smoky voice called Honor Moore.

As Matthew Prior sat fidgeting in his airplane seat just above O'Hare, Honor was on the telephone following up a lead for her latest exposé.

"Harris, what's happening with...? What? ... Leaving? ... God, that's all I needed. ... No, that's no good, I'll have to do it myself ..... What, by rail? Why the hell by rail? ... Phobic about air travel? Humph! ... All right, Harris, just get me a first-class sleeper. I'm on my way."

She hung up, swung herself out of her chair, and walked

over to her office closet. The Louis Vuitton bag she kept packed with essentials was there. She grabbed it, flung on her lightweight Donna Karan coat, and sailed out of the office, hurling a few final instructions to her secretary as she left. Two minutes later she was in a cab racing for Union Station.

3

"Hey, isn't that Glamora?"

The excited voice belonged to a teenage boy with a shaved head, and rings through his ears and nose. His companion, who had a long switch of black hair growing from the top of his scalp and eyes rimmed with purple lines, struck a pose of exaggerated amazement.

"It sure as shit is!" he rasped. "Ho-lee fuck!"

The figure who had aroused so much interest was an unusually tall woman with fire-engine red hair, wearing an oversize pair of gold-framed sunglasses and dressed in an *outré* outfit made of vinyl in shades of black and magenta. She had just exited from a stretch limousine outside Union Station and was crossing the sidewalk to the entrance, accompanied by a phalanx of young men, none of them her equal in height. She flashed a mechanical smile at the group of onlookers who were hanging around waiting to see her go by, and a more animated one at the two or three photographers who had suddenly appeared on the scene.

"Where to this time, Glamora?" one of them yelled as she whirled past.

"None of your fucking business," she yelled back off-handedly.

"I wish you wouldn't do that," whispered one of her escorts.

"Screw you," she said. "When did you join the language police?"

As the group entered the main hallway of the station, more people turned to look and to comment. It wasn't every day that they saw a celebrity as currently notorious as Glamora in person. In another sense, they saw her constantly: she turned up on their favourite talk shows, confronted them on the covers of magazines, appeared in the gossip columns and supermarket tabloids they read, and probably haunted them in their dreams at night. What was she? She was everything — an actress, a model, a sometime singer, a would-be dancer, a video artist, a writer, and above all a shrewd entrepreneur. Her exercise tapes — "Glamora's Good Moves Guides Volumes I to VI" — were best-sellers. Glamora's signature perfume — Satanic — was in all the best stores. Glamora's CD-ROM, "The International Sex Atlas", was rated one of the year's ten best educational software programs.

The young men who surrounded her were curiously alike: all had sleek dark hair, conspicuous eyelashes, designer stubble on their faces, and perfectly tailored pin-stripe suits. They were also, clearly, very much her *cavaliers serventes*. Several of them were carrying pieces of her matching set of Italian leather luggage. One of them dashed ahead to the newsstand to buy her some magazines; another rushed to a candy store to grab a box of Belgian chocolates; a third followed the first to tell him to get a copy of the *L.A. Times*. If it wasn't for the fact that she was a famous anti-smoking advocate, they would have been flocking around with cigarette cases snapping open and lighters clicking.

When they reached the Metropolitan Lounge (Amtrak's first-class waiting room), she waited until they had stacked her bags by the door, found her a comfortable seat on an overstuffed sofa, piled up her reading materials and chocolates, and then, as they stood attentively as if waiting for some sign of favour, she dismissed them with: "OK, guys, you can get lost now. See ya in the funny papers!" They didn't seem at all surprised by this curt and uncivil dismissal but made their adieus and left with every appearance of equanimity. Glamora, without one further glance in their direction, settled herself on the sofa and picked up a copy of the *New Republic*.

4

Approaching the station from the opposite direction was another absurdly long stretch limousine. It was a deep thundercloud blue, had tinted windows, and carried on the front of the hood the yellow and green flag of the African nation of Zwamali. Prince Achmed lounged in the back seat wearing the characteristic robes of his country and listening to Def Leppard on his Sony Walkman. On the seats facing him were Harrison and Morrison, two of the security officers who had been assigned to guard him during his visit to the U.S. The other two, Jackson and Jones, were in the seat behind the chauffeur. All four of them were bored with each other and with the prince, who kept asking them questions they couldn't answer about American culture.

Achmed was a handsome man with skin the colour of polished teak, eyes that glowed like black opals, teeth that would have made new snow on a raven's back look dingy, and deep black hair as tightly curled as the wool on a merino sheep. He was tall even for someone of his warrior tribe, broad-shouldered, slim-waisted, long-legged, and high-buttocked. His feet were so long and narrow he had to have his shoes custom made by an Oxford boot-maker he had favoured since his student days. (The boot-maker prized highly among his many royal endorsements the one that read "By appointment to the Royal House of Zwamali.")

As he listened to the music, he moved his body rhythmically in his seat, jerking his shoulders forward and back alternately and clicking his fingers to the beat. Harrison looked at Morrison and raised his eyebrows. Morrison shrugged and turned to gaze out of the window.

"This is good," said the prince. "You men don't like Def Leppard? What then is your favourite group?"

He took off his earphones so he could hear their answers.

"Favourite group?" asked Harrison wearily. "I guess the Beach Boys, Your Highness."

"Ha! And what about you, Mr. Morrison?"

"Me?" Morrison seemed startled as he turned back from the window. "Er ... well ... I'd have to say the Mormon Tabernacle Choir."

"Interesting," the prince murmured. "The Mormons have many wives, isn't that so? We who follow the Prophet are allowed only four."

Morrison shook his head. "I think that's a thing of the past, Your Highness. Since women's lib and all that."

"Ah, yes, that begins to affect us in Zwamali. Western

ideas have brought many troubles to our people. But I suppose we cannot be open to Western trade without also opening ourselves to Western thought."

Trade had been very much on Achmed's mind lately. His country was rich in minerals, but poor in agricultural produce. His people could not eat minerals, so many foods had to be imported. This had led to a serious trade imbalance. Now he was on his way to a World Trade Conference in Los Angeles, which was to be attended by the President of the United States. Achmed had met the President when they were both studying at Oxford. He hoped that this old acquaintanceship could be renewed to the benefit of his country. However, the President was sure to make any trade deal contingent on improved civil rights for the Zwamalians. This would not be popular with Achmed's uncle, King Habib, or indeed with most of his relatives and friends.

"Ah, well, wasn't it your President Lincoln who said that you cannot please all of the people all of the time."

"Not exactly, Your Highness," Harrison answered, raising his eyebrows again, but by this time they were pulling up in front of the station. Further conversation was cut short as they attended to the unloading of the prince's bags.

5

"No, I can't appear on the Oprah Winfrey show next month. I am booked solidly till next year. Yes, yes, if a gap appears unexpectedly in my schedule, I'll let you know."

Dr. Vartan Kadourian hung up the phone and turned to

his assistant, Rosemary Peach.

"Besides," he said to her with a mischievous grin, "I hope to have my own talk show before next year. No point in spreading myself too thin, is there?"

Spreading himself too thin was almost a way of life with him, Rosemary thought wryly. First there had been the breakthrough book, *Mind/Body Fusion*, then there had been the six follow-up volumes, *The Meeting of Body and Mind, Your Body, Your Mind and You, Out of Your Mind, Into Your Body, Releasing Body/Mind Power, Bridging the Body/Mind Gap*, and the latest, *The Mind's Body, The Body's Mind*, which had sold six hundred thousand in hard cover and two million in paperback. In the meantime, there had been the phenomenal success of the audio-tape set, *Kadourian's Way to Physical and Mental Balance*, the endless seminars all over the corporate world, the consultations sought by the eminent, including the President of the United States and great tycoons like Sir Mortimer March and Rupert Murdoch, and, of course, the countless appearances on television. If he were spread any thinner, he'd be invisible.

Rosemary's cynicism was an attempt to cover up her own unwilling admiration for the man. There was no question that he was charismatic. His eyes were those of a martyr in a Spanish painting, full of conviction and ecstasy. His mouth, framed in the black contours of his beard, was both sensual and firm. He had a voice with the deep, dark tones of a church organ, and hands as sensitive and supple as a violinist's. Sometimes Rosemary thought he was a complete charlatan, but at others she knew he had a strong belief in his own mission. Inevitably, critics had raised questions about his background: a medical degree from the University of

Smyrna, some involvement with a government health research institute in the Balkans, a period in Switzerland on the staff of the dubious Eisenbach Institute, a year of private practice as a therapist in New Zealand, and a decade ago his arrival in the United States. with the manuscript of that best-seller-to-be, *Mind/Body Fusion*, under his arm. While he tried to find a publisher for it, he had made his living writing an advice column for a newspaper syndicate, which had led to two things that raised him above the rank and file of popular pundits. One was the fervent commendation of his wisdom by a Hollywood star noted for her preoccupation with the transcendental. The other was his testimony at a famous murder trial, which was largely responsible for convincing the jury that the accused murderer had been suffering from a dissociation between mind and body at the time the crime took place — the famous sleep-walking defence. Now, ten years later, he headed a highly profitable organization that marketed his various products and fed the media a multitude of news stories about his various pronouncements and successes.

"It's twenty past. Hadn't you better go?" asked Rosemary.

Kadourian looked at his watch.

"Yes, I'd better," he said.

"You have your travel documents?"

He felt in the inside pocket of his jacket, then nodded. A faint frown ruffled Rosemary's brow.

"I honestly wish you'd go by air. It would save so much time," she argued.

He put his hands on her shoulders and fixed her with his compelling gaze.

"It's kind of you to be concerned, but you know what I

believe: body/mind synchronization isn't compatible with air travel. Neither the human body nor the human mind was meant to be subjected to excessive speed."

He really did believe it, she acknowledged helplessly. To her way of thinking, once humanity had moved from horse and buggy to the Model T, it had already overshot its natural speed limit, and the Flying Angel was to the Model T what the Starship Enterprise was to the Spruce Goose.

"I guess you know what's best for you," she conceded finally.

"Rosemary," he said with a repeat of his mischievous grin, "I know what's best for everybody."

Just as he was about to go out of the door, Rosemary noticed what she assumed to be his black medical case on the chair under the window.

"Did you mean to take this?" she said, picking it up.

He glanced back and a look almost of panic came into his eyes.

"Oh ... yes," he said, crossing the room and almost snatching it out of her hands. "Thank you ... I'm ... I'm glad you noticed it."

There was a noticeable clinking sound from inside the bag as he hurried back towards the door.

"Goodbye. Take care," she called after him.

He stalked down the corridor to the elevator, his black Burberry draped over his shoulders and his black felt hat tilted at a dashing angle. Rosemary sank down in her swivel chair with a despondent sigh. She had an uneasy feeling that she might not see him for a long time.

6

Of all the people in Chicago that day who were heading for the railroad station, Aldo was probably the most miserable. The relationship he had been having with Tanya, the former *Playboy* centre spread, had deteriorated to the point where she had taken the scissors to his two favourite Gianni Versace suits and thrown eggs at his vintage Ferrari. When he tried to figure out how it all started (drawing his heavy eyebrows down in a frown and getting that puzzled look in his eyes like a St. Bernard who's lost his brandy-keg), all he could think of was the time he accidentally sat on her Burmese kitten and smothered it. Had things started to go into the toilet at that point? All he knew was that lately he couldn't say or do anything without her calling him a pig.

It wasn't as if Tanya was one of those feminists or anything. Still, she kept insisting that she needed more respect, that she had to make her own decisions, that she would not be taken for granted. Somewhere or other she had learned the word "empowerment" — probably from watching one of those afternoon talk shows where women dumped on their husbands and boyfriends. But the most worrying manifestation of the new Tanya was that she wanted to get on top of him when they were having sex. It made Aldo feel very weird, lying there naked on his back with her bouncing up and down on his dick. What he felt was the opposite of empowerment: all wimpy and exposed to such a degree that he would wilt and shrivel inside her, and then he would feel like a jerk and she would accuse him of having come already with somebody else. Who could blame him if he got mad then and took a pop at her?

Maybe it was just as well that he had to go away for a week or two. He'd put some space between them and meanwhile he would be doing what he liked best, the thing that made him feel most like a man. He'd be fighting. First he'd be working with his old trainer, going some rounds with a few sparring partners, and then he'd have the important fight, the one that would qualify him as one of the challengers for the World Heavyweight Title. He could visualize the posters, plastered all over L.A.: "Tonight at the Forum! The Big Bout! Aldo Bracciano v. Emmett Townes — The 'Italian Thunderbolt' and the 'Delta Panther.'"

He straightened his shoulders in the back of the taxicab and smiled. He was beginning to feel better already.

7

The conference had ended that morning. The delegates had had their farewell breakfast, and a final session with the representatives from D.C., Marvel National Periodical Publications, and half a dozen other comic-book publishers. The story guys, the artists, the fans, and the business people had met and mingled at social events over the last three days. There had been a rare comics exhibition, and display stands for all the current titles, and stalls for the vendors of comic books and comic-book memorabilia. All in all it had been a very successful event. Eddie Tsubouchi and Sven Sanchez hadn't known each other before they met at the convention, but it turned out that they were near neighbours in the San Bernardino area and that they were both train buffs. So it wasn't altogether surprising when they discovered that they were both booked to go back to California on the Flying Angel. Rather than stay in the regular roomettes they had reserved, they decided to splurge and share a deluxe bedroom.

Sven was the older of the two, a middle-aged half-Scandinavian/half-Spanish comic-book artist who drew *Warrior Lords*, one of the old standbys published by Prime Comics of Pasadena. Eddie Tsubouchi was about half Sven's age, a second-generation Japanese-American and one of the up-and-comers of a rival publisher, Warp Books. Eddie's major invention so far was the Spirit Shifter, a strange unworldly creature who was not only capable of moving his spirit into other people's bodies but also able to switch other people's spirits from one body to another. The Warrior Lords, on the other hand, were a group of old-style super-heroes on the model of Superman and Captain Marvel.

The two had met at breakfast the first morning in the Marriott Hotel. Sven was carrying his dish of Rice Krispies from the breakfast buffet when he collided with Eddie, who was carrying a plate of scrambled eggs and toast. Somehow the scrambled eggs and the Rice Krispies got hopelessly intermingled and they both had to start all over again, but they both behaved with civility and ended up sharing a table. Sven was fascinated by the younger man's energy and imagination, while Eddie found Sven's measured good sense and well-grounded expertise reassuring. As with many such relationships between men of disparate ages, there was a certain nervousness that neither they nor anyone observing them should misconstrue their regard for each other as in any way homoerotic. The result of this was a certain boisterous candour in their dealings with each other.

"You're stuck in history, old man," Eddie would say. "You belong in *Jurassic Park* with the rest of the dinosaurs."

"And you, Mr. Whiz Kid, should remember what Oscar Wilde said — beware of being too up to the minute: you'll find you get old-fashioned all of a sudden ... or words to that effect. Now me, I'm a classic like a Brooks Brothers suit. I never go out of fashion."

"Sure, sure — a Brooks Brothers suit. That just about sums you up. All line and no style."

So it would go on. However, this morning at breakfast, Sven had been preoccupied and downcast. Eddie tried to engage him in their usual banter without much success. Finally, Sven produced a telegram that had come for him that morning. Prime Comics' distributor had been bought out by a competitor, and the new owners planned to drop a number of lines, including *Warrior Lords*. They would carry it until the end of the year but after that either Sven would have to come up with a more innovative concept or he and his Warrior Lords would have to find a new way of getting into the hands of a dwindling band of fans.

"Oh, shit, I'm sorry, Sven," said Eddie. "If there's anything I can do to help —"

"Don't worry — I'll be OK. If the worst happens, I can always sign on with the Cartoonists' Correspondence College. Spend the rest of my life teaching housewives from Iowa how to draw bodies in motion."

"Well, hey, you've got a couple of days on the train to think about it. Maybe if we put our heads together we can come up with something really incredible!"

Sven wondered whether that might not be the answer — a collaboration between experience and ingenuity. Maybe the Warrior Lords had had their day and needed to be killed off, like Superman (only for them there would be no reincarnation). Maybe he could get excited again about starting from scratch with an untried idea. Or maybe he was just getting too old to pump any more octane into his creative fuel tank. Still, Eddie had a lot of energy and a lot of confidence, and a transfusion of some of that might re-animate him. It was worth a try.

"C'mon," he said to Eddie. "Let's get our bags and get on this goddam train."

8

"Dad?" said Buzzy Nash. "Who's the black guy getting out of that limo?"

"Eddie Murphy," said his father.

"G'wan, that's not Eddie Murphy. Eddie Murphy's littler than that."

"I don't know who he is," Anderson Nash said with a tinge of exasperation. "He could be Superfly for all I know."

"Superwho?"

"I guess he was before your time. Let's not go into that now. We need to get to the right track and get on the train."

It was great being able to spend more time with Buzzy, but it could also be an effort. Buzzy had been staying at his place in Washington for a month, and Buzzy's mother, his ex-wife, had been good enough to allow them both to extend that by taking a train back to L.A. rather than flying. She worried about Buzzy flying anyway, especially since her neighbour had lost a son in an air crash in Colorado. Nash and his wife had been divorced three years now, and she had custody, so Buzzy and his father didn't get to spend a lot of time together. When they did, a large part of the first few days together was spent simply trying to get to know one another again. There were always surprises: the boy who had been an ardent fan of the Teenage Mutant Ninja Turtles one year was completely dismissive of them the next, having transferred his loyalties to the Mighty Morphin Power Rangers, or Bart Simpson would have been elbowed aside by Beavis and Butthead, or a taste for McDonald's hamburgers would have been replaced by an addiction to tacos from Taco Bell. One constant seemed to be his devotion to the L.A. Dodgers. He wore a Dodgers T-shirt, a Dodgers baseball cap, drank out of a Dodgers mug, even had Dodgers pyjamas. Another constant was his absolute allegiance to a series of comic books about a group called X-Men. In fact, he often fantasized about becoming a member of the group, taking on an identity of his own invention — Scopeman, Seer of the Universe. Scopeman had the ability to see events on distant planets and could look into both the future and the past. Occasionally, to make things complicated, his vision would be clouded by the Black Mist, an interstellar force of mysterious origin.

Much of this Anderson Nash knew, because Buzzy confided in him, although some of the more outlandish stuff he had pieced together from Buzzy's private monologues accidentally overheard, or from comics that Buzzy had drawn himself in emulation of the artists who drew his heroes. Buzzy wasn't at all bad with a pencil — streets ahead of most kids his age, with their stick figures or shapeless blobs. There might even be a future for him as some kind of artist, preferably the kind who wouldn't raise the blood pressure of Republican congressional leaders.

They were passing through the main concourse of the station, Anderson with two suitcases and Buzzy struggling with his own Dodgers duffel bag.

"Would you like some candy to eat on the train?" Nash said.

"Sure," said Buzzy.

Nash handed him a couple of bills.

"Go and get some while I get a newspaper."

Buzzy was delighted, but at the same time suspicious. Getting candy out of his dad wasn't usually that easy. He wandered over to the candy stand, casting backward glances to where his father was headed. There were newspapers right by the candy display, so why did his father have to go all the way over to the bookstore? Buzzy paused at the counter and made a careful selection — a couple of Three Musketeers, a packet of chocolate-coated raisins, and a Butterfingers. When he started back towards the bookstore, he saw his father was talking to a woman who looked like an off-duty nurse — hardly any makeup, hair hidden under some kind of pudding-basin-shaped hat, big horn-rimmed glasses, and a shapeless coat made of a greenish-brownish cloth. By the time he reached his father, she had gone.

"Who's that you were talking to, Dad?" he asked with an attempt at nonchalance.

"Talking to?" Nash looked startled. "Oh, her. I wasn't really talking — just giving her directions."

"Where to?"

Nash sighed exasperatedly.

"What's this? The third degree? She wanted to know what track the Flying Angel was on."

"So she'll be on our train."

"Unless she just wants to see someone off," his father said. "Anyway, we'd better make tracks ourselves."

"Make tracks for the track," Buzzy snickered, but he wasn't entirely satisfied by his dad's explanation. After all, when you had a father who worked for the CIA in Virginia, you couldn't help wondering sometimes whether he was a kind of super-spy. Licensed to kill, even. That little innocent-seeming encounter might have been a contact with a counter-spy. The woman hadn't looked glamorous enough to be a part of the world of international intrigue, but then she could have been in disguise.

"That's it," he said to himself as he followed his father through the station. "Nobody dresses like that unless they're trying to hide what they really look like."

So, stimulated by the possibilities this opened up for the train journey, he hurried towards the Flying Angel.

9

Aubretia Adams was having one of her bad mornings. She woke up in an unfamiliar room and immediately began to panic. Surely to God she hadn't been so stupid as to pick up some perfect stranger and go back with him to his place? Taking a survey of her surroundings, she noted with relief that she was in what was quite obviously a hotel room — a rather expensive one, judging by the decor. Furthermore, there were no crumpled pyjamas on the other side of the bed, and there were no gargling and spitting noises coming from the bathroom. She raised her head cautiously from the pillow and immediately let it fall back again. Ouch! Hydraulic drills were battering away at her skull and her eyeballs were being squeezed by sharp tweezers. It didn't take a rocket scientist to figure out that she'd tied one on the night before. Tied one on? Hell, she'd *nailed* one on!

Gradually recollections began to seep back through all the noisy interference inside her head. She was in Chicago. Ha! that was a start. "Chicago, Chicago, that toddlin' town." Why the hell would she be in Chicago? For an opening at the Art Institute? Don't get smart! All right, who did she know in Chicago? Chauncy Wimbush, the Gaffrey brothers, Mayor Daley, Studs Terkel, Saul Bellow? Maybe only a nodding acquaintance with the last three. Hi there, Dick, Studs, Saul — stop that, for heaven's sake. Concentrate! Why in God's name would anybody be in Chicago? Or maybe the better question is: why would anybody stay in Chicago? Ah, that was it! She wasn't staying, she was just passing through. Passing through, passing out — it's all the same. "I did but see her passing out, and yet I'll love her till I die." Whoa! Getting off track again. Track! Track! That rang a bell. Bell. Bells on their toes. "I'll be right there with bells, when that old conductor yells: All aboard! All —" that was it! A train. She was here to catch a train.

Easing her eyes open again, she squinted at the clock-radio by the bed. It was after four. But was that after four in the morning or after four in the afternoon? She struggled from beneath the covers, defying the hydraulic drills and the tweezers and all the other assorted tortures of hell that were triggered by this movement, and made her way to the window. With her last ounce of strength, she dragged the heavy drapes open and staggered back as a flood of sunlight poured into the room.

"Oh, God, it's afternoon," she wailed, and then as the recollection that the Flying Angel left in an hour forced its way into her consciousness, "Gotta get out of here!"

She flung herself into the bathroom, showered, did a hasty makeup job, tied her still-damp hair in a canary-yellow scarf, threw on some underwear, slacks, a blouse, and a jacket, grabbed up her bags, and ran for the elevator. There was no way she could miss this train. If she did, it would mean that Natalie (who was joining the train at Kansas City) would be left high, dry, and swinging in the wind. She was counting on Aubretia to be there. After all, she was a foreigner and presumably didn't speak the language very well.

As she staggered into the elevator with her two suitcases, Aubretia wondered, not for the first time, why she had let herself get stuck in this particular situation. It had all begun when she met that friendly couple in Europe. They were Austrians or Hungarians or some such thing, but very much upper crust. Since they didn't speak much English, Aubretia had summoned up her schoolgirl French, which was surprisingly efficient considering its years of disuse. Soon they had been chattering away like old friends. She'd enjoyed them so much that she travelled with them for a week or two, visiting German schlosses and Italian palazzos. They had all had a particularly good time in Tuscany, even making it to Siena in time for the *palio*, an historic horse race held twice a year. Anyway, she and the — er, what was it? Lindenhoffs, that's right — had kept up a correspondence, and when their daughter, Natalie, had come to the U.S. to go to school in Kansas City and subsequently found herself involuntarily pregnant, Aubretia had promised to take her on a scenic train trip to the west coast to take her mind off her troubles. It was too bad that it had to coincide with one of Aubretia's spectacular headers off the wagon. God knows this shouldn't happen to her at the mature age of thirty-nine (or thereabouts). But it had, and that was that.

The elevator doors opened and Aubretia flew across the lobby to the reception desk, checked out in record time — mainly by elbowing everybody else out of the way and talking very loudly — then dashed out of the hotel just in time to snag a taxi from under the nose of a very annoyed corporate executive.

"Union Station — and there's an extra five dollars in it if you can get me there in fifteen minutes!" she screeched at the driver, flinging her bags in ahead of her.

"It's just around the corner, lady. You could walk it in five minutes!"

"Not with this hangover, I couldn't," she muttered.

Her sincere tone must have impressed him, because he gave a sympathetic "tsk, tsk" and pulled immediately away from the curb, causing her to collapse sideways on the back seat. True to his word, he had her at the station in three minutes and, almost speechless with gratitude and dyspnea, she gave him ten dollars more than the meter registered. Crossing the sidewalk she almost tripped over a tall man who had just been knocked over by an in-line skater, but recovered herself and made it to the Metropolitan Lounge without any further mishap. Panting like a foxhound, she waved her ticket at the attendant behind the counter, only to be told in a maddeningly calm tone that the train was delayed an hour.

"Hell," she said, stomping over to one of the overstuffed armchairs and sinking into it. "I could have stopped off for a facial and a manicure and still made it."

The plain bespectacled woman in the pudding-basin hat sitting next to her, who looked like a nanny on holiday, gave her a rebuking glance, folded up her copy of *Good Housekeeping*, and moved to the other end of the lounge.

"And pooh pooh to you too," said Aubretia to herself, before settling down to wait till they were called for boarding.

10

In that interlude between the end of the lunch rush and the beginning of "happy hour," the cocktail bar at the Palmer House was as quiet as a held breath. Jorge, the barman, noticed that there was only one customer left, a pretty woman of about thirty sitting at a table near the lobby entrance. She had a half-drained strawberry daiquiri in front of her and she seemed in no hurry to finish it. One of her slender hands toyed with the straw, stirring it around in the pink foam. Jorge couldn't quite figure her out. She looked foreign, but her darkness wasn't a Hispanic darkness. There was something Slavic about her cheekbones, but the rest of her features were more delicate than those of a typical Slav. Her eyes were very dark, almost gypsyish, so perhaps she was of Magyar descent. Her expression had the serenity of the faces one sometimes sees in early Flemish paintings. Having come to the end of his conjectures, Jorge shrugged and picked up his copy of *A Short History of Time* from behind the bar. He might be a bartender but he was also a physics major at the University of Chicago, and he knew the difference between productive and fruitless speculation.

Had Delia known what was going on in the bartender's mind, she might have been diverted or even flattered. Her background was, in fact, almost as cosmopolitan as his musings had suggested. Her father had been a career diplomat in the service of the Galinian Republic, until recently a part of the Soviet Union. In his youth in London, while working at the embassy there, he had met and married Delia's mother, an English girl who had Welsh and Cornish ancestry. They had returned to the Galinian Republic in the early 1960s and Delia and her brother Fedor had been born soon after in the capital city, Solonitza.

Delia's father, Igor Hentzen, was a well-established member of the apparatchik class, so the family had lived privileged lives, hardly touched by the deteriorating economic situation in the Soviet world. Delia and Fedor had excellent educations — he at the University of Solonitza, and she at the State Theatre School. Their privileged lives began to show signs of unravelling, however, when a political coup replaced the current head of state, Marshal Evreinev, with a younger, more charismatic, and more dangerous leader, Istvan Golovyov. Golovyov and his wife, Luba, soon became notorious for exploiting their position and for the harsh measures they took against dissidents. The poorer sector of the population became poorer still under their regime.

About a year before the fall of the Berlin Wall, Fedor,

who had become increasingly radicalized at university, joined an underground resistance movement. The Golovyovs' punishment fell not upon him but upon his father, who was publicly disgraced with some trumped-up charges of illegal influence peddling. Igor never recovered from his treatment by the secret police and died of an overdose of narcotics within months of his trial. This drove Fedor to greater and greater extremes in his attempts to unseat Golovyov, and after the fall of the Berlin Wall, his group organized a coup, in which they planned to trap the Golovyovs in their palace. The television footage of Luba Golovyova's attempt to escape was disturbing: her frantic eyes as she was dragged out of her car, the animal-like sounds she made as she darted from side to side trying to escape the fists and weapons of the mob. She could not save herself. The husband she had stood by for fifteen years somehow managed to arrange his own escape in all the confusion, leaving her to die on the street.

Delia grimaced and took another small sip of her daiquiri as if to neutralize with its sweetness the unpleasant aftertaste of Luba Golovyova's death. She had been a detestable woman, but her husband's abandonment of her had been even more detestable. The irony was that he had managed, with the help of the new Russian criminal gangs, to transfer a sizable share of the Galinian state treasury to secret bank accounts and overseas investments, and was now living a life of luxurious seclusion on an expensive Malibu property.

But it wasn't Golovyov's treachery, or even his greed, that had brought Delia Hentzen halfway across the world in pursuit of him. It was what had happened to her brother.

She stood up abruptly, almost upsetting the small table. She couldn't bear to think of Fedor just at that moment. A glance at her wrist told her that in any case it was time she started towards the station. It wasn't many blocks, but she had decided to walk, and that meant leaving herself plenty of time. She would think about Fedor later.

As she left the bar, the bartender glanced up from his book and watched her, mildly curious about where she was going, where she had come from, and what kind of life she led. But she was less substantial to him, in fact, than a character from a movie and he soon forgot he had ever seen her.

11

There was one more passenger on her way to Union Station that afternoon, one more who would be a travelling companion for Matthew, Honor, Glamora, the two Nashes, Dr. Kadourian, Prince Achmed, Sven and Eddie, Delia, and Aubretia. Her name was Teresa Shaughnessy and she was being followed by a man who looked like a creature from another era — some post-First-World-War Kafkaesque time-warp — with his long dark overcoat, his black Homburg hat, his stiff-collared shirt, his rolled umbrella, his gold-rimmed pince-nez, his drooping, walrus moustache, and his narrow almost bloodless face. Was he an employee of a Central European bureaucracy, a violinist from a state orchestra, a translator of obscure scientific treatises, a schoolmaster from a village somewhere in the Urals? He was none of those things. He was, in fact, Konstantin Marminski, a paid assassin for the so-called Russian "mafiya."

As he moved through the crowded streets of Chicago, he

attracted many curious glances but seemed oblivious to all of them. He was focussed on one thing and one thing only: the figure he was following. Weaving between groups of idling teenagers, middle-aged shoppers, and young mothers with baby-carriages, he forged onwards, never losing sight of his prey. This was a very important assignment for him, because it meant a chance to wipe out a couple of unfortunate blunders he had made in the past, one involving a bungled attempt to eliminate an absconding bank official and another the killing of a bystander during the assassination of a Moscow businessman.

The person he was following seemed quite unaware of any pursuer. She was a plain-looking woman of about middle height, bespectacled, and dressed in a hat like an upturned bowl and a coat in a muddy indeterminate shade that might have been mushroom or taupe. Her upright posture and firm tread suggested that she was someone who was used to being obeyed — a hospital matron, for instance — and though she moved with confidence and purpose, she did not hurry. In fact, she paused frequently to look in shop windows or to examine the menus posted outside restaurants.

Marminski had picked up her trail about twenty minutes earlier in the crowded lobby of a large chain hotel. While she was busy paying her bill, he managed to exchange her dark-brown leather travelling bag for an identical one he was carrying. That was step one. Now he meant to carry out step two, which was to kill her in such a way that it looked like an accident, before she reached the station. Carefully keeping far enough behind her that he would not be caught off guard by her intermittent pauses, he was able to dart quickly into a doorway or pretend interest in the array of magazines on a newsstand any time there was a danger that she might spot him.

In this fashion, he and his quarry continued their journey through the city, drawing ever closer to the great railroad terminal. Their route took them past the Civic Opera House, past the Mercantile Exchange, down Wacker Drive to the Sears Tower, and then right along Jackson. It was along this stretch that Marminski temporarily lost sight of her. A crowd of people had disgorged from a tour bus and blocked his way. A minute later, he spotted her again at the corner of Jackson and Canal. The flow of traffic had caused a buildup of pedestrians waiting to cross the street. Between the shoulders of two teenage boys, he glimpsed the woman at the curb's edge, looking towards the oncoming traffic. Marminski managed to squirm and sidle his way through the pack of bodies until he was directly behind her. At that moment, a news van delivering the afternoon edition came hurtling down the road. Marminski couldn't have asked for a greater stroke of luck. In a second he had encircled the woman's ankle with the handle of his umbrella, and given her a sharp blow in the small of the back with his fist. She gave a startled yelp and toppled forward, straight into the path of the onrushing van.

It was all too quick for anyone in the crowd to see exactly what had happened. Before anyone had time to take note of the man in the long overcoat, he had melted back into the crowd as they all pressed forward in open-mouthed, grisly curiosity. The driver of the van was shaking noticeably and repeating to himself over and over again: "She just came out of nowhere." The body lay on its back, half under the van's wheels, while its face, frozen in an expression of dread, looked up with sightless eyes at the crowd of sensation-seekers. If Marminski had waited a second or two longer, he would have noticed that this woman was not carrying a brown bag and that her face was not that of the woman he had followed from the hotel. But, by the time a member of the Chicago police force had arrived and covered the body with his coat, Marminski was walking unperturbed across the main hall of Union Station towards the track where the Flying Angel waited, happily confident of the success of his mission.

He passed the entrance to the Metropolitan Lounge. Waiting for him by a newsstand was a woman dressed almost identically to the one he had been pursuing. She was looking at her watch and frowning.

"You've cut it very close this time, Konstantin," she said reprovingly.

He handed her the brown leather bag.

"I had to await my opportunity," he said. "You still have plenty of time to board."

"And you'll meet me at the other end?"

He patted the front of his overcoat.

"I have my airline ticket right here. I leave tonight, which gives me two days to set up our cover. I'll be at the Los Angeles station when you arrive."

She nodded brusquely.

"I will see you then."

Marminski lifted his Homburg to her in mock courtliness.

"Have a safe trip, Varya," he said. "They say the Flying Angel is the last word in rail travel, but I've heard rumours about its control system."

"So?" said the woman, raising her eyebrows. "I've survived worse things than a train crash."

"But if you were to die in it...?"

She looked directly into his eyes and gave him a very unpleasant smile.

"Ah, Konstantin," she said, "we all have to die some time."

Marminski's pallid face seemed to grow even more ashen, and then, abruptly, he saluted her with his umbrella, wheeled around, and marched away towards the exit. When he was out of sight, Varya began to hurry towards the train. Realizing she might have to present her ticket, she stopped and opened the bag to look inside. There was a moment's panic when she couldn't find the ticket among the neatly folded clothes. Then she checked the side pockets on the outside of the bag and found it: a ticket on the Flying Angel in the name of Teresa Shaughnessy. She breathed a sigh of satisfaction, but a moment later it turned to a gasp of dismay when she straightened up and saw a woman who looked very much like Teresa Shaughnessy — alive and unharmed — walking towards the Metropolitan Lounge, carrying a brown suitcase just like the one Marminski had brought her.

"What has the fool done?" Varya muttered to herself savagely. "Now I've got to switch the bags back before she notices."

Hastily, she snatched the unattractive bowl-shaped hat off her head and stuffed it in the nearest trash-can, took off the heavy-rimmed spectacles and thrust them in with the hat, fluffed up her hair, and carrying the brown bag, hurried to catch up with the woman she had thought was dead.

12

It would hardly be true to say that she had never been followed by a man before, but it certainly hadn't happened since the summer she turned thirty and realized she would probably never be a bride. In a way, she supposed, it was flattering, but she didn't feel flattered; she felt spooked. There was this tall, stony-faced character, dressed like O'Hanrahan the Undertaker, stalking her through the streets of an unfamiliar city. At home in Derry, she would have known how to deal with him; he'd have felt the sharp edge of her tongue. Here in a foreign city that she associated with gangsters and machine-guns, she didn't know what to do. The sharp edge of her tongue wouldn't be much good against a fusillade of bullets.

Taking advantage of a sudden surge of people descending from a tourist bus and interposing themselves between her and her stalker, she darted ahead to the next corner, turned it, and ducked into a doorway on her right. She waited for a moment, pressed against the wall and breathing rapidly. Holy Mother of Jesus! This was more exciting than a stroll along the River Foyle. She felt like one of them fu-jitsu girls in "The Avengers." As she waited, listening for the sound of footsteps, her eyes caught a notice-board just inside the door. It said: "Cafe Zelda — 2nd floor — Your Fortune Told!"

To Teresa Shaughnessy, a sign like that was catnip. She could no more resist it than she could resist a bag of mint humbugs or a bunch of pink and white carnations. With a glance at her wristwatch to make sure she had enough time, she made her way up the stairs.

The entrance to the Cafe Zelda was an archway covered with a bead curtain, which made a chinking, rattling sound as she pushed through it. Once inside, she saw she was in a room about the size of Father Sheehan's parlour back home — bigger than most people's parlours but not really grand. It held about five small tables set for tea, and a small counter at one end with a hot water urn, some plates of sandwiches and buns, and a mixed collection of china. There wasn't a soul to be seen in the entire place.

Undaunted, Teresa crossed to a table, put her bag under it, loosened her coat and sat down. When nothing happened after about a minute, she cleared her throat loudly and rapped on her teacup with her spoon. The results were immediate: from a doorway behind the counter a fat, dark-haired woman with a large white cat in her arms appeared. She didn't look much like Teresa's idea of a gypsy fortune-teller, given the fact that she was wearing a Chicago Cubs T-shirt and red stretch pants.

"I was just feeding Petulengro," she wheezed. "Didn't hear you come in, honey."

"That's all right, but I've got a train to catch, and I just wanted a quick reading," said Teresa.

The fat woman, who was presumably Madame Zelda, put the cat on the floor and gave it a little pat on the rear. It hunched itself up, looked over its shoulder at her with a sort of weary disdain, and disappeared back through the door.

"Palm or tea-leaves?" asked Zelda.

"Tea-leaves," Teresa answered without hesitation. "I could do with a cup to steady me nerves."

Zelda went behind the counter and busied herself with the tea things, while Teresa looked around and took in more of her surroundings. There was one window, which was heavily draped in burgundy-coloured velveteen and had a wilting cactus in a pot on the sill. The walls of the café were painted a sort of pale puce and stencilled with characters from the Tarot deck. Teresa gave a shudder when she saw the Hanged Man. There was also a tariff of charges on the wall behind the counter. A strange light fixture with a bluish globe of opaline glass hung from the ceiling.

"There we are, honey," Zelda wheezed, placing the steaming cup in front of her. "Anything to eat?"

Teresa shook her head and applied herself to the tea. It was awful, but drinking it was just a means to an end, so she didn't linger over the task.

"There," she said, shoving the emptied cup towards Zelda, who had seated herself on the other side of the table.

Zelda lifted the cup in both hands, turned it a few times this way and that and said finally: "I see a journey."

Teresa remained unimpressed — after all, she had told her she had a train to catch.

"I also see a tall dark man — or anyway a man in dark clothes."

That was better. It could be the man who had followed her. On the other hand, fortune tellers always saw tall dark men.

"You've come a long way," wheezed Zelda with a note of vexation in her voice.

Teresa didn't respond. She knew her accent and her clothes marked her as a recent arrival.

"And you've much further to go ... Much, much further. I see the journey stretching ahead of you ... but I see no end ... no end to it. And there's something here near the bottom of the cup ... some kind of danger."

This time she did get a reaction from Teresa, which gratified her. Teresa gulped and leaned closer to the cup, simultaneously going a little white around the nostrils.

"What kind of danger?" she breathed.

"It's hard to tell. The signs are murky ... but, wait. There's something else here. See it? This little thing here that looks like a V. It could be a bird flying —"

"Beware of some bird flying over and doing his business on me head," Teresa thought derisively.

"— or it could be the first letter of somebody's name. Yes, honey, I think that's it. Watch out for somebody whose name starts with a V."

This time Zelda's voice held more conviction. In fact, she seemed genuinely concerned. She looked up at Teresa and fixed her with her dark eyes.

"I mean that, honey. It's important. It's not just the tea-leaves either. I've got a feeling, and when I get one of my feelings ... Well, I don't want to scare you. Just be careful, honey, please."

Teresa was shaken. She tried to dismiss the crawling fingers of dread that were walking up her spine like the itsy-bitsy spider climbing up the spout, but she had seen the light of truth in the fortune-teller's beady eyes.

"All right," she said. "Thanks. I will."

She dug into the pocket of her coat for her money clip, paid Zelda, retrieved her bag from under the table, and made her way out of the cafe and down the stairs. Zelda stood at the door of the cafe, as Petulengro rubbed his white fur against her ankles, and watched Teresa go. Then she shook her head and went back inside.

13

There were two or three people ahead of Teresa at the reception desk inside the Amtrak first-class lounge. She set her bag down on the floor by her feet and waited as they showed their tickets and confirmed their reservations. As usual there was, as Teresa put it to herself, "a lot of argy-bargy" about whether the accommodations the passengers had requested were the ones they had been given, and why the train was delayed. She shifted from one foot to another as she stood. All that walking had made her legs tired, and she'd be glad of a chance to sit down. Suddenly, she felt someone bump against her from behind and turned around with some indignation.

"Oh, please excuse me. I'm very sorry. I lost my balance for a moment."

It was a woman of about her own height, with tousled hair and a face that was un-made-up except for a hasty daub of pink on her lips. She was dressed in a plain grey frock and her coat, which was slung over her left arm, was almost exactly the same colour as the one Teresa was wearing. In her right hand she was carrying a brown leather bag that was almost identical to the one at Teresa's feet. As she glanced down at her own bag, it seemed to her that it had been moved out of position. Perhaps the woman had knocked against it when she stumbled.

"No harm done," she said.

"I'm glad. It's been such a day, rushing about here and there, no wonder I'm dizzy."

The woman's voice had a foreign intonation, but Teresa

couldn't tell whether it was French, German, Russian, or Scandinavian.

"Have you got far to go?" Teresa asked, prepared to be sympathetic.

"Oh, yes, right to the other side of the country. It's quite an adventure."

"Me too. I'm off to California, and me who's never been further from Ireland than Calais, and that was when I was working in London."

The tousle-haired woman peered at her and gave her a sympathetic smile.

"I know what you mean," she said. "I'm from Belgium, myself, and I've never been further abroad than Paris."

"You're pulling my leg, so you are," said Teresa. "You can surely wrap your tongue around our language, and no mistake!"

"Thank you, but I'm not unusual. Many Belgians have English as their second language. So are you travelling on the Flying Angel?"

"I am that," said Teresa, "and what's more I'm going deluxe. All paid for by me new boss."

"He must be a wealthy man. And what kind of work do you do?"

"I'm going to be the nanny for his two little tykes."

At this point their conversation was interrupted because Teresa had reached the front of the line and had to present her ticket. She picked up her bag, plunked it on the counter, and unzipped a side pocket. There was the ticket with her name on it, just as she'd left it. She handed it to the man behind the reception desk, who glanced at it cursorily.

"Everything's in order, madam," he said. "Car 10,

Room A. I'm afraid the train's been delayed, but it should be ready to go in just over an hour. Just take a seat in the lounge and you'll be called when it's time to board."

She thanked him, smiled at Varya, and went to find a seat. Varya presented her ticket, which the Amtrak official seemed to scan a little more closely than he had Teresa's. There couldn't be anything wrong with it, she told herself. She had bought it under the false name she had used to rent the Chicago apartment, and there was no way anyone could have connected that name with the name of Varya Krasna.

"Thank you, Miss Verhaeven. Your ticket's in order. You'll find your room in the rear section of Car 10," the official said, and repeated his message about the delayed departure.

Varya (or, to use the name on her ticket, Katharine Verhaeven) left the counter with a more settled mind. Marminski may have blundered but she had two days and two nights on the train to put things right. She also had time before the train left to buy some things she would need. The contents of her brown bag, which had been intended to be found with the dead Teresa, would not be appropriate for Katharine Verhaeven. Fortunately she had noticed a couple of shops in the station that would provide her with what she wanted. She even had time to go to the dry-cleaners, which wasn't far from the station, and pick up her brown dress. Since she hadn't brought her camera, maybe she would buy herself one of those Polaroids. She liked to keep a photographic record of her work.

After that, she could relax and give her mind to the problem of how to get Teresa Shaughnessy out of the way without attracting any suspicion to herself. For an operative with her kind of record that should be — what was it the Americans said? — a cakewalk. With a self-satisfied grin, she left her brown suitcase in the luggage area of the Metropolitan Lounge and went off on her shopping expedition.

Two

The Journey Begins

1

When Matthew regained consciousness, he was lying on a comfortable couch in Amtrak's Metropolitan Lounge with two captivating blondes gazing down at him.

"Oh, God," they were saying in a rusty croak. "I am so sorry. I hope you haven't broken anything."

He looked around and saw he was in a spacious room full of armchairs, sofas, flowers, magazines, TV sets, and announcement boards for train departures. Perhaps there weren't quite as many of these things as he saw, considering that he seemed to be suddenly afflicted with double vision. Slowly as he turned his head back towards them, the two blondes swam together into one.

"I'm Honor Moore," she said. "You aren't going to sue me, are you?"

"This is a dangerous country," said Matthew. "I've only been here a couple of hours and already two people have tried to cripple me."

Honor Moore's eyes widened.

"Oh, you're English!" she said. "I just love a man with an English accent — Jeremy Irons, Daniel Day-Lewis, Hugh Grant — they all sound so marvellous — and look so marvellous!"

Matthew reflected that at least she hadn't mentioned Dudley Moore or Eric Idle.

"You don't sound so bad yourself," he said. "Do you have a cold or do you always speak like that?"

"Always — and I don't smoke or drink whisky either. People always assume that with a voice like this I must lead a pretty dissipated life."

Matthew laughed, and then groaned and put his hand to his forehead. Honor immediately looked concerned.

"Hey, are you OK? Can I get you anything?"

He shook his head and then wished he hadn't as the room blurred on him again. He squeezed his eyes shut and then opened them and focussed on his wristwatch. The face was indistinct for a second or two; then it cleared and he saw the time.

"Oh, Lord! I guess I've missed it," he muttered.

"Your train? Which one were you booked on?"

"The Flying Angel to L.A."

She patted his arm reassuringly.

"Then you're fine. It won't be leaving for another hour. Something about a rupture in the air-hose."

"You seem to be very well informed."

"I'd better be. It's how I make a living."

"What? Driving trains?"

She made a face at him.

"I guess you don't recognize me, huh?" she said. "Oh, well, it figures: you just got here from England..."

"Let me guess. You make your living being well-informed. Hmmm ... I know! You're a futurist, like Faith Popcorn. You write books about upcoming trends."

"I suppose that's the dry English wit we're always hearing about. Faith Popcorn! God! As a matter of fact, I'm a reporter on a TV show. How about you?"

It was typically American, Matthew thought testily, to exhibit such a frank curiosity about any stranger you happened to run into, or in this case trip up. Besides, he hated telling people he was a playwright: either they assumed he was his more successful brother, Paul, or they had never heard of either of the Priors, which was worse.

"I'm an accountant," he said, and saw disappointment, hastily masked, pass across her face.

"Great! Where would we be without you guys?"

"Thanks."

He raised himself to a sitting position slowly and warily, fearful that his head would start spinning again. The tentative movement seemed to produce no unpleasant side effects, so he proceeded to unfold his long, angular body until he was standing up. Apart from a dull throbbing at the back of his skull, he felt reasonably unimpaired.

"Well, it was very nice to meet you," he said, holding out his hand. "Though unexpected. Maybe we'll meet again ... less violently, I hope, next time. Anyway, I'd better make my way to the train."

"Wait!" she called out as he began to move away. "There's plenty of time. I'm going on that train too. I can help you get over there."

There was something almost desperate in her voice, which made him pause and look back at her. But she wasn't looking at him; in fact, her eyes seemed to be fixed on a group of people at the other side of the passenger lounge. One was an unusually tall red-headed woman, dressed to attract attention in a vinyl outfit of black and magenta. Two of the others were talking to her — one a dark bearded man with heavy eyebrows with a Burberry draped over his shoulders, and the other a young Japanese-American with a long pony-tail. Standing nearby, but not taking part in the conversation were a middle-aged, tight-lipped father with his gawking pre-teen son, a thirty-something, muscular Italian in a well-cut suit, a plain-faced thirtyish woman who looked like a nurse, a very haggard-looking *grande dame* with a yellow scarf around her head, and a handsome African in robes, flanked by four tough-looking men who might possibly be his bodyguards. Close by, on the other side of the vinyl-clad redhead, were a silver-haired, olive-complexioned man with a black moustache and a young, dark-eyed woman with an almost gypsyish look.

As he took in this scene, Honor Moore hurried up to him and clutched his arm.

"Listen, will you do me a favour?" she asked.

He began to say something about being glad to if it were at all possible, but she interrupted him.

"Will you pretend to be my fiancé?"

Matthew goggled at her, dumbstruck.

"I know it sounds crazy," she went on hurriedly, "but it's very important. There's someone who's going to be on that train who's kind of chasing me ... wanting to be a bit too friendly if you know what I mean. I thought if it looked like we were together, he'd back off."

Matthew had a feeling that he was heading down a road that would lead him deeper and deeper into a morass, but he felt too stupefied to think of a graceful way of refusing.

Grudgingly he said, "Oh, I suppose so, but isn't he going to be suspicious when he finds we're in different sleeping quarters?"

As he spoke, they were walking towards the main door of the lounge where the luggage was stacked. When Honor didn't respond immediately, he glanced at her and saw that she was looking at him with an almost shamefaced expression.

"Yes, well, that's another favour I meant to ask," she said.

2

"This is the sort of situation they used to exploit in those old madcap Hollywood comedies in the thirties," mused Matthew as he and Honor reached the platform and got their first sight of the Flying Angel — which with some modifications wasn't unlike something from a thirties Hollywood comedy itself. In fact one could almost see Busby Berkeley choreographing one of his elaborate dance numbers around it. Sleek and silver, its high, two-level coaches stretched away into the distance where, far ahead, Matthew could just make out the bullet-like engine.

At the door of the rear coach waiting to greet them was a cheerful-looking black man in an Amtrak uniform.

"Afternoon, folks. You in this coach? OK, I'm your attendant, Lincoln Madison — but you can call me Scats. Got your tickets there? Travellin' together? Fine, fine! Here, let me help you aboard with some of that stuff."

Scats Madison took Honor's weekend bag and

Matthew's suitcase and led the way on board and up a narrow flight of stairs to the second level. At the top of the stairs he turned left along the upper corridor and conducted them to Room B. It was an L-shaped compartment with a long bench seat to the right of the window and a single seat to the left.

"OK. Here it is. Let me stack these bags. Well, now, let's see ... have you travelled with us before?"

Both Honor and Matthew signified that they hadn't.

"Fine, fine. Well, your sleeping accommodations are here."

He indicated the bench seat and a slanting hatch above it that was fastened to the roof of the compartment.

"The bottom one opens up to make a decent-sized bed and this bit up here folds down — and you've got an upper berth. It's a bit tricky to climb into and there's not much headroom, so the smaller party should probably sleep up there."

Next he pointed to a unit by the door.

"Here's your washbasin, mirror, power points, small closet. And you also got your own private shower."

He opened a door in the smaller section of the L. Matthew looked over his shoulder and saw a tiny coffin-like space, encased in what looked like sheet metal. There was a diminutive toilet, taking up much of the space, with a shower head in the ceiling above it. Clearly anyone taking a shower would have to do it sitting down.

"The john flushes automatically when you put the seat down," said Scats, demonstrating.

As he lowered the seat, there was an alarming roaring sound as if some enormous suction device had been activated. Matthew flinched. It would certainly take some getting used to.

"Oh, and here are your light switches, and down here is the call button. If you need me anytime, just press it and I'll be with you as fast as I can. There's just me to handle thirty roomettes here, so sometimes I'll be a bit longer gettin' to you."

"We'll be patient," said Matthew, pressing a few dollar bills into his hand. "So there are thirty compartments in the coach?"

"You're in the deluxe section of the coach here. There's five bedrooms on this floor and five below. You'll notice they're all on the left hand side of the corridor. The rear section of the coach has a centre corridor on both levels with five rooms on each side of it. No private showers in those, of course."

"I guess not," said Honor. "You have to be anorexic to get into this one."

Scats laughed indulgently.

"C'mon, it's not that bad. At least you don't have to line up to use the washrooms like the folks at the back. Anyway, I'm outta here. I see somebody out on the platform needin' my help. Catch you later," and he was gone, bustling off towards the staircase.

"Cheery sort," said Matthew.

"He sure is."

Matthew looked around the compartment.

"Clearly, it's going to be rather tight in here for two. I suggest we make some rules. Who gets to use the bathroom when — that sort of thing."

"You're not going to be like Claudette Colbert in *It Happened One Night*, are you?" said Honor disbelievingly. "You're not going to hang a big bed-sheet down the middle of the compartment and tell me to stick to my side of it?"

Matthew raised his eyebrows.

"No, I don't believe that will be necessary. I'll merely lay my cavalry sabre on the bunk between us."

"Oh, hah hah — more of that dry British wit," said Honor in her husky drawl. "If only I had Dorothy Parker's talent for repartee."

"She'd probably have said something like 'The only thing drier than British wit is their roast beef.' In any case, I've never understood this American nonsense about British wit being dry. What, in God's name, is wet wit?"

"Well, at least I'm thankful you didn't say 'What's wet wit, eh, what?'"

"This conversation is getting very silly," said Matthew censoriously. "And frankly I'm beginning to wonder about this man who is supposedly following you."

"Oh, you are, are you? You mean that I'm not worth following, is that it? You wouldn't follow me if I was the last woman on earth, I suppose."

To her surprise, Matthew burst into song at this point.

"If you were the only girl in the world," he sang,

"And I were the only boy,

Nothing!"

Honor scowled and then burst out laughing. Relieved, Matthew joined in.

"That's the most ridiculous thing I ever had sung to me," she said when she had recovered.

"Well, it's not the most ridiculous thing I ever sang. The most ridiculous thing I ever sang was..."

"Never mind," said Honor hastily. "Look, if you feel uncomfortable about the sleeping arrangements, I still have the couchette I booked originally. As long as I can establish that we're together — for the record — so that this guy won't bother me, I can sneak off to it when everybody's bedded down for the night."

Matthew gave her a slow, considering look. She was an extremely attractive woman he decided — a little more overbearing than he usually cared for, but intelligent, nicely put together, and generally pleasing.

"Never let it be said," he pronounced, "that I kicked a lady out of my bedroom."

But the effect wasn't quite what he expected.

Honor snapped: "Oh, you really are the most infuriating man!" and slammed out of the compartment.

"Now, what on earth got into her?" he wondered, but just at that moment he was thrown slightly off balance as the train lurched forward and began to move away from the platform, and for a time at any rate, he forgot about Honor and her capricious behaviour.

3

"And away we go!" yelled Buzzy Nash, bouncing up and down on the seat.

"Watch the upholstery," said his father. "Do you realize this is brand-new rolling stock, and we're its first passengers? I don't want people pointing a finger at me and saying — 'It was his kid who trashed the train.'"

Buzzy glanced anxiously at him, thinking not for the first time that it was hard to be sure always whether his father was joking or not.

"Ah, c'mon, Dad," he said when he had determined that Nash's impassive face was lightened by a hint of levity, "you know I wouldn't trash a whole train."

"Just selected bits, huh? Well, anyway — say goodbye to Chicago."

The train had passed out of the station and was sliding sleekly through the marshalling yards. The only notable thing in view seemed to be a huge burned-out warehouse at the side of the tracks.

"I think I'll get my camcorder out and take some shots through the window," said Buzzy.

The camcorder was one of Buzzy's latest enthusiasms, of which he had many. It had been given to him by his father just after he arrived for his Washington visit, and he'd already taken reams of videotape of everything from the Washington Monument to the National Air and Space Museum, much of it — to his father's mind — redundant, since it consisted of long sequences showing essentially static things. However, apart from offering a few gentle hints about going easy on the zoom and relying more on tracking shots, Nash had kept his own counsel. In this case, shooting from the train would at least give the scenes he captured the added interest of motion.

Buzzy concentrated on keeping the camcorder steady as he captured the passing scene: mainly expressways, gravel heaps, and automobile graveyards. Presumably the landscape would improve as they moved further into the countryside. In the meantime, as the Flying Angel picked up speed and winged south-westward, the most exciting thing to be seen was the flaring red burn-off from the oil-treatment towers just outside Romeoville, Illinois. While Buzzy was occupied in this fashion, Anderson Nash took out a copy of *Newsweek* and began to read a long report on the man who had replaced the former head of the CIA, and wondered as he did so if this would mean a new beginning for people like himself in the organization, people who had been, not tainted exactly, but subtly compromised by the Aldrich Ames spy case.

Just after they had passed Joliet, the public address system hummed on with an announcement about sittings for dinner. They realized simultaneously that their stomachs were rumbling, which was not surprising considering neither of them had eaten anything more substantial than a sandwich at the airport since eight that morning. Buzzy was hoarding the candy bars he had bought in Union Station.

"How about some chow, pardner?" Nash said, doing one of his mediocre John Wayne imitations.

Buzzy, who would normally have responded to this ancient piece of buffoonery by holding his nose and pulling an imaginary chain, chose for once to let his father off the hook and said merely: "Sure thing, old timer." Quite amicably, they left the compartment together and headed for the dining car.

4

"Joliet! Jeez, I never hoped to see that place again."

The sound of his own voice startled him. It wasn't like Aldo Bracciano to talk to himself, but in the circumstances it was perhaps understandable. In his younger days, he had —

as he put it — "gotten himself in dutch with the law" while passing through the state of Illinois. It was actually a matter of car theft, slightly complicated by the fact that he had chosen the car of a state prosecutor to steal. He ended up doing a three-year stretch in Joliet, but got out after eighteen months because of good conduct (or what passes for good conduct in prison). Life in prison had taught him some enduring lessons, but it had also given him time to develop his physique and had left him with some useful contacts, not least of whom was a Mafia-connected fight promoter called Vito Salvadini.

Vito had taken a slightly more than fatherly interest in Aldo while they were both incarcerated, which presented Aldo with a dilemma. If word got out in the prison population that he and Vito were, as the inmates colourfully put it, "playing patty cakes," his reputation would be shot. If, on the other hand, he turned Vito down, Aldo would be shot. Fortunately, Vito had the ability and the power to make sure that things were handled very discreetly, and if anyone ever gossiped about their relationship it never came to either Aldo's or Vito's ears. Certainly Aldo never saw anyone in the prison look at him with that particular kind of veiled derision that would have suggested they knew his secret. Nevertheless, that brief period of situational homosexuality had made Aldo sensitive about his maleness, which was probably part of the reason why Tanya's assertiveness was giving him such trouble.

From Tanya, his mind shifted to an encounter he'd had earlier, just after he boarded the train. He had just stacked his bags when he heard a voice from the corridor say: "Hey, big boy, you want to help me with this fucking door?"

He looked up and there was that tall red-headed broad — what was her name? — Glamora, signalling to him from the corridor. As a matter of fact, she looked pretty hot in that vinyl outfit. Nice curves and bulges all in the right places. Too bad she was taller than he was. But he jumped up and went to her assistance with some alacrity.

"Is it stuck?" he said as he joined her in the corridor.

"No, I just forgot to say 'Open, Sesame.' Of course it's stuck. What are you? A comedian?"

"No, a boxer," he said. "Here, let me at it."

The door was stuck, so it hadn't been a come-on. It took Aldo two or three good tugs to get it to move.

"Here. Let me get these bags for you, too."

Glamora stood aside as he carried her four-piece luggage ensemble into Room J.

"It's kinda tight in here, isn't it? Wouldn't you think deluxe accommodation would be bigger than a fucking broom closet?"

"She has a nasty mouth," thought Aldo, who wasn't used to being around women who talked like men. "She'd be right at home in a locker room."

"Yeah, they are kinda small," he admitted.

"Small? That's like saying Marlon Brando needs to lose a few pounds! This place is so small I wouldn't keep a june-bug in it."

Not only did she talk dirty but her mind leaped all over the place. Marlon Brando? Junebugs? Aldo was beginning to get a look on his face that usually appeared only after he'd taken a hard left to the side of the head.

"What's your name, slugger?" she asked as she proceeded to arrange her things around the compartment.

Aldo couldn't take his eyes off her. Not only was she tall, she was stunning. On most women that fire-engine red hair would look ridiculous but on her it looked legitimate. What's more, it didn't overwhelm the rest of her. Her eyes were large and vividly green. Her mouth was red and luscious. She had a skin that in spite of the immoderate use of makeup looked healthy and flawless. Above all, she seemed to radiate sexual warmth.

"Er ... it's Aldo. Aldo Bracciano..." he stammered after a pause.

"Aldo? Well, I'm Glamora ... but that's my working name. You can call me Vikki."

"Sure. Well, I did recognize you. I mean you're a star and all that. But anyway ... hi, Vikki."

He gave her his goofiest smile, and in the inexplicable way these things happen, the stupid smile sped right through her tough-girl carapace and entered the soft spot in her heart.

"Hi, Aldo," she said, answering his smile with one that was almost as absurd. "Take the weight off your Oxfords. Sit down and talk to me while I get this crap sorted out."

He sat on the small seat facing her as she hung a couple of outfits in the diminutive closet by the door and started to hold up and shake out various items of female underwear of a very diaphanous and erotic type. A faint blush appeared on Aldo's sallow cheeks as he swallowed and turned his eyes away. He didn't want to look like a creep who got his kicks eyeballing women's panties.

"Hey, I said 'talk,'" Glamora ordered. "You're a boxer. Your name is Aldo. Go on from there."

"Er ... hmm ... I ... uh ..." Aldo began.

"It's gonna be that hard, is it?" said Glamora, shaking a pair of sheer black stockings at him. "Let's see if I can get you started. Where're you from?"

"Er ... Asbury Park," he managed.

"You're kidding. In New Jersey? 'Is it Granada I see or only Asbury Park?'"

"Huh?"

"It's a line from a song. Cole Porter — 'At Long Last Love'?"

"Oh, yeah ... sure."

It was clear that sophisticated song lyrics were not something he had a connoisseur's knowledge of, but he dimly realized that she was doing her best to charm him.

"Doesn't The Boss come from there?" Glamora continued.

"Springsteen? Yeah, he went to the same high school I went to."

"No shit! Did you do good in high school?"

"Nah. I dropped out as soon as I could."

Suddenly, as an awful possibility occurred to her, Glamora narrowed her eyes at him and rapped out: "You're not a smoker, are you?"

"Jeez, no," Aldo protested. "It ruins your wind."

She beamed at him.

"Good!" she said. "Guys who smoke are a real turnoff. So what's your family like? Any brothers or sisters?"

"My family's OK. My old man runs a fruit market. Yeah, I've got two brothers and a sister. How about you?"

For the first time since they had started talking, Glamora hesitated; a darkness seemed to gather behind her eyes.

"I had a sister," she said. "She's dead."

"Jeez, I'm sorry," said Aldo, but something bright and effortless had gone from between them, and pretty soon Glamora ended the conversation and indicated that she wanted to be alone.

So here he was back in his compartment as the train passed through Joliet, thinking about prison, and Vito, and Tanya, and wondering whether he'd get another chance to talk to Glamora and call her Vikki and find out more about her life.

5

Harrison, Morrison, Jackson, and Jones, plus two porters and a small group of curious children, followed Prince Achmed as he made his royal way through the station to the track where the Flying Angel waited for the departure signal. At the door to the rear coach, they were met by Scats Madison, who took one look at Achmed and groaned inwardly. These foreign, high-powered blacks were always a pain in the ass. Still, it wouldn't do to show any lack of accord in front of all these white folks. So he stepped forward, smiling amiably.

"Welcome aboard the Flying Angel, Prince," he said.

Prince Achmed frowned and turned to his bodyguards.

"His Royal Highness doesn't like to be referred to as 'Prince,'" said Morrison. "He's not a rock star."

"No," said Scats to himself, "he's not a rock star; what he is is a turkey." But aloud he spoke more diplomatically.

"Sorry, Your Royal Highness. Us folks over here have a

hard time keepin' the forms of address straight. Let me show you to your accommodation."

The prince signified with the barest of nods that he would allow Scats that honour, and followed him up the steps of the coach.

"This is my accommodation?" he huffed as he surveyed the interior of Room F.

"It's the best on the train, Your Royal Highness. These are our deluxe bedrooms."

The prince looked around him again with an air of total disbelief.

"Where will all my luggage go?" he asked finally.

"Well, Your Royal Highness, we can stow some of it in the baggage car. It'll be safe there. Just keep what you need for a couple of days — underwear, socks, shaving stuff."

Why was this man talking to him about his underwear? Achmed wondered. Did Princess Di get this kind of treatment? He shrugged his shoulders in resignation.

"Very well, tell the porters to take this one, this one, and this one. I'll keep these two here. Now, Mr. ..."

"Madison. Lincoln Madison."

"Now, Mr. Madison, what is the security like in this coach?"

"The what, Your Royal Highness?"

"Is this coach accessible from the rest of the train at night? Do you lock the doors between the coaches?"

Scats looked at him quizzically.

"No, sir, Your Royal Highness. We never do that. Some folks like to stretch their legs durin' the night. Might want to stroll into the observation car."

The prince turned to his bodyguards, who were standing in a cramped cluster in the corridor.

"This coach must be secured," he said. "Mr. Harrison, Mr. Morrison, you two take the first shift, one guarding the upstairs door and one down here. Mr. Jackson and Mr. Jones, take the second shift, midnight to six in the morning."

The bodyguards were unprepared for the change in the prince's tone. In the limousine, he had shown an almost naive curiosity; with the sleeping-car attendant he had been self-important; now he was crisp and decisive, like someone used to handling power confidently and without challenge. As professionals themselves, they recognized the assurance of someone who could probably handle himself well in a tight situation.

"Fine, Your Royal Highness," said Morrison. "We'll see to it that the coach is protected. I guess first we'd better take a survey of the passengers to see who has a legitimate reason to be back here."

"Right," said Harrison. "It's lucky it's the last coach, so we only have one end to worry about."

Scats and the four bodyguards left to make their rounds of the other compartments, and Achmed sighed and closed his eyes for a moment. It might have seemed to an onlooker that he was praying, but in fact he was wondering whether the face he had glimpsed in the crowd, as he and his entourage made their way from the Metropolitan Lounge to the train, belonged to an old acquaintance.

6

When Delia Hentzen climbed the steps to Coach 10, she caught one of her heels in a tread and almost fell. Would have fallen, in fact, if a pair of strong arms hadn't grabbed her and held her upright. She turned to offer her thanks and saw a tall, darkly bearded man, wearing a black felt hat at a rakish tilt and with a black Burberry draped over his shoulders. He smiled and gazed at her intently through a pair of lustrous and bottomless eyes.

"You must be more careful," he said. "There might not always be someone there to catch you when you fall."

His voice was almost self-consciously rich and resonant, like the voice of a radio evangelist, or a Welsh actor, or a charlatan. Delia distrusted him immediately. The voice and the eyes were consciously used to create an effect, to suggest mastery and magnetism, in fact to dominate. There was also something disquietingly familiar about them.

"You're right," she said. "I must watch my step. You know, I have a feeling we met once — a long time ago."

By this time, they were edging along the corridor on the lower level towards their rooms. To Delia's discomfort, she discovered that hers — Room H — was directly next to his — Room G.

"I think I would have remembered that," he said, making his eyes crinkle impishly. "Perhaps you recognize me from my television appearances."

Delia shook her head.

"I don't think so. I haven't been here long enough to see much American television."

The impish sparkle in his eyes faded, though the smile remained resolutely in place.

"Ah, well, perhaps you've seen my face on a book jacket."

"Not unless you write books about acting. Or biographies of actors. That's all I read."

Even the smile was beginning to slip a little now.

"Then I think you must be confusing me with someone else," he said rather stiffly.

Delia smiled consolingly.

"You're probably right. I do that all the time. I have a terrible memory for faces. Anyway, thank you again for helping me. I'm sure we'll run into each other again, since we're neighbours."

She turned to go into her room and then on an impulse turned back.

"You haven't ever been in Solonitza, have you?"

There was a moment when the dark, luminous eyes seemed to look out on an utter void. Then the studied twinkle reappeared.

"Solonitza?" he said. "Where is that? I've never been good at geography, I'm afraid."

"It's the capital of the Galinian Republic," said Delia. "They call it the Paris of the Black Sea."

"Sorry," he said. "The only Paris I'm familiar with is the one on the Seine. Well ... until later, then. Perhaps I'll see you at dinner. Oh, by the way, my name is Kadourian, Dr. Vartan Kadourian."

"I'm Delia Hentzen."

He nodded and retreated into his room. Delia went into hers and slid the door closed. "That was an odd encounter," she thought, "and did his eyes really go dead when I mentioned Solonitza? Or was he just looking blank? In any case, I'm almost sure I've seen him before somewhere. But wherever it was, I don't think he called himself Kadourian."

7

The woman with the bright yellow scarf around her hair seemed to be having trouble with her luggage. She would take several rather unsteady steps, then put down one bag, pick it up, take a few more steps and then put down the other.

"It'll take her the rest of the day to get to the train at this rate," said Sven. "Come on, let's give her a hand."

He and Eddie quickened their pace until they were abreast of her and then Sven said: "Excuse me, do you need some help?"

Aubretia stopped, put down both bags and looked rather blearily at the two of them.

"Help?" she said. "I need more than help: I need counselling. What makes me get myself into these things? I hate travel."

Eddie hefted one of her bags and Sven took the other.

"I take it you're heading for the Flying Angel?" said Sven.

"You take it right. Hey, this is really nice of you, and I'm being such a bitch. The name's Aubretia. It's a damned silly name I know, but it's a family name."

Sven and Eddie exchanged a glance that said, "Boy,

what did we get into?"

"Which end of the train are you heading for?" asked Eddie, hoping it wasn't all the way down towards the engine.

"I'm in the last coach. Deluxe accommodation. Nothing but the best for Aubretia. Though, God knows, what's best for Aubretia right now is a quiet weekend with her head in an ice-bucket."

"Hung over?" Sven asked diffidently.

"...doesn't begin to describe it. Words cannot express — et cetera, et cetera — blah, blah, blah. It even hurts to talk, but when I'm in this state I can't stop."

"You don't say," said Eddie to himself.

"And are you two fellows on this damned train, too?"

"Yes," said Sven. "I'm Sven Sanchez and this is Eddie Tsubouchi."

"God, tell me again when I'm sober. My mind can't handle it now. Anyway, whoever you are, you're good guys. There aren't many of you left."

She was beginning to sound a little maudlin now, and Sven was alarmed to see a tear roll down one cheek. Fortunately, they had now arrived at the rear coach and they helped her to board and carried her bags up the narrow stairs to the second level. Sven and Eddie were in Room E, but they settled Aubretia in Room B and were thanked profusely before they retired to their own accommodation.

"Sheesh," said Eddie, throwing himself into the single seat by the window, "that's one strange lady. I wonder what she's doing on the train if she hates travel?"

"Maybe that's why. They say it's good therapy, confronting the thing you hate most or fear most."

"And what's that for you, old buddy?"

Sven looked at him dourly for a moment. "Being expendable," he said.

8

"This is a whole lot cleaner than the Belfast trains," Teresa Shaughnessy said to herself, as she inspected her deluxe bedroom. "Everything's spotless, and oh, won't it be lovely to relax all by me ownsome, after all that flurry and scurry."

She had opened her suitcase and removed what she needed for the night: a pink flannelette nightgown with little blue flowers on it, a pair of travel slippers, and a toilet bag. These she had placed in the rack by the window before stowing her suitcase on the floor by the single seat. Then she had plumped herself down on the long seat opposite and opened her copy of the latest Maeve Binchy paperback. Maeve was her favourite writer. She loved the way she could get right to the heart of her women characters.

Her eyes had scanned less than half a page when she heard a little tap at her door and then the sound of the door sliding open. She looked up and saw the woman she had encountered in the Metropolitan Lounge.

"You're all settled in, I see," said the woman. "I was just passing down the corridor on the way to my compartment and I happened to see you in here."

"Come in ... er ... Miss ... ?" Teresa said, though without notable enthusiasm.

"Verhaeven. But you can call me Katharine."

"Come in, Katharine. I'm Teresa. Teresa Shaughnessy."

"I won't just now, thanks. I'm going to freshen up a bit before dinner."

She looked around at Teresa's accommodation with some envy.

"I can see the difference between first class and deluxe now. My room is quite tiny. And your new employer paid for this?"

Teresa was becoming slightly annoyed. There seemed to be an implication that somehow she had been handed an unfair advantage over this Katharine woman.

"Well, yes," she said. "It's very comfy. Me new boss wrote and said it would make up for the length of the journey. Not that I mind that. I'm looking forward to seeing the scenery."

The woman smiled.

"I agree. That's why I took the train. You don't see any of the country from the air, and I wanted to make the most of it. Who is your new ... er ... boss, by the way?"

"For sheer nosiness," thought Teresa, "this one has Mrs. Hanratty back home beat by miles."

"He's a foreign gentleman," she said. "A political fellow. He's got one of them names that's hard to pronounce. Something like Govvleyov or Gollyvov. I'll get used to it, I dare say."

Varya had her mouth open to correct Teresa's pronunciation, then thought better of it. At least, she was now absolutely certain that this was the same Teresa Shaughnessy that she and Marminski had been instructed to eliminate.

"You don't have a cigarette, do you?" Varya said. "I left mine in my compartment."

"I don't smoke," said Teresa primly. "I always say: 'If

the Lord had meant us to smoke he'd have put chimneys in our heads.'"

"I'd better get along, then. Perhaps I'll see you in the dining room."

"And perhaps you won't," Teresa said to herself as soon as the woman was gone. She had begun to feel that this Katharine Verhaeven was pushing herself on her for some reason, and that reason was probably not a straightforward one. She picked up her Maeve Binchy again and began to read, but she hadn't reached the bottom of the page before another thought occurred to her.

"There's the 'V' Madame Zelda warned me about, or I'm a Dutchman! Verhaeven! Well, if it is, she'll find it's not so easy to put the wind up Teresa Shaughnessy."

Three
Dinner in the Diner

I

The skies were already darkening over the Illinois country-side when Matthew left his "deluxe bedroom" to make his way towards the restaurant. It too was on the upper level of the train but in the next coach, and to get to it he had to pass through the observation lounge. As he did so, Matthew noted that it was sparsely populated and that the few passengers who were sitting there, watching the Illinois landscape streak by, were elderly Westerners in bolo ties and rimless glasses. At the far end, at the entrance to the restaurant, a cluster of people waited to be seated. When Matthew joined them, the woman in front of him turned and smiled.

"A bit of a crush, isn't it?" she said in a pronounced Northern Irish accent. "It's because there's only the one sitting tonight. Ah, well, it'll taste all the better when we do get it."

"A delight delayed is a delight doubled," Matthew answered aphoristically.

"Are you after being some kind of poet?" asked the woman, her plain, bespectacled face wearing a look of sly amusement.

Matthew beamed back at her.

"Ah, is it after teasing me you are, with your Irish

levity? No, as a matter of fact, I'm a playwright. Though why I bother I don't know, when everyone knows the best playwrights in the world come from Ireland."

By this time the brisk, middle-aged blonde who was seating the diners had approached them with two menus in her hand.

"Two?" she asked.

Teresa looked at Matthew inquiringly.

"Of course we'll share a table," he said. "I hate eating alone."

"Good. I hate it too."

The restaurant was new and gleaming like the rest of the train, and seemed wider than the dining cars Matthew was used to on British Rail. The tables on either side of the central aisle were set with crisp linen and well-polished cutlery, and the waiting staff were equally crisp and well-polished, in white shirts, maroon vests, and black trousers or slacks. The steward who came to the table Matthew and Teresa were sharing was a black man with a very shiny bald head and large ears. The little badge pinned to his vest announced that his name was Pete.

"What can I do for you, folks? A drink before dinner?" He sounded both friendly and aggressive and the pitch of his voice was just a tone or two below soprano.

Matthew as usual ordered the most outrageously sweet and sticky of the cocktail specials and Teresa asked for a glass of white wine.

"So are you going all the way through to Los Angeles?" asked Matthew when the drinks had arrived.

"I am," said Teresa. "What about yourself?"

"Yes, all the way. I've been there before but this is the

first time I've done it by train."

"Oh, it's me first time ever. First time in America, too. I was as pleased as Punch when they told me I had the job."

"And what is the job, if you don't mind my asking?"

"I'm going to be the nanny for a foreign family. There's three kiddies: a boy about seven, a girl about four, and a baby they've just adopted."

"Are they a nice family? Do you know anything about them?" Matthew asked, remembering stories of the ill-treatment of imported nannies in the United States.

"Just that he was some kind of political big-pot — over in Russia or somewhere. He's got a name like Gollyvov — or at any rate that's as close as I can get to it."

"Golovyov?"

"That sounds right."

Some kind of political big-pot was right, Matthew thought bleakly. Golovyov was almost in the same league as Ceausescu in Romania, but he had been sharper than Ceausescu, or more responsive to the winds of change. He had modified his principles to harmonize with the doctrine of glasnost and had steered his country towards a kind of democracy, not out of conviction but because he saw advantage in it for himself. Eventually, an uprising of young idealists had turned rapidly into a very ugly bloodbath. Matthew well remembered the television footage of Golovyov's wife, Luba, being pulled from her car and beaten to death by a raging mob only days after the jubilant scenes at the Berlin Wall. Golovyov wasn't in the car. In fact, nobody knew where he was until he turned up in California some months later, living very lavishly. There had been questions raised in the press about his presence in the United States but for some reason he was allowed to remain. Not long after that, he married a wealthy Texas divorcee with two children. This was the first Matthew had heard of them adopting a third.

"I hope you'll be happy in your new job," he said after what he hoped was not too awkward a pause.

"Well, it's always been me ambition to go to California."

"Why California particularly?" he asked.

"It's not California so much as Hollywood," she said with a faint flush appearing on her cheeks. "I'm a terror for the films. I've been a fan since I was a little tot."

She actually said "fillums," a pronunciation that struck Matthew as somehow deliciously and authentically Irish.

"Be careful in Los Angeles," warned Matthew. "Someone may spot you and offer you a screen test."

"Oh, that's very likely," she scoffed. "And if he did, I'd run a mile, thinking he was a white slaver or something."

"What kind of films do you like?"

"All kinds. But I like romantic ones best — like *Sleepless in Seattle*."

Matthew couldn't resist the opportunity to enhance his standing in Teresa's eyes by modestly disclosing his own reasons for going to Los Angeles.

"Is that right?" she said with something like awe. "You'll be writing a fillum! You've got to tell me who's going to star in it."

"It's a little bit premature to talk about that, but I believe the producer has his eye on Julia Roberts for the female lead."

"Julia Roberts! Oh, God, would you listen to the man? You'll be meeting Julia Roberts?"

Matthew diffidently allowed that he might.

"I know it's asking a lot, but do you think you could get an autograph for me, if you do? Here, I'll give you me address in Los Angeles. You could send it on to me there."

She opened her saddle-leather tote, pulled out a notebook and pen and hastily scribbled something.

"Here," she said, tearing out the page and handing it to him. "Don't lose it."

Matthew folded it and slipped it into his pocket without looking at it. Meanwhile the routine of dinner continued. Pete brought their drinks and took their food order, and with admirable celerity soon had their first course on the table.

2

Diagonally across the aisle from the table where Matthew and Teresa were sitting, Eddie and Sven were sharing a table with Aubretia. They had just passed through Chillicothe, Illinois, and were commenting on how unscenic the scenery had been so far, when a pretty, dark-haired woman with an exotic, almost gypsy-like appearance approached them.

"Do you mind if I join you?" she asked, smiling pleasantly. There was a trace of an accent in her speech that none of them could readily identify.

"Join us?" said Aubretia. "Help yourself. We're not an exclusive group, are we, boys?"

Eddie and Sven indicated that they weren't, and the woman took a seat opposite Eddie.

"Thank you," she said. "I hate dining alone and you looked like such a friendly group. Are you all going all the way through to Los Angeles?"

Sven and Eddie nodded, and Aubretia murmured affirmatively.

"I think I might, too," said Delia. "This trip was quite spontaneous and I haven't quite decided. I might stop off somewhere along the way."

"You don't have many choices," Aubretia advised. "There's Kansas City and then nothing till we get to Caliente, Nevada. Wonderful scenery, of course — through the Rockies and the desert — but nowhere much to just hang out."

"Hang out? I'm sorry, I'm new to the U.S. and I'm not used to the idioms yet. Oh, by the way, my name's Delia Hentzen."

"Hi, Delia. I'm Aubretia and these two hunks are Eddie and Sven. 'Hang out' means sort of loiter about, have fun doing nothing — or at least I think that's what it means. It's the kind of thing teenagers here do a lot of."

Just then, Roberto, their waiter, came by to take the dinner orders, and asked Delia if she'd like a drink first.

"Yes, I think just a glass of white wine, thank you."

Eddie, Sven, and Aubretia ordered a second margarita each.

"I know, I know," said Aubretia. "I shouldn't, given that I'm still reeling from the effects of last night. But the hell with it. I'll sober up again before Kansas City."

"That's only a few hours away," said Eddie. "Anyway, why do you need to be sober in Kansas City?"

Aubretia winked.

"Because I'm meeting someone there. Someone is joining me in my classy little deluxe bedroom."

Eddie's Japanese-American skin went an interesting shade of pink, and Sven gave an embarrassed grin. Aubretia waved her napkin at them.

"Oh, it's not what you think! It's the daughter of some friends of mine."

"Ah, you're giving the little girl a treat — a trip to California! Isn't that nice?" said Delia.

"Little girl, nothing! She's an unmarried mother — or soon will be. This is her."

Aubretia dug in her purse, produced a photograph, and passed it around. It was a colour shot, showing the pre-pregnant young woman sitting on the rim of a fountain in some park or other. She was ripely pretty, though somewhat over made-up. She wore her brown hair drawn straight back from her forehead and fastened in a ponytail behind.

"I'm not really giving anything away. You'd probably guess as soon as you see her that she's pregnant. She's in her fifth month."

As Sven passed the photograph back, it slipped out of his hand into the aisle. A woman in a brown dress at the next table picked it up and handed it to him. He gave it to Aubretia with a worried frown.

"Should she be travelling so far in her condition? What if there's some kind of problem?"

"Yeah, especially if it happens between Kansas City and Caliente?" said Eddie.

Aubretia looked concerned.

"That's unlikely," she said. "And if it does, there are always people around to help. I saw a kind of nurse-like woman getting on the train. In fact, she's over there."

Delia turned to look and saw behind her across the

aisle a plain-looking woman with large, heavily rimmed spectacles, sitting with a tall, thin man in a well-cut grey suit.

"She does look like a nurse, but that doesn't mean she is one."

Aubretia craned her head to the side, and caught Teresa's eye just as she was lifting a spoonful of soup to her mouth.

"Hello, dear," she called to her, "are you a nurse?"

Teresa swallowed the soup and dabbed her mouth with her napkin.

"A nanny. But I've had hospital training."

"There," said Aubretia with satisfaction. "I've got a nose for nurses. Have you any experience with expectant mothers, dear?"

Teresa looked nonplussed.

"Why? Surely you're not expecting, are you, missus?"

Matthew spluttered uncouthly into his soup.

"Me?" said Aubretia. "Have a heart. The only thing I'm expecting is another hangover. No, I've got a young woman joining me in Kansas City who's into her fifth month. I just wondered if, in a pinch, you could help out."

"Well, missus..."

"Call me Aubretia."

"Well, Aubretia, I won't say I couldn't. Mind you, the conditions'll hardly be ideal. But I once delivered a preemy on a bus in Carrickfergus, and after that anything else would be a picnic."

"There," said Aubretia. "It's all settled then."

At that moment, the waiter brought Delia's white wine, and the first courses for the other three, so conversation at their table became more sporadic until the end of dinner.

3

From the table opposite, Varya had heard enough of the conversation to suspect that Delia, judging by her accent, was most probably a Galinian like herself. This was troubling. It could be a coincidence, of course, but how likely was it that two exiled Galinians would be travelling in the same coach of the same train? The exchange between Aubretia and Teresa also worried her, because she didn't want too many people on the train to remember Teresa clearly, particularly if her plan was to work out.

Worse was to come. She had taken an aisle seat when she came into the dining car, and had hoped by looking unwelcoming to discourage anyone from sharing her table. Unfortunately, it hadn't had the desired effect. She had barely begun to sip her vodka and tonic when a rather hunted looking man of about thirty-five and a young boy of about ten took the two seats at the other side of the table. This was going to make things difficult, because her ability to concentrate on the conversation between Matthew and Teresa would be threatened by any exchanges she would have with her table-mates. The man on his own she could have frozen out quite easily, but little boys weren't as alert to subtle social signals, and to be cold and stand-offish with him would only bring unfavourable attention to her. Her chief tactic, if her plan was to succeed, was to remain as inconspicuous and as unmemorable as possible. Which is why she did what she did next.

"Enjoying your trip so far?" Anderson Nash asked her

after he had ordered a scotch and water for himself and a soda for Buzzy.

Varya peered at him blankly.

"I'm sorry," she said. "I'm a little deaf. What did you say?"

"I said 'Are you enjoying your trip so far?'"

"Am I what?"

"ENJOYING YOUR TRIP!"

"My trip?" she repeated, smiling uncertainly. "Yes, thank you."

"Going all the way to Los Angeles?"

"Sorry?"

"LOS ANGELES! ARE YOU GOING ALL THE WAY THERE?"

"Oh! I'm not certain. I may break my journey."

"Where did you think of breaking it? Kansas City?"

"What do I think of ... what?"

"ARE YOU GOING TO BREAK YOUR JOURNEY IN KANSAS CITY!"

Varya looked pained, as if Nash's persistence was giving her a headache.

"Possibly," she said, and began to stare out of the window.

Nash gave up. He wasn't going to spend the entire meal bellowing questions across the table. Besides, the woman was plain and in an odd way neutral. Apart from the slight foreign accent there was nothing to distinguish her. So he turned his attention to Buzzy.

"Well, how goes it so far, pardner?"

Buzzy put his hand to his ear and said, "Eh? What?"

"That's enough of that," Nash said, glancing uneasily at the woman opposite. She seemed not to have heard.

"Isn't that the woman I saw you speaking to outside the bookstore in the station, Dad?" Buzzy whispered.

Nash glanced at the woman again. She was still staring out of the window at the gradually darkening landscape.

"No," he said. "That woman had heavy spectacles. More like the one at that table over there."

Buzzy looked in the direction his father had indicated and saw Teresa Shaughnessy taking a swig from a glass of wine.

"Yeah, you're right. But that wasn't the one you spoke to."

"How can you tell?"

"Well, I was so surprised to see you talking to somebody that I took a good look at her. I mean you sent me for candy and you went to the bookstore for a newspaper. But there were newspapers at the candy stand. I thought you'd got rid of me so you could have a secret meeting with one of your undercover agents."

"Buzzy!" Nash put his finger to his lips. "I've told you before about weaving these fantasies about my work."

"But you do work for the CIA, Dad," Buzzy said, in what he cheerfully assumed was a barely audible whisper. "Nash of the CIA."

"Shut up!" his father hissed. "I certainly don't want you to go broadcasting it all over the place."

"Heck, Dad, I'm sorry. I only whispered it. Anyway, I still say if you put glasses on this lady, she'd look like the one you met in the station."

Again Nash cast a worried glance at his table partner, but she seemed lost in her own world of deafness. Now that he looked more carefully, it seemed that Buzzy might be right. Put a big basin-like hat on her head to cover the colour of her hair, wipe off the lipstick, and give her some heavy-rimmed glasses and she would look quite a bit like the woman in the station, and, come to that, quite like the woman sitting at the table across the aisle. But so what? He knew from experience that people tended to focus on the more striking superficialities of appearance. People with few noticeable features to begin with can make themselves unrecognizable to all but their most intimate friends by changing their appearance in some quite minor ways: short hair instead of long, coloured contact lenses, cheek pads, facial hair — even something as simple as a big basin-shaped hat and a pair of eyeglasses.

"Anyway, Dad," said Buzzy. "You never explained about the newspaper."

Anderson brought his attention back to his son with an effort.

"Newspaper? Oh, they just had the Chicago papers at the candy stand. I wanted the *L.A. Times*."

Buzzy bought the explanation, but reluctantly. The idea of having caught his father in the act of carrying out some covert operation was too appealing to be turned loose without some regret. For one thing, he hadn't seen a *Los Angeles Times* in his father's possession, which meant that either the bookstore had been out of stock or his father was lying. Buzzy didn't want to believe the latter possibility.

Looking at him from the other side of the dining car, Delia Hentzen saw a worried-looking boy of about ten in a Woody Woodpecker T-shirt, baggy jeans, and a baseball cap worn backwards. The boy had a snub nose and slightly pro-truding Bugs Bunny-ish teeth, held back by a gleaming brace. He also had an amazingly penetrating whisper, which carried quite clearly to her seat just across the aisle. Delia mentally filed away two impressions from the conversation she had overheard. One was that the boy believed his father to be an undercover agent, which of course might be simply his fantasy. The other was even more interesting to her at that moment, however: it was that the woman the boy suspected his father of having met clandestinely in the station had spoken with a faint but unmistakable Galinian accent.

4

Under normal circumstances, Prince Achmed would have been quite content to dine in solitude in his compartment. Jackson had even offered to see that dinner was brought to him and had borrowed a menu from the dining car. But Achmed was bored. He didn't want to sit there by himself, and to dine with any of the four security men would have been, to say the least, lacking in novelty. So, despite protests from Harrison, Morrison, Jackson, and Jones that it would compromise his security, he determined to join the other passengers — like Haroun al Raschid mingling with the commoners of Baghdad.

As he started through the observation car, followed closely by Jackson and Jones (Harrison and Morrison being at their respective posts at the upper and lower levels of the coach), he saw ahead of him a figure he recognized. It was no-one he had ever met, but someone for whom he had a great deal of admiration. The prince had found much to impress and enlighten him in *The Mind's Body, The Body's Mind*, and he had found that practising the mental and physical exercises from Kadourian's series of tapes had greatly increased his sense of well-being. Here was an opportunity to meet the guru himself.

"Excuse me," he said as he caught up with Kadourian at the door to the dining car. "It is Dr. Kadourian, is it not?"

Kadourian turned with a less-than-welcoming look on his face, which was swiftly replaced by one of gratification when he heard this exotically dressed black man say: "If I may introduce myself — I am Prince Achmed, and a great admirer of your work."

"A pleasure, Your Royal Highness," oozed Kadourian. "I had heard of your visit to our country. I hope that you have found us hospitable."

"Perhaps you would do me the honour of dining with me. I'd very much like to discuss your post-Cartesian hypothesis."

Kadourian nodded graciously.

"Delighted, Your Royal Highness."

The hostess showed them to a table and gave them menus. After they had sat down and ordered drinks, the prince said: "By the way, doctor, in this situation there's no need for formality. You may call me Achmed."

"In that case," said Kadourian, hugely pleased with himself, "I can't have you calling me 'Doctor.' My name is Vartan.'

The prince reached across the table, and the doctor allowed his slender violinist's hand to be swallowed in Achmed's large black grasp.

"Agreed then, Vartan?"

"Agreed, Achmed."

The drinks arrived quickly. Kadourian had treated himself to a margarita, but the prince made do with a Shirley Temple, since he took the proscriptions of his religion very seriously.

"I am a great admirer of Descartes," said Achmed, plunging immediately into serious matters. "My favourite quotation occurs early in the *Discourse on Method*, where he says: 'It is useful to know something of the manners of different nations, that we may be enabled to form a more correct judgment regarding our own, and be prevented from thinking that everything contrary to our customs is ridiculous and irrational — a conclusion usually come to by those whose experience has been limited to their own country.'"

"Amazing," Kadourian said. "To be able to quote so extensively from such a source shows a remarkably retentive memory!"

Achmed waved a hand modestly.

"I studied PPE at Oxford, you know."

Kadourian looked blank.

"Philosophy, Politics, and Economics," explained Achmed. "Then I went on to Patrice Lumumba University in Moscow to study the Marxist interpretation of history."

"Fascinating," said Kadourian.

"But I must give some of the credit to you," Achmed went on, grinning at Kadourian. "It was the exercises in *Releasing Body/Mind Power* that taught me how to develop my powers of memory."

If Kadourian had been instantly elevated to the Zwamali nobility, it would hardly have given him more gratification than to be told that a member of royalty had practised his teachings to such evident effect. His whole person seemed to exude self-satisfaction.

"It's very kind of you to say so, and if Your Royal Highness wishes, I'd be happy to come to Zwamali and give some lectures."

"Ah-ah, Vartan!" Achmed said wagging his finger. "Not 'Royal Highness,' remember? Achmed!"

"Achmed!" Kadourian was swimming in billows of affirmation.

The two men beamed at one another, lifted their glasses and clinked them.

"To the balance of body and mind!" said Achmed.

"To the future of Zwamali!" Kadourian rumbled.

"Will you guys be having soup?" chipped in Pete, their waiter.

They both fixed him with looks of Olympian disapproval.

"We need another minute to study the menu," said Kadourian.

"Take your time, guys. There's only one sitting tonight so we won't be rushing you out."

"Democracy has its imperfections," said Kadourian when the waiter had moved on.

"Ah, well," Achmed answered, "when one chooses to mingle with the *demos*, one cannot expect the manners of the court."

The meal proceeded with many comments from both of them about the inadequacies of the chef and from Kadourian about the inferiority of the wines. Then just before the dessert course, Achmed fixed Kadourian with an intense gaze.

"Tell me, Vartan," he said. "I hear that you have been consulted by the President. Is he worried about his prospects in the next election? I ask because he is by way of being an old friend. We were at Oxford together, and he visited me in Moscow the year after I graduated."

"Really! That's most interesting. I had no idea you and the President were acquainted. Yes, I'm afraid he is worried — and with reason. The Republicans are making a very strong showing in Congress and with the right nominee for the presidency, they could easily be in charge of the White House and Congress after the election. However, he and the First Lady have both adopted my programme of aerobic meditation, and there are already signs that his power quotient has intensified. So I have hopes..."

Achmed nodded thoughtfully and poured himself another glass of mineral water.

"I was relying on my acquaintanceship with him," he said, "to gain some small advantage for my poor country. We need a better trading relationship with the U.S. However, it might be wise, given the uncertainty of his political future, to cultivate some prominent members of the opposition."

"The opposition? Yes, they are growing more and more isolationist, I'm afraid. Of course, there's always Senator Lugar."

"Is he the President's most likely successor?"

Kadourian shook his head and listed several candidates who were more likely than Richard Lugar to win the Republican nomination.

"In my country in the bad old days," said the prince, "the answer would have been so simple. A few beheadings, an assassination or two, and you could guarantee that the government would be run as you wished."

It was on the tip of Kadourian's tongue to say that he

too had experienced very similar bad old days in various parts of Eastern Europe, but he thought better of it.

"I think you'd better pray that the President is re-elected if you want your country to profit," he said instead.

"I'm not sure that Allah would intervene on behalf of an infidel," the prince answered in a colder tone than he had used until now, then added in a sly aside, "but I will direct my mind/body energy towards the President's mind/body nexus and we can leave Allah to his eternal tasks."

Kadourian bent his head in a politic bow of acquiescence and the next moment the waiter arrived with the dessert.

5

When he heard the announcement over the public address system that dinner was about to be served, Aldo Bracciano summoned up the nerve to go and tap on Glamora's door.

"Yeah, waddya want?" she yelled from inside.

"Uh ... It's me — Aldo. I just thought maybe you'd want to eat?"

The door slid open and she stood surveying him. She had changed since he saw her last. Instead of the outrageous vinyl outfit, she wore a tight clinging dress that seemed to be made out of dark-blue cobwebs, trimmed around the neck and sleeves with silver thread. The tops of her firm, creamy breasts climbed out of its neckline like volcanic islands erupting from a sunless sea. Nobody since Kim Novak, Aldo thought, had breasts like that.

"Whatsa matter?" Glamora mocked. "Never seen tits before?"

"'Scuse me for starin',"' Aldo said, turning pink. "I ... er ... was just kinda surprised you changed. I didn't think they'd be that, you know, formal. You think I should put on my tux?"

"Tux? You're taking a tux to L.A.? Who're you planning on fighting? Gentleman Jim Corbett?"

Aldo looked blank. His knowledge of the history of pugilism didn't extend much further back than Muhammad Ali.

"Never mind. No, you don't need to wear a tux. You look gorgeous just the way you are. C'mon, what're you waiting for? Let's get our asses in gear here!"

She swept past him into the corridor, and started up the staircase to the second level. He closed the door of her compartment and followed, wondering resentfully why he kept letting her make a sap of him. It was like Tanya all over again. Always putting him in the wrong, making him feel like a jerk, fucking with his mind. On the other hand, he knew very well why he put up with it. They were both awesome, and when he saw them his dick took charge and self-respect went out the window. Broads! Why did God have to create them? They were nothing but trouble!

As soon as they were at the table, however, he forgot these grievances, because Glamora had switched to another channel of her multiple-choice personality. Suddenly, she was all mystery and romance, drowning him in a hazy, sea-green gaze.

"Know something?" she said. "You may be a big palooka but you've got the kinda mug I like on a guy: sulky and boyish and ... well, I guess, lonesome-looking. I'd like to stick my tongue right between those pouty lips and kiss you stupid."

Aldo half-grinned, half-grimaced. "Hey, hey!" he chided her. "Where I come from, the guy's supposed to come on to the girl."

"Oh, we're playin' by the Asbury Park rules? Get the hell on with it then."

Aldo winced.

"Er ... uh ... well ... I ... er ... think you're pretty sexy."

"Good. Go on. Let's hear your best line."

"Huh? Oh ... er ... You're a terrific-lookin' babe."

Glamora sighed. "And this is where I say, 'Gee, mister, I bet you say that to all the girls.'"

Aldo sensed that her interest in him was beginning to wane, and he knew he'd have to deliver the goods if he wanted to score later on that evening. He began to sweat with the effort of racking his brains.

"Jeez, I ... er ... I'm ... you've got me so wound up I don't know what I'm sayin'. You're outa sight. You ... turn me on! I wanna stick my face right between your boobs and lick your —"

"Excuse me, folks," said Pete the waiter. "You want to give me your drink orders?"

Glamora loved the mortified expression on Aldo's face. This little trip was getting to be fun.

"I'll have a bourbon on the rocks," she said. Then, batting her spiky eyelashes at Aldo, she asked him sweetly, "How about you, honey?"

"A ... a ... a ... a beer, a cold beer ... "

He pulled his handkerchief from his breast pocket and began to mop his fiery face.

"You want a Bud or a Schlitz?" Pete asked, grinning, his pencil poised above his order pad.

"Schlitz!"

Aldo waited until Pete was out of earshot and then said: "Jeez, Vikki, d'you think the guy heard me?"

"So what if he did?" she said. "You didn't say nothing he wasn't thinking himself, probably. You freak out too easily. Don't sweat it, slugger."

She slid her hand across the tablecloth and put it over his. He started, then looked down at their hands lying together, looked back up into her eyes again, and smiled.

"Anyway, what I was saying," he said, "I meant it all. I'd like to — "

"All right, Casanova, we can talk about it later. That is, if you're coming back to my place after the eats."

His smile broadened and he squeezed her hand.

"You bet," he said.

The rest of dinner was uneventful for them, except that at one point, right out of the blue, Glamora began to talk about her sister.

"She's the one person in the world I really miss," she said. "We were real close when we were kids back in Idaho. Then she went away to study in England, married this guy, and I never saw her again."

"You weren't at the wedding?" asked Aldo.

"No, she got married abroad and I couldn't get away. I was on tour and I didn't want to break my contract. She sent me some of the wedding pictures, though. The guy was a real Continental type, dark hair, dark eyes, kind of like a gypsy."

"How come you never saw them after that?"

"They died."

"Jeez, I'm sorry."

"All right, shut up! I don't want to talk about it."

Aldo shut up. He didn't want to risk another one of Glamora's personality changes, especially not one that would result in him being shut out of her room that night.

6

Matthew had begun his meal with vichyssoise, while Teresa tucked into a bowl of New England clam chowder. Both of them followed this with beef tenderloin, washed down in Matthew's case by a decent Californian cabernet sauvignon, and in Teresa's by another glass of chardonnay. After that came rich, gooey desserts: amaretto cheesecake for Teresa and pecan pie drizzled with chocolate sauce for Matthew.

"I haven't enjoyed meself so much since Tommy Muldoon's wake," Teresa said as the meal approached its end. "Bless you, Matthew, for keepin' me company. I'd have felt sinful eating all that on me own."

"Then why don't we meet again for breakfast tomorrow? What time do you think you'll be up?"

"I'm always up with the lark. But let's say eight o'clock. Or is that too early for you?"

"How about eight-thirty?"

They raised their coffee cups in agreement. At the same moment, the woman sitting at the table behind Matthew rose to leave. The train, which had picked up speed over the last stretch of track, suddenly jolted, throwing the woman off balance so that she collided with Matthew's shoulder. If he hadn't reacted quickly, his coffee would have gone all over the table. As it was, a certain amount of it slopped out onto the table cloth and Matthew's tie. The woman was cumbersomely apologetic and dabbed at the tablecloth and Matthew's tie with a tiny embroidered handkerchief, which she took out of a tapestry-covered bag. She fussed with his coffee cup and Teresa's, moving them so that she could get at the spill, while Matthew protested that there was no significant damage done.

"Still a bit dizzy — eh, Miss Verhaeven?" Teresa joked.

The woman gave her a startled glance.

"Oh, it's you, Miss Shaughnessy. I didn't recognize you for a moment. Please let me buy you both another coffee."

"That's OK, ma'am. Refills are free," said Pete the waiter, arriving with a cloth to mop up the remaining drops.

The woman nodded, made some further faltering gestures of contrition, and departed, still apologizing, down the aisle towards the exit. Pete topped up the cups and moved on to the next table.

"What a very nervous lady. You've met her before, apparently," Matthew said.

"She bumped into me in the Metrowhatsit Lounge. I don't know about nervous, but she's got a nerve all right. She turned up in me compartment before dinner, and talk about nosy! She wanted to know all me whys and wherefores. There's something funny about her, if you ask me."

While they had been eating, the train had left Illinois, crossed a corner of Iowa, and was now clattering through Missouri, though it was too dark now to see much of the countryside. The public address system crackled into life to announce that the next stop would be La Plata, at approximately eleven o'clock. Matthew yawned and apologized.

"I must be tireder than I thought," he said. "I don't

usually conk out quite this early."

Teresa began to gather herself together, picking up her bag and smoothing down her dress. Suddenly she too was racked with a colossal yawn.

"Glory be," she said. "I'm near enough to nodding off meself. Well, we'd both better be getting a good night's rest."

Matthew was just about to get up, when Honor Moore suddenly appeared in the door of the dining car, looked around anxiously, saw someone she clearly wanted to avoid, then, spotting Matthew, rushed over to him and kissed him before sitting opposite him at the table.

"There you are, darling," she croaked to cover his dumbfounded reaction. "I've been looking everywhere for you."

"I'll say goodnight, then," said Teresa, winking at Matthew. "Leave you two lovebirds together. See you for breakfast!"

And off she went with a cheery wave.

"Who's that?" asked Honor. "She looks like an Irish version of Miss Marple."

"More like an Irish version of Miss Froy."

"Froy?"

"Yes, she's a character in a Hitchcock movie, *The Lady Vanishes*. In fact, she's the lady who vanishes."

"Never saw it. How come you know so much about it? Are you a Hitchcock freak?"

"That's not exactly how I'd describe myself. I'm a great admirer of Hitchcock movies, yes. The earlier ones particularly."

"Sounds like an odd obsession for an accountant."

"Oh? I've known accountants who were experts on

Japanese porcelain. Anyway, I lied to you earlier. I'm not an accountant."

Honor's eyes gleamed in triumph.

"I knew it!" she said. "I said to myself 'No man who sounds like Jeremy Irons could be an accountant.' So what do you do?"

"I'm a writer."

"Oh."

If anything this latest revelation seemed to depress her more than his earlier claim to be an accountant.

"If you're after the same story I'm chasing, I'll kill you," she said without much conviction.

"Ah, I thought so. You're not dodging some admirer. You're pursuing a lead and you want me as camouflage. If they think you're innocently on a trip with your fiancé, they won't suspect you're after them."

"Them! There isn't any 'them.' There's one story, one person ... right on this train. And it's going to blow my audience right through the walls of their living-rooms when I break it on "Hot Flashes"."

Matthew waved to the waiter, then turned back to Honor and smiled.

"You seem to have a very sadistic attitude towards your audience. Anyway, there's no need to worry about me. I'm not that kind of writer. I deal strictly in unreality, and I have no ambition to blow an audience through any kind of walls."

Pete approached the table with his usual geniality.

"A drink for the lady?"

"A drink and then some food. Can I get a dry martini, a steak medium rare, and a salad with vinaigrette?"

Pete nodded, removed Teresa's used dishes, and reset

the place for Honor before going off to the kitchen.

"So what kind of writer are you?" Honor continued after Pete had gone. "And what do you want to do to an audience if not blow them through the walls?"

Matthew explained about his commission to write the script for a remake of *The Lady Vanishes* and even gave her a brief synopsis of the plot.

"Hmmmm," said Honor when he had finished. "I suppose it might work with the right cast, but it's a tad old-fashioned, don't you think?"

"So was *Murder on the Orient Express*, but that did all right at the box office."

Pete arrived at this point with Honor's martini, and Matthew took the opportunity to order a snifter of Grand Marnier.

"I'm sorry about the way I behaved earlier," said Honor, after she had taken a sip of her drink. "Back in the compartment, I mean."

"Don't worry about it. I was probably being pompous and obnoxious."

"You were, but that's not the point. The point is I overreacted. Anyway it's absolutely vital that this person I'm tracking shouldn't think I'm on to anything. So if you wouldn't mind going on with ... well ... you know..."

Another yawn contorted Matthew's face. He couldn't remember feeling this tired in a long time.

"Please excuse me. I must be suffering more from jet lag than I usually do. Yes, of course I don't mind pretending to be your fiancé."

Honor's steak and salad were placed on the table along with Matthew's liqueur. Matthew picked up his glass and held it up to the light, admiring the rich dark amber colour, then he let a trickle of it roll down his tongue. It felt like sweet fire in his mouth and down his throat.

"It's been very boring hiding in the other couchette," Honor said, slicing into her steak. "Besides, I left my case in your compartment."

"No problem. As soon as you've finished dinner just come along."

Impulsively, Honor reached out and grasped his hand.

"You're a nice guy, Matthew," she said.

Matthew finished his drink and rose to go. As he did so, he staggered a little. The train wasn't to blame this time; it was riding smoothly on the tracks.

"Oops," he said. "Must have drunk more than I thought. I feel quite woozy. Not to worry; I'll make it. See you later."

"I hope you're not suffering from concussion."

"Who, me? No, I'll be fine."

She watched as he made his way unsteadily out of the dining car and decided he must have had a good bit of wine before she arrived at the table. In about twenty minutes, she had finished her steak and salad, swallowed a couple of cups of decaf, and settled her bill. Then she set off after Matthew.

On her way through the observation lounge, she noticed about halfway along on her left a staircase down to the lower level. On an impulse, she decided to investigate what lay below. Descending, she found herself in the bar area, which had tables on both sides and a counter at the far end. There were half a dozen people sitting around talking and drinking, and at the back in a small confined space, a group of smokers huddled miserably in one of the few areas on the train, apart from the private compartments, where their anti-social behaviour was tolerated. The door at the rear of the smoking section led to the lower level of the first-class coach.

Again, curiosity prompted her to go through that door, and as she approached it she noticed a man sitting there in a dark suit, white shirt, and striped tie. He gave her a hard stare. It wasn't a sexually appraising look, she thought; it was more as though she were being checked out against a mental card-file. If that was his intention, she must have passed his scrutiny because she went on through the door without any challenge and entered the lower corridor. What she had expected to find there, she didn't quite know, but it was disappointingly similar to the upper corridor: a row of five deluxe bedroom compartments to her right; a row of five windows looking out onto the rushing darkness of the Missouri countryside to her left.

The blinds of the first compartment were drawn so she couldn't see inside. In the second compartment, a black-bearded man with intense eyes was reading a magazine. She had no trouble identifying him as Vartan Kadourian, the self-help guru, and moved swiftly past before he could look up and see her. In the third compartment was a young woman with glossy dark hair and the face of an aristocratic gypsy. The next compartment was empty except for a suitcase and a copy of the *Sports Illustrated* Swimsuit Edition. The last compartment's blinds were also drawn, but she could hear from inside the sound of two voices: one was a man's with what sounded like a New Jersey accent; the other was the unmistakable voice of Glamora. Honor allowed a smile of gratification to hover on her lips before passing on. She had heard enough to know that Glamora had the man, whoever he was, wound tightly around her little finger.

After Glamora's compartment came the staircase to the upper level, and beyond that the less-expensive first-class accommodations, similar to the one she had upstairs. In this part of the coach, there were five compartments on each side of the corridor. As she made her way idly towards the door at the back of the train, the door of one of the compartments slid open and a woman of about thirty-five in a plain brown dress came out and moved off in the direction Honor had just come from. Honor barely looked at her before turning her attention to the view out of the train's rear door. But since all she could see was a few yards of retreating tracks lit by the train's safety light, she didn't linger long over it.

She retraced her steps to the staircase and began to climb. Perhaps part of the reason for this whole detour, she pondered, was to delay actually going to Matthew's room. Her feelings were confused, to say the least. Certainly, he was an attractive man, though rather older than those she was usually drawn to, but on the other hand it was questionable whether there was much point in sleeping with someone she might never see again after they reached Los Angeles. On the whole, she wasn't a promiscuous person, and if past experience was anything to judge by, a casual sexual encounter would only leave her feeling depressed and annoyed with herself.

Still grappling with this dilemma, she reached the top of the stairs, passed Scats, who was fiddling with something at his work station, and turned down the corridor towards Matthew's compartment. There was the woman in the brown dress again, just disappearing into the furthest compartment.

So she wasn't the only one wandering into other people's bedrooms. Perhaps being on a train was like being on a cruise, which from her experience meant a continual game of musical beds. She took a careful glance up and down the corridor. Scats was out of sight around the bend in the corridor to her left, and no-one was approaching from the observation car on her right. She tapped at the door of Room B and waited. There was no sound. She tapped again and whispered "Matthew?" Then she put her ear to the door. There were sounds now all right: muffled, prolonged snores, interrupted by the occasional sudden snort. She tugged at the door and it slid open. "At least he hasn't locked me out," she thought bitterly.

Inside, she found Matthew, fully clothed except for his jacket and shoes, sprawled out on the lower bunk, sunk into what was clearly a profound sleep.

"Matthew, damn it!" she hissed through her clenched teeth and shook him by the shoulder.

He moaned and rolled away from her but didn't progress one inch towards wakefulness.

"MATTHEW!" she whispered loudly, her lips close to his ear.

"Another first-class entertainment," he mumbled. "Mr. Prior has done it again..."

Then he flung out one arm, almost catching Honor across the head, and relapsed once more into a kind of protracted droning.

She was furious. She grabbed up her overnight bag and slammed out of the compartment, letting the door crash behind her.

"Silly fool," she muttered to herself. "I wouldn't be

engaged to him if he was the last man on earth."

Then she remembered him singing "If you were the only girl in the world" and couldn't restrain a snort of laughter. Scats raised his eyebrows as she passed him, and watched her disappear, still laughing, down the rear corridor towards her own room.

"Now, what goes on with them two?" he asked the coffee machine, which of course had no opinion on the matter at all.

Four
Sleepless in Kansas City

1

"We should be in Kansas City soon."

The two men in Room E on the upper level had still not retired for the evening. Sven Sanchez was sitting on the lower bunk with a sketch pad intently recording a face he had seen earlier that evening. Eddie Tsubouchi was sitting cross-legged in the single armchair opposite, reading Will Eisner's *Comics and Sequential Art*.

"What're you drawing, Sven?" he asked, glancing up from the page.

Sven put down his pencil, stroked his black moustache, and said: "Just some guy I saw in the dining car. I thought his face might do for a character in the new *Warrior Lords*."

"You do that, huh? Take models from life, I mean."

"You don't?"

"Nah! It cramps my style. I like to let them swim up from the deepest, darkest, nastiest depths of my subconscious."

"You can say that again. Going by the last *Spirit Shifter* I saw, if I had a kid I wouldn't let him read it. Talk about sick and perverted!"

He said this with a regretful chuckle to let his companion know that though he was serious it shouldn't poison their friendship. Eddie snorted in response. He thought of himself as being on the cutting edge of comic book art, way beyond such current favourites as *X-Men*. His influences weren't so much the old DC Comics as the Japanese *manga* and such artists as Sato and Tezuka.

"If you had a kid," Eddie retorted, "he'd be too much of a geek to appreciate my stuff."

Sven sighed.

"Geek or not, I kinda wish I had one."

Eddie had learned in the last few days that Sven had felt disconnected all his life. With a father who was a Mexican bandleader and a mother who was a Swedish physiotherapist, he hadn't known which bubble in America's melting pot he belonged to. So he had grown up an outsider and a loner. But Eddie's father, who was about Sven's age, had been born in an internment camp for Japanese-Americans during the Second World War, so if alienation was the issue, his old man had it in spades. Still, old Junji Tsubouchi at least had the reinforcement of a cohesive ethnic group. He'd married a Japanese girl and Eddie and his brother and sister had been brought up to be proud of their heritage. Poor Sven didn't know whether to eat tacos or Swedish meatballs.

"It's not too late, is it? Lots of guys get married at your age and start families. Get one of those mail-order brides from the Philippines."

Sven looked at him reproachfully.

"That was tasteless," he said. "What if I said I was going to find me a nice geisha? Anyway, I've been married. Twice. And I got dumped twice. It doesn't exactly encourage you to try again."

"You shouldn't go for those tall blondes with the long legs. You oughta know by now that's a recipe for disaster. They're towering over you all the time, so naturally they get the idea they're the boss. Then you try to assert yourself and it's: 'I'm outta here, baby.'"

"So you're saying I should marry a midget? What about you? You're no Wilt Chamberlain."

"And I don't go out with no girls who look like Wilt Chamberlain. I've got this Korean chick who comes just up to my shoulder. Neat and petite."

Sven smirked.

"I bet your family love that. I know how you Japanese feel about the Koreans. Like Mexicans feel about the Indians in Chiapas."

"OK. So my folks are old-fashioned that way, but they're trying. We all went to a Vietnamese restaurant the other day."

"Neutral territory."

"Yeah. They thought she was sweet — for a Korean. Anyway back to you and the blondes. How about the woman from the TV show, the one we saw in the restaurant?"

"Not tall enough," Sven said wryly.

"OK. How about Glamora — the tallest blonde in the entire hemisphere. Or she was until she dyed her hair bright red. Now there's a natural for a character in *Warrior Lords*. Or why not start a new comic called *Superbitch*?"

Sven laughed, but sadly and unwillingly. To him, super-bitches were not a matter for jest.

"I don't think so, Eddie. It'll take more than that to pull my nuts out of the fire."

Eddie stuck a marker in his book and put it on the fold-down table by the window.

"Well, I think it's time I turned in; I don't know about you..."

The rhythm of the train began to change at that moment. There was less sway and the regular clatter of the wheels on the track grew slower.

"We must be getting close to Kansas City," said Sven. "Why don't we wait till the train stops? I hate trying to undress in a moving train. It always waits till you've got one leg out of your pants to give a sudden lurch and throw you on your ass."

"You've got a point there. Yeah, let's wait. I'm in no hurry."

So they sat and gazed companionably out of the window as the lights of the city grew brighter on the dark horizon.

2

Next door, in Room D, Anderson Nash was snoring. He lay sprawled on his back, head lying at an angle half off the pillow, pyjama top dragged up to reveal some inches of lean but hairy abdomen. His son, Buzzy, wide awake, stared down at him from the upper bunk. "Wow, grown-ups sure look gross when they're sleeping ... and all that honking and snorting! Not too cool," he thought. He hadn't often seen his father asleep before and it was hardly an appealing sight. Before the snoring started, he had been trying to read one of his X-Men comics by the beam of a flashlight, a practice that both his mother and father had forbidden on the ridiculous grounds that it would ruin his eyes. No way — his eyes were like lasers, penetrating even the strongest defences thrown up by evil-doers. After all, was he not Scopeman, Seer of the Galaxies?

On the whole, Buzzy was glad to be with his dad on the train. So far the trip had been a satisfying one for both of them, except — in Buzzy's case — for the lack of pizza in the dining car. But watching the countryside flying past while they commented to one another about the various sights had been what Buzzy's child therapist would have called "a positive bonding experience." Even the sight of his father's ungainly slumber didn't negate that.

For Buzzy, sleep seemed far away. To be truthful, he wouldn't have welcomed it if it tried to sneak up on him. He was afraid he would miss something, and he didn't just mean the rushing panorama beyond the train windows, which in any case was obscured now by darkness. No, he didn't want to neglect the possibility that something might be happening on the train itself. Everyone knew that Buzzy was nosy. Even his best friend at school, Wingy (Wingfield Lathrop Pendleton III), had been known to call him Snoopy occasionally. And he wasn't suggesting a resemblance to Charlie Brown's dog. However, Buzzy preferred to think of his curiosity as a highly developed investigative talent.

Anyway, lying in his bunk reading *X-Men* and listening to his father snore suddenly seemed unbearably tame. It would be far more interesting to explore the sleeping train and see what people got up to on an Amtrak express in the middle of the night.

It was tricky getting down the ladder from the top bunk

without making a lot of noise. Then he had to slide into his clothes in the semi-darkness. At one point, as he hopped about trying to pull on his sneakers, the train's lurching almost made him lose his balance and bump into the lower bunk. But finally he was ready. He cautiously edged open the door of the compartment and squeezed out into the corridor. A reassuring snore came from his father as he clicked the door shut. Turning first to the right, he moved towards the back of the car.

The attendant, Scats, was sitting by his counter with its coffee machine at the top of the stairs, reading a copy of the *National Enquirer*. He looked up and grinned when he saw Buzzy.

"Hey, there. Want some coffee?"

"No, thanks," said Buzzy seriously. "It'll keep me awake."

Scats gave him a quizzical glance.

"Ri-i-ight," he said. "We wouldn't want that, would we? Not in the middle of the night."

"So why aren't you asleep?"

"Well, partly it's 'cos I'm on duty, but mainly it's 'cos my back's givin' me the miseries. So what's doin' with you?"

"Oh, nothin'. My pop's snoring and I just thought I'd take a walk and see out the back of the train."

"Well, don't go openin' that door back there or you'll find yourself shakin' hands with Casey Jones."

Buzzy promised to be careful and moved on down the other corridor. He walked slowly and listened hard but there were no screams or gunshots, though he did hear someone talking in his sleep. When he reached the rear door of the train, he looked out and could see by the train's tail lights the twin rails of the track endlessly retreating. He stood there for some moments, but soon the spectacle palled and he returned to where Scats was sitting.

"See anything interestin'?" asked Scats, turning a page of the tabloid and shaking it flat again.

"Nah. Just like the track and stuff. I'm gonna head up the other way."

"OK. Take care now."

Buzzy gave Scats the high five, and moved back along the corridor in his own section of the car. He walked past his compartment and on towards the observation lounge in the next coach. As he entered it, he noticed that there was a dark-suited man sitting very close to the door. He wore a white shirt and a striped tie, and his suit-jacket had a tell-tale bulge under the left shoulder. Buzzy had been in Washington often enough to have seen Presidential bodyguards on ceremonial occasions with the same bulges and, on some rarer occasions, he had seen his father's jacket pulled out of shape in the same way. The man noticed him looking and stared back icily.

"You packin' a gun?" asked Buzzy.

"Get lost, kid," the man said in a pained voice. "What were you doing in there, anyway?" he continued, jerking his head towards the first-class sleeper. "No visitors allowed past this point."

"I'm not a visitor," Buzzy answered indignantly. "I'm with my dad."

"Who's he?"

"Anderson Nash."

"Oh, Nash's kid," the man said. "I guess you're OK. But go on back to your compartment. You shouldn't be wandering all over the train."

Buzzy had half a mind to ignore the order, but something about the cold, blank determination in the man's face made him change his mind.

"OK," he said, "I'm goin'. But it's just 'cause I've seen enough."

In fact, there wasn't much more to see in the observation car except a few nerdy-looking middle-aged guys, a couple of them asleep in the seats and some others playing cards. And, anyway, he suddenly did feel quite tired. He decided he would leave exploring the rest of the train till the next day.

On the way back, just as he entered the rear car and drew level with the door of the first compartment, he thought he heard something. Pausing, he listened. There was a thud, a muffled gurgle, another thud, then a dragging sound. This was followed by a rapid whisper, but he could make out no words. At that moment, the train lurched again, throwing him against the door. There was a sudden silence beyond it, and before anyone could open it and ask what the hell he was doing, Buzzy scurried on to his own compartment and scrambled inside as fast as he could.

"Buzzy?"

His father had opened one eye and was staring at him.

"Oh, hi, Dad."

"What's going on?" asked Anderson Nash, flicking on the light.

"Nothin'. I just took a walk."

Nash squinted at his watch.

"It's past one o'clock in the morning!"

Buzzy chewed on one of his nails and studied his

father's expression. He was irritated, he figured, but not really mad.

"Dad, if you heard somebody being murdered, what would you do?"

"Heard? What d'you mean, heard?"

"Like if you were outside the door and you heard some sounds like somebody being murdered inside."

Nash had a sinking feeling that Buzzy had inadvertently overheard not a murder but an encounter of another sort.

"Son," he said heavily, "just because you hear some moaning and bumping around doesn't mean a murder is taking place. I mean — it's the middle of the night and folks are in their bedrooms. You're old enough to know what goes on in folks' bedrooms."

Buzzy thought for a minute.

"Oh, that," he said tolerantly. "Well, I guess it could have been. But it sounded more like a murder to me."

"Your imagination will land you in trouble one of these days. Now go to bed, for Pete's sake. And no more reading comic books."

Buzzy changed back into his pyjamas and climbed back up the ladder. He lay on the bunk with his hands behind his head, listening to his father's breathing gradually become more rhythmical and segue eventually into snores.

"I shoulda brought some ear plugs," he muttered to himself before turning off the light. "And anyway I still think it was murder."

He was still awake when the train pulled into the station in Kansas City, and thinking this might offer some interesting shots for his travel video, he reached down and grabbed his camcorder from the little table by the window.

There was hardly anyone on the platform, which was not surprising at 1:15 in the morning, and those few who were there seemed to be meeting arriving passengers. Undeterred, Buzzy raised the viewfinder to his eye and pressed the record button.

3

They had started an hour late, of course, Aubretia thought, but still they must be getting to Kansas City soon. In about half an hour, in fact, if the train hadn't lost more time en route. She looked again at the timetable and saw that they were scheduled to spend twenty minutes in the station before departure, and then once they had left Kansas City, as she had told that girl who had shared their table at dinner, there would be no further stops until Caliente — a thousand miles away. According to the route map, though, the train did at one point pass between Colorado Springs and Pueblo, which were only fifty miles apart, so if there was an emergency of any kind, it shouldn't be difficult to get help from one of those places.

To tell the truth, all this consulting of timetables and maps was a reflection of her uneasiness about the consequences to Natalie of any unforeseen complications in her pregnancy at a time when they were far from any first-rate medical facilities. Maybe it had been a mistake to agree to this trip in the first place. She'd never forgive herself if anything happened to the baby. It didn't bear thinking about.

"What's all this doom and gloom?" she asked herself testily. "Your problem, old girl, is that you're too damned sober. That's when you always start thinking like this — thinking about that other baby — and about poor little Christopher."

The tears were already trickling down her face again as she reached into the side-pocket of her suitcase and pulled out a bottle of Jack Daniels. She unscrewed the cap, lifted the bottle, and tilted it into her mouth. A couple of gulps and she'd be as good as new. Whatever the hell that meant. Had she ever been new? At the moment, she felt older than the pyramids ... older than the goddam Rockies. Thirty-nine and holding. But holding what? That's what she needed all right: a little warm bundle with tiny fists and tiny screwed-up eyes to hold and hold and hold.

Well, she was going to get it. Those damned doctors had screwed things up last time. Talking of damned doctors, that one in the bar tonight was a sonofabitch if she'd ever met one. But this time no damned doctor was going to get in her way. Forget that whole business in Eastern Europe. This time it was Aubretia's turn to win.

She took another gulp of bourbon as she heard the tempo of the wheels begin to slacken.

"I'm goin' to Kansas City,' she sang. "Kansas City here I come."

If she wasn't careful she would be really smashed by the time she met Natalie. She looked at the bottle, picked up the cap to screw it back on, and then stopped. What the hell! She was always better value with a few drinks under her belt. She took another slug and smiled dimly out at the Missouri moon, which was, after all, almost as high tonight as she was.

4

"OK, Aldo! Take it easy!"

Aldo was perspiring with the effort not to make some clumsy and utterly self-defeating physical attack on Glamora. He was stretched out on her bunk in his under-shorts, while she, still wearing the dark-blue cobweb dress, massaged his chest.

"You've got to relax, slugger, otherwise nothing's goin' to work. Performance anxiety really kills the libido."

"The which?"

"The libido. You mean you've never read Freud?"

"Give me a break, Vikki. All I read is the sports news."

Glamora smiled soothingly.

"Well, you should read Freud. It's wild. You can learn all about your psycho-sexual development. Like, for instance, I bet you don't know whether you're oral, anal, or phallic."

"Listen, I've never gone for that kind of stuff. And anybody who says I did is a liar."

He flinched as she dug her fingers deeper into his pecs.

"Whatsa matter, big guy? Am I hurting you?"

"Hurting me? Are you kidding? I just wasn't expecting you to do that."

Glamora looked down at him. He really was, she reflected, a good-looking guy. That kind of half-boyish, half-brutish Mediterranean hunk that really pushed her buttons. The sulky, almost pouting mouth was offset by the deeply cleft chin and the slightly flattened nose. The hazel eyes with their thick black lashes were counterbalanced by the scar that bisected one of his eyebrows. And as for the body ...

well, it would certainly do. With abs like that, he'd be the perfect TV pitchman for her exercise tapes. But there were a couple of other ways he could be useful too. Setting aside his sexual potential, he looked as if he might have had, at one time, some experience as an enforcer for the mob. That made him particularly interesting to her, considering the action she was contemplating.

Running the tips of her scarlet nails down his hairy chest, she leaned closer to him, her mouth only inches from his. His eyes grew wider as they looked up into hers, and he began to breathe faster. He reached up with his arms to pull her body closer, but she shook her head.

"Uh-uh. Not yet, lover. Remember, we're trying to get you to relax."

"This ain't no way to do it, Vikki," he moaned. "I'm freakin' out here!"

"Here, put your hands behind your back," she ordered.

"What the—"

"Just do it."

Reluctantly he complied, only to find his wrists swiftly bound together with a silk scarf.

"Hey, come on, Vikki!" he protested.

"It'll help, I promise. Now, close your eyes," she said softly. "Go on, close 'em."

He let his eyelids fall, the thick lashes almost brushing his cheek.

"Now take a deep breath, and let it out very slowly. Good! Now another one. That's it. And another. Let your body go, as if it was sinkin' into the bunk. Keep breathin' those deep breaths. Feel all your muscles going slack. There now, doesn't that feel better? Just like you're floatin'."

It did feel better, except for not being able to use his hands. All the tension seemed to be draining out of his limbs, and a wonderful warmth spread through his veins. He felt open and attuned.

"We could be so much better friends, Aldo," Glamora breathed, "if only I could be sure."

"Sure?" he mumbled like someone talking in his sleep. "Sure about what?"

"Sure that you'd be there for me when I need you."

This was not unfamiliar territory to him. He had heard those words from Tanya and other women before her. Usually it meant not getting pissed off when they were acting cranky because of their monthlies.

"'Course I will," he purred. "There for you? Sure—"

"Because I need your strength, slugger. I'd like to feel that if somebody or something was threatenin' me, you'd deal with it."

"Deal with it? No prob, Vikki—"

"Even if it got to be kind of a life-or-death thing."

"Mmmmm ... ri-i-ight. Life or ... WHAT!"

His eyes snapped open and he half raised his body off the bunk.

"Death!" she said, shoving him back. "You heard me. Death!"

"What the f- ... What the hell you talkin' about, Vikki?"

All the springs inside his body that had been luxuriously uncoiling suddenly contracted.

"I'm talkin' about protectin' me, you clunk. Whatsa matter? You're gonna chicken out when somebody tries to give me a hard time?"

"No, but ... hey, I'm no hit-man. You're talkin' like you

want me to blow somebody away."

"Did I say that?"

"You said 'life and death.'"

Glamora stood up, hands on her hips, glaring down at him contemptuously.

"OK, Mr. Toughnuts. I see we don't have as much in common as I thought."

The train was slowing down at that moment and they could hear the screech of brakes being applied. Lights began to flow past the window.

"So what I'd like you to do is get the hell out of my compartment. Go on, get up and get out. Now!"

She ripped the scarf loose from his wrists, and he leapt to his feet, seeing that she was suddenly as fierce as a rabid vixen. Before he had time to react, she had grabbed up his clothes, yanked open the door, and thrown them out, pushing him out after them. The door banged shut behind him and he was left in his under-shorts in the corridor, scrambling to pick up his pants and shirt, as the train slid majestically into Kansas City station, where a handful of interested spectators on the platform witnessed his predicament. Suddenly there were footsteps coming down the stairs from the upper level and the sound of a voice.

"Goddam broads!" he wailed in a sweat of embarrassment, and darted into the security of his own compartment before whoever was coming downstairs could see him.

5

Matthew couldn't stay awake long enough to get his clothes off. He took off his jacket and shoes and collapsed on the lower bunk. The rocking motion of the train may have had something to do with it, but on the other hand there was something about the absoluteness of his surrender to unconsciousness, like falling limply off a cliff into a black chasm, that seemed not quite natural. Or so he fuzzily thought when he woke up a couple of hours later to realize that the train had stopped.

Groggily, he stumbled over to the window and peered through a gap in the curtains. Since he was on the upper level of the car, he had an excellent view of the platform and station buildings, on one of which he could see the words "Kansas City." He had studied the Amtrak timetable and its passenger system map closely enough to know that this was Kansas City, Missouri, and not Kansas City, Kansas, which lay just across the border. Another of those confusing American things, he grumbled mentally, like having to pronounce Boise, Idaho, "Boy-zee" instead of "Bwahs."

As he watched in his foggy state of half-consciousness, he saw a large troop of boy scouts being marched onto the platform from the ticket office and marshalled outside the train by a couple of scout leaders. They were of all ages from about eleven to seventeen and of all shapes from short and fat to tall and scrawny. Matthew shuddered as he contemplated the train being overrun by them. Robert Baden-Powell had a lot to answer for.

Once the boy scouts had been safely loaded aboard, the

platform remained empty for some minutes, except for Scats and another attendant from the train, talking and smoking. Beyond them on the far side of the station was an ill-lit parking lot fenced off from the platform by a high chain-link barricade. Matthew wondered vaguely if it was the same parking lot where the Kansas City Massacre took place back in the thirties, when the would-be rescuers of the bank robber Frank Nash killed four lawmen and Nash himself in a spray of machine-gun bullets.

He could see, lurking dimly in the shadowy area between the parked cars, a teenage male in cutoff jeans and a baseball jacket. Waiting to meet somebody from the train, Matthew supposed. Then, looking at his watch and realizing it was after two in the morning, he wondered if his purpose might not be more sinister. After all, it looked as if everyone who might be getting off the train had already done so.

Five more minutes went by and the train showed no sign of moving. Finally someone else appeared in the parking lot, a man in the uniform of some kind of railway functionary. The boy greeted him and they climbed into a car and drove away. "So much for my sinister imaginings," Matthew thought. "Just a boy meeting his father from work." As he watched, Matthew's eyelids began to feel heavier and heavier. "I didn't drink that much, I know I didn't," he said to himself resentfully. "So why am I feeling as if I'd been whacked over the head with a sandbag?"

Babbling internally in this fashion, Matthew returned to his bunk just as the train gave a warning shudder and began slowly to move out of Kansas City station. The last thought he had before he drifted off again was, "Mustn't be late for breakfast with Teresa."

Five

The Morning Run

1

The sun was up and shining on the Kansas plains long before Matthew struggled awake the next morning. In fact, by the time he had showered (an operation that was distinctly taxing in the confines of the tiny bathroom cubicle), shaved, dressed, and made his way to the dining car for breakfast, the train was already crossing the border between Kansas and Colorado. If he had been aware of the fact at the time, it would have been hard to restrain him from quoting his favourite line from *The Wizard of Oz*: "Toto, I don't think we're in Kansas any more." As it was, he seated himself in silence and began to study the menu.

It was just after eight-thirty, so he wasn't altogether surprised that Teresa Shaughnessy was not already in the dining car. She had said she was an early riser, but she might have decided to stretch her legs by walking the length of the train and back. In any case, he had no premonition that anything was wrong. Minutes after he sat down, he was joined, not by Teresa, but by Honor.

"Good morning, darling," she said in her throaty drawl. She kissed him on the forehead. "How's your poor head this morning?"

Matthew looked up startled as she sat opposite him.

"Fuzzy. And where did you get to last night?" he said.

"Why would you care?" she answered, fixing him with a look of mild animosity. "You obviously found sleep too attractive to postpone until I showed up. I got to your compartment about forty minutes after you left the dining car and you were already zonked out."

"You should have woken me up."

"Don't think I didn't try. I yelled at you and shook you, but all you did was mutter something in your sleep about first-class entertainment. God knows, I wasn't even getting third-class entertainment."

Matthew frowned.

"You really couldn't wake me?"

"No, you were absolutely comatose. As if you'd been drugged."

"That's what I thought," he said, gnawing nervously at his lower lip. "I've never slept like that before, and — Lord! — when I woke up, it was as if I was still fighting my way through layers of cotton wool."

Pete the waiter came by at that point to take their breakfast orders and pour some coffee. When he had gone, Honor looked at Matthew with a more tolerant expression.

"I hardly think you would have been drugged," she said. "It was probably a reaction to your accident in Chicago. You did get a nasty whack on the head, and it may have caused a mild concussion. And then you probably had too much to drink. Besides, why would anyone want to drug you?"

He took a slow, thoughtful swallow of coffee. Simultaneously the train lurched and coffee slopped over the edge of the cup onto the tablecloth.

"I don't know why," he said as he dabbed at the spill with his napkin, "but I think I know how."

He then proceeded to give Honor an account of the incident at dinner before she arrived, when the woman in the brown dress had lost her balance and bumped against him, spilling coffee on the tablecloth.

"Moreover," he said. "She fussed about with the cups, mine and Teresa's, moving them about and dabbing at things with her handkerchief. She could have had some kind of soporific drug hidden in her handkerchief, possibly in the form of pills, and dropped some into our coffee cups as we were distracted by the waiter."

"But didn't he take the cups away and give you new ones?"

"No, he just refilled the cups we had. I wonder if he noticed anything in them."

Pete was back with their breakfast plates a few moments later and Matthew put the question to him.

"I did notice something," he said immediately. "Little white tablets. I thought they must be artificial sweetener — Equal or something like that."

"Were they in both cups?"

"Yup, I think so."

"So you see," said Matthew to Honor, "I could have been drugged and so could Teresa. She was starting to yawn last night at about the same time I did."

"Or the little white tablets could have been just sweetener, and both of you could have been yawning because you were tired. I don't see the point in creating a mystery about it."

Matthew shook his head impatiently.

"Why would a perfect stranger drop sweetener into our

coffees? I tell you, it had to be something else, and judging by how I felt last night, it must have been a sleeping pill of some kind. It also explains why Teresa's late. She told me she was an early riser, but that she would meet me at eight-thirty — as a sort of concession to my slothfulness. It's nearly nine o'clock now."

Honor stabbed a piece of pineapple on her breakfast fruit plate and raised it to her mouth. After chewing it thoughtfully for a moment, she said: "Maybe she forgot she was having breakfast with you. Maybe she got up early, had breakfast and went back to her compartment."

"Possibly. In any case, that's exactly what I'm going to find out as soon as I've finished. I'm going to go to her compartment and knock her up."

"Matthew!!" Honor said, scandalized.

"Oh, sorry. Another one of those British/U.S. confusions. When we say 'knock someone up,' we mean wake someone. Surely you don't think I have a secret passion for middle-aged Irish nannies."

"I don't know what to think about you sometimes," Honor grumbled. "You certainly don't seem very interested in my problems. You haven't asked me a thing about this story I'm working on."

"Would you tell me if I did?"

"No."

"Well, there you are then. I'm sharing my mystery with you and you won't even give me a hint about yours."

Honor gave him an agonized look.

"I ca-a-an't, Matthew. I might be totally wrong about it and then I'd look like a total fool."

"Oh, all right," he said. "But just to show how generous

I am, I'm going to let you come with me when I start to explore the mystery of the missing nanny."

Her lips crinkled into a sour little smile.

"Oh, joy," she said.

As they continued with breakfast, the Colorado plains — not really distinguishable from the Kansas variety — flowed uneventfully past the train windows. The sun beat down starkly on scrubby earth and dried-up creeks and the occasional small town with its quota of feed-mills, truck dealerships, and fast-food restaurants. Anything in the way of spectacle would have to wait until they reached the western part of the state. Meanwhile a party of boy scouts straggled into the dining room. They looked as if they had slept in their uniforms and boycotted the shower facilities. Several of them had hair that had been disarranged by their pillows and consequently stuck out at odd angles. Subdued and self-conscious, they crowded around two tables at the end nearest the observation car and began a nudging, whispering consultation about the menu.

"That's a relief," said Matthew. "I didn't dream them anyway."

"Dream who?"

"The boy scouts. I saw them boarding in the middle of the night in Kansas City. A great gang of them. But I was so dazed I didn't know whether I was asleep or awake."

"I'm glad you didn't dream them, too. I'd be nervous if I thought you went around dreaming about boy scouts."

"I suppose that's an example of your soggy American wit," he said with an air of having settled a score.

"You bring out the juvenile side of me," sighed Honor. "I haven't had conversations like these since I was at

Evansville High. For the Lord's sake, let's go and investigate your mystery before we're both reduced to infantile drooling."

Suitably crushed, Matthew paid the bill and followed Honor out of the dining car. The observation lounge also had its complement of boy scouts, watching the scenery go by, arguing, play-wrestling, or simply snoozing with their mouths open. Right by the door leading from the observation lounge to the first-class sleeper, a man in a dark suit, white shirt, and striped tie was sitting, but Honor noted that though he was dressed almost identically to the man she had seen last night on her wanderings, he was clearly someone else. Come to think of it, the one last night who had stared at her so deliberately had been on the lower level, at the back of the bar-lounge. Still, it was odd that there should be these clone-like characters, apparently guarding access to the first-class coach.

"Teresa's in Room A," Matthew said just after they had entered the corridor where the deluxe bedrooms were.

"Go ahead and knock. She's probably overslept."

Matthew tapped at the door of the compartment. When there was no answer, he rapped on it loudly.

"Hello? Teresa? What happened to our breakfast date?"

There was no answer. Matthew tugged at the door handle and the door slid open. The compartment was empty, the bunks had been returned to the daytime position, and there wasn't a sign that Teresa Shaughnessy had ever been there.

"That's damned odd," Matthew began, then spotting Scats Madison coming along the corridor called to him: "Scats! Do you know what happened to Miss Shaughnessy?"

Scats lumbered up to them with his usual cheerful smile.

"Sure do," he said. "She got off the train in Kansas City."

Matthew stared at him disbelievingly.

"She can't have. She was supposed to have breakfast with me at eight-thirty."

A suppressed snort of laughter from Honor made him turn and glower at her.

"Just listen to yourself," she said. "It sounds like breakfast with you would outweigh all other attractions. Perhaps she just got an urge to visit Kansas City. People are allowed to make stopovers on this trip, you know."

"But she was going straight through to L.A. She said so."

Scats coughed.

"Excuse me, Mr. Prior, sir. The other lady said Miss Shaughnessy was getting a little train-sick, and she was going to spend the night in a bed that didn't shake all the time."

"The other lady?"

"The one who helped her off the train. She was a lady from the back of the car. They seemed to know each other."

Matthew turned to Honor with a look of perplexity. She raised her eyebrows and shrugged.

"Sounds plausible to me," she said.

It sounded plausible all right but Matthew wasn't convinced. After all, he had heard Teresa say that her employer was meeting her at the station in L.A. She didn't seem like the sort to risk inconveniencing a man of Golovyov's status because of a little train-sickness.

"How did she seem?" he asked Scats.

Scats scratched the back of his neck and wrinkled his

forehead.

"Well ... she did look kinda poorly. The other lady had to help her down the steps, and she had some kind of scarf wrapped around her chin."

"Did she say anything?"

"Nope. The other lady did all the talking."

Honor yawned.

"I must say it sounds all above board, darling. She felt ill and her friend helped her off the train."

"What did this friend look like?" Matthew persisted.

"Ordinary. Could have been late twenties early thirties. Had on a kind of greeny-brown coat over a brown dress."

Matthew snapped his fingers.

"There!" he said. "I bet it was the same woman. The one who made me spill my coffee. She was wearing a brown dress. Do you know her name, Scats?"

Scats paused and thought for a moment.

"It was a foreign sort of name. Van Hoven or something like that. I saw it on her ticket but I didn't know how to say it."

"And was her ticket to Kansas City?"

"No," Scats was sure about that. "She was booked through to L.A. as well."

"Well, I'm damned if I don't think that's very odd behaviour. Two perfect strangers going to L.A. suddenly decide to get off the train at Kansas City."

"Perfect strangers? Scats just said they seemed to know one another."

Matthew was silenced for a moment, not just because of Honor's remark but because he had suddenly remembered another detail of that incident in the dining car. When the woman had collided with him and then started trying to mop up the coffee, Teresa had said something like "Dizzy again, Miss Van Hoven" or Von Haven … or whatever the name was. Then she had told him something about this same woman stumbling against her in the Metropolitan Lounge in Chicago, and had made it clear that she found the woman intrusive and inquisitive. It hardly seemed likely that she would have turned to her for help when she was feeling unwell. He had been in the next compartment. Why hadn't she called on him? Or perhaps she had, and he hadn't heard her because he was sunk into a drugged sleep.

"The more I think about this, the less I like it," he said. "I'm going to see if anybody else along the corridor saw or heard anything."

Scats smiled and waved them both past.

"Go right, ahead, Mr. Prior. The folks is mostly back from breakfast now. Here, start with Room C next door to you. I know Miss Adams and her friend are in there."

So Matthew tapped gently on the door of Room C. It was the first interview in what was to be a long series that day, as the train carried them further from Kansas City and closer to the Rocky Mountains.

2

Looking at herself sternly in the mirror above the washbasin, Aubretia Adams resolved to put a strict limit on her intake of alcohol while Natalie and the unborn baby were in her charge. She had been quite befogged when the girl had joined the train last night, and she could scarcely have made a very good impression. As for her impression of Natalie? Well, that was just it, she remembered getting off the train to help her board, though in the end it was the attendant, Scats, who had lent his arm to her and supported her up the steps. It had been all Aubretia could do to get herself back on board. She couldn't remember much after that. There seemed to be a whole blanked-out period, followed by dim memories of undressing and getting into her bunk. Then she had woken up this morning with the usual Godzilla-sized hangover and found Natalie already up, freshly bathed, though looking rather wan.

"Hi, Auntie Aubretia," she said. "How are you this morning? Personally, I've never felt worse. I'm so tired of this pregnancy thing!"

Auntie Aubretia? She guessed she must have told Natalie to call her that last night. Anyway, she hated to hear it this morning. It made her feel like Margo in the last reel of *Lost Horizon.* Then all that youthful self-absorption on top of it: "How are you? Wait till I tell you how sick I am first."

"I'm doing as well as can be expected, dear, given my advancing years," she said caustically.

"Oh, you're not that old, Auntie. Why, I was surprised to see how young you looked!"

She'd obviously been expecting something that looked as if it had crawled out of the Valley of the Kings, Aubretia fumed. The girl didn't look all that good herself, if the truth were told.

Pregnancy had certainly wiped the bloom from her youth. Her ponytailed hair was lank and drawn back from a rather spotty forehead; her cheeks were puffier than they had been; she was wearing far too much make-up; what's more, she had the shape of a goose-neck squash.

"Thank you, dear," said Aubretia, attempting to inject a tinge of sweetness into her tone. "I think we're going to be great friends."

Natalie gave her a look damp with gratitude.

"My mother and father told me you were a good, generous person," she said, then suddenly winced with pain and grabbed at her back.

If there was one thing that brought out the best in Aubretia, it was seeing others in trouble. All her resentments about the girl's youth and self-centredness dwindled in the face of her suffering.

"My dear, are you all right?"

"It's just this pain in the lower part of my back. It's like being stabbed with a bayonet."

"Perhaps you'd better lie down. Here, stretch out on the long seat here and I'll sit over there in the single one. Let me get a blanket for you. There, I'll tuck it around your legs."

"Oh, don't look at my legs. They're so swollen."

While Aubretia was busying herself getting Natalie settled with a pillow, a blanket, and a copy of *Cosmopolitan*, there was a tentative rap at the door.

"Yes, who is it?" she called.

"It's Matthew Prior. I'm from the next compartment."

"Yes?"

"I wonder if I could trouble you for a moment. A friend of mine seems to have disappeared and I thought you might have seen something."

Aubretia slid the door open and beckoned Matthew and Honor inside.

"I can only spare a moment. My young friend here isn't feeling well and I want her to rest."

Matthew looked at the girl lying under the blanket. Her face was half turned to the wall as she read her magazine. She lifted a limp hand and waved at him.

"This is the friend you were meeting in Kansas City?"

"Yes, Natalie Lindenhoff. Poor child, she's not feeling quite herself. Well, you know how it is at this stage in a pregnancy. You never feel quite right."

Matthew did know. His wife, Henrietta, had been particularly afflicted both times. Honor, who didn't know, felt glad that she hadn't yet shared Natalie's experience.

"I'm sorry, and I'll make this as fast as I can. Did you happen to see two women get off together from this coach in Kansas City?"

"Two women? What were they like?"

"I think you spoke to one at dinner last night. She was sitting at my table and you asked her whether she was a nurse."

Aubretia nodded.

"The one with the Irish accent. Yes, I remember her."

"The other one was a sort of nondescript woman with rather messy hair, wearing a greenish coat and a brown dress."

There was a pause while Aubretia made a sincere attempt to remember whom she had seen last night on the platform, but all she could remember was Scats and Natalie. Everything else was shrouded in a Jack Daniels haze.

"No ... No, I'm sorry. I really don't remember seeing anyone."

"I think I did," said Natalie weakly from her prone position. "Was one of them wearing a funny hat shaped like a basin upside down and a pair of big heavy-rimmed glasses?"

She had an oddly indistinct voice, Matthew noted, and an accent that was a peculiar mixture of North American and Central European — the sort of sound Meryl Streep might produce if she were playing one of Chekhov's three sisters.

"I'm not sure about the hat," Matthew answered. "But certainly one of them — the Irish nanny — was wearing glasses like you describe."

"I'm sure about the hat," Honor said. "I saw her wearing it in the Metropolitan Lounge. I thought then I hadn't seen a hat like that since I went to parochial school."

Matthew turned to Natalie again.

"So you think you saw them?"

"I think so. There were two women in the station and one seemed to be helping the other. I don't remember much about the other one, though. They were both carrying similar bags, I noticed, and the one who wasn't wearing spectacles had a brown dress on and a sort of greeny-grey coat. They were going towards the taxi-stand."

"Did you notice anything else about them — or hear anything either of them said?"

Natalie seemed about to say something, then stopped.

"You hesitated?" Matthew said to her.

"Well, I'm not sure. But I think the one in the brown dress said something about trying the Holiday Inn ... or it might have been Quality Inn."

There was some strain in her voice and her face showed a sudden twinge of pain.

"Really," said Aubretia, "I'll have to ask you to excuse us. She's not feeling at all well. And I'm not exactly brimming with health myself."

Honor tugged at Matthew's sleeve.

"Come on, darling," she said. "Let them rest," and then with a smile at both of the occupants of the compartment: "Thank you so much for your help. I'm sure there's nothing to worry about. Matthew has a tendency to go overboard sometimes."

3

Matthew allowed himself to be pulled out into the corridor and propelled along to the next compartment, Room D. Inside he could see a man in his early middle age and a boy of about ten. He knocked on the door and the man gestured for him to enter.

"Sorry to bother you," he said, "but I'm a bit concerned about a friend of mine who seems to have disappeared from the train."

"Come in. Have a seat."

The boy moved a litter of comic books out of the way to make room for Matthew and Honor. After they had gone through the formalities of introduction, Matthew focussed on the father.

"I think you were sitting behind us at dinner last night. I was with a woman with an Irish accent wearing heavy spectacles."

"Yes, I noticed you both when we first came in," said Nash.

"Did you notice the woman who bumped into me and spilled my coffee?"

Nash's son, Buzzy, nudged his father.

"The deaf lady at our table," he said.

"Oh? Was she deaf?" asked Honor.

"She was, wasn't she, Dad? You had to nearly shout in her ear to make her hear you."

Nash grimaced.

"She wasn't an easy dinner companion," he said. "I began to wish there was somewhere else to sit but the dining car was pretty full."

"It's odd. She didn't seem deaf. At least she didn't seem to have any difficulty hearing Teresa," Matthew said. "Was she sitting directly behind me?"

"Yes. You were back to back."

"So she could have overheard our conversation?"

Nash looked doubtful.

"Not if her hearing was as bad as it seemed to be."

"Did you see them together at any point later in the evening?"

"No, we came back here right after dinner and didn't go out again ... or at least I didn't," Nash said, turning a baleful paternal eye on Buzzy.

Buzzy squirmed a bit in his seat, but he didn't look unduly repentant.

"Ah, c'mon, Dad, give me a break," he groaned.

"Did you see something?" Matthew asked the boy.

"I didn't see anything, but I heard something," he said.

Nash sighed patiently.

"Now, Buzz, son, if we're going to have all that stuff about somebody being murdered in the middle of the night — "

"What?" Honor exclaimed.

"Buzzy reads too many comic books. He's always imagining murders and conspiracies and visits from interplanetary aliens."

Indignation made Buzzy turn an interesting shade of pink.

"That's not fair, Dad. I did hear something."

"Maybe you'd better let him tell me the story," said Matthew.

So with Nash's reluctant consent, Buzzy gave Matthew a somewhat embroidered version of his late-night excursion through the first-class coach.

"You're sure it was the first compartment after the observation lounge where you heard the noises?" asked Matthew.

"Positive," Buzzy said. "Room A. I couldn't see anything because the blinds were down and I didn't hang around after I heard somebody coming towards the door. But I did hear noises — bumping and dragging noises like I said. And whispers and a kind of choking sound."

With some embarrassment, Nash reminded Buzzy that he had suggested the noises could have been associated with some other activity than murder.

"Jeez, Dad, did you see her?" Buzzy protested. "The woman in that compartment looked like my fourth grade teacher."

"So you knew whose room it was?" Honor said.

"Well, I didn't then. That's why I thought Dad might be right. But now I know it was the woman who had dinner with Mr. Prior, I can't believe she was doing what Dad said."

Matthew felt it wasn't the time or place to give a lecture on the sexual potential of the middle-aged, so he changed the subject.

"Did you see anyone else on your travels?"

"Yes. Scats — the attendant. We talked for a bit. And there was a guy just inside the observation lounge. A guy in a dark suit with a gun in a shoulder holster."

"You never mentioned that, Buzzy," said his father. "Is this another one of your tall stories?"

The pink flush of indignation rose in Buzzy's face again.

"No, Dad. He was, like, guarding the entrance to our car. He knew you, too. He called me Nash's kid."

"That's interesting," said Matthew. "Do you have any idea who this could be, Mr. Nash?"

"No, I don't," Nash replied firmly.

"It could be one of your CIA men, Dad," Buzzy blurted out.

His father frowned and his nostrils pinched together as they did sometimes when he was angry with Buzzy.

"You're with the CIA, Mr. Nash?" Honor asked.

"I suppose I could tell you that Buzzy's just fantasizing again, but I know it wouldn't take you long to find out otherwise, Miss Moore. I've seen your programme and I know you must have a strong research team. Yes, I'm a CIA officer, but I'm strictly off duty. I'm on holiday with my son, taking him back to join his mother in Los Angeles. So I'd appreciate it if this went no further."

Honor gave him a reassuring smile.

"No problem, Mr. Nash. I can be very discreet, and I certainly wouldn't want to antagonize a potential source. You wouldn't mind if I put you in my file, I hope?"

"As a potential source? I'll certainly give that some thought."

There didn't seem to be much more to be learned from either of the Nashes at that time, so within moments

Matthew and Honor had thanked them both and moved on to their next interview.

4

The knock at the compartment door interrupted Sven and Eddie in the middle of a game of penny-a-point Gin Rummy. Eddie had just scored 107, so with his bonus 100, that meant Sven owed him another two dollars and seven cents, putting Eddie's total gain for that morning at nine dollars and thirty seven cents. The interruption came as a welcome diversion for him, though Sven scowled when he heard the knock.

"Who is it?" he yelled.

"I'm a neighbour down the corridor. Matthew Prior. I wondered if I could ask you something."

"Come on in," said Eddie.

When they saw that Matthew was not alone but accompanied by a good-looking, leggy blonde, their greetings were a great deal warmer.

"This is my — er — fiancée, Honor Moore," Matthew lied, ushering her in ahead of him.

"Good to meet you," said Sven, offering Honor an unnecessarily prolonged handshake.

"Sit down. What can we help you with?" Eddie said.

Matthew looked around the compartment, taking note of the sketch pads and other artistic paraphernalia that were strewn about.

"Something a bit puzzling has happened," he said. "Honor here thinks I'm making too much of it, but I'm not so sure. Did you notice me in the dining car last night?"

"Yes, you were at a table near ours," said Eddie. "With a ... well, I think she said she was a nanny."

"That's right," Sven said. "A woman who was sitting at our table asked her if she was a nurse, and she said she was a nanny but she'd had hospital training. She sounded Irish."

"She was. And now she's gone. She told me very distinctly that she was travelling all the way through to Los Angeles on this train and that her employer was going to meet her at the station. But instead she seems to have left the train in Kansas City."

Sven got up, grabbed one of the sketch pads, flicked through it till he got to a particular page and then handed it, open, to Matthew. With a remarkable economy of line, Sven had drawn a woman in a strange bowl-shaped hat, eyes hidden behind heavy eyeglasses, and with the lower part of her face swathed in a scarf. Next to her, and seeming to support her, was another figure — a hatless woman with rather disordered hair and a decorative bag hanging over one shoulder. The face of this figure looked somehow taut and wary as if expecting to be challenged. Both of the figures were carrying similar pieces of luggage.

"That's her," Matthew said excitedly. "When did you draw this?"

"While the train was standing at the platform in Kansas City. I sketch a lot of different faces and figures ... for reference. I'm a comic book artist but I like to base my characters on real people."

"So you actually saw them getting off together?"

"Right. And they headed straight for the main station building."

"Did you recognize the other woman?" Honor broke in.

"Yes, I did. She was sitting across the aisle from us with a man and a kid. This woman at our table, Miss Adams, dropped a photograph she was showing us. It landed in the aisle and this woman in the drawing picked it up and handed it back."

"You don't know who she was?"

Sven thought about this briefly and then shook his head.

"No. I think I saw her earlier in the Metropolitan Lounge in Chicago, but I'm not certain."

Eddie snorted scornfully.

"That's 'cause you were so busy eyeballing Glamora. He usually goes for tall blondes," he explained to Honor with a smirk, "but the occasional redhead gets his attention."

"I'd think that particular redhead would get anyone's attention," Honor said with deadly sweetness.

None of the men seemed to disagree with this, and Matthew hurriedly changed the subject.

"Getting back to these two women who left the train, did it look as if they were both leaving voluntarily? That is, did one of them seem to be coercing the other?"

"Not really," said Sven. "They were walking very close together so I suppose theoretically one of them could have had a gun in the other one's back. Since they were both carrying bags, that wouldn't have been easy."

"It wouldn't have been impossible, though," Matthew mused.

Honor, who had been getting more and more impatient, opened the door onto the corridor and began to leave.

"Come on, darling. I think we've kept these fellows

from their card game long enough."

Matthew thanked Sven and Eddie and followed Honor out. Now that everyone in the upper level of the deluxe sleepers had been canvassed, he pondered what his next step should be. All the information so far pointed to the fact that Teresa and this Van Hoven woman had left the train together. Yet he had heard Teresa tell him directly that she was going straight through to Los Angeles, and also that she didn't care for this mystery woman, had in fact described her as "nosy." On top of all that, she had made a clear commitment to meet him for breakfast. Even if she had become train-sick later that evening, it didn't seem likely that she would turn to the Van Hoven woman for help.

"I think you're wasting your time," said Honor as they stood outside Room A. "You're letting your *Lady Vanishes* scenario run away with you."

"I just don't believe that Teresa would have left the train with that woman."

"Obviously she did."

By this time they had turned the bend in the corridor leading to the less-expensive accommodation. Scats was there at his work station, checking some kind of list. He looked up as they passed.

"How's the investigation goin', Mr. Prior?" he asked.

"It's going nowhere. This Miss Van Hoven ... you said her compartment was back here?"

"No. In the back part of the car but on the lower level. You want me to show you?"

Scats led them down the narrow staircase, turned right at the bottom and ambled along the centre corridor to a door about halfway down on the right. He pulled the door open and stood aside to let them in.

"Here it is. I cleaned it up this morning. She hadn't even slept in her bunk."

Matthew looked around carefully. Finally his eyes rested on the sloping underside of the upper bunk, which was in the closed position.

"The top bunk wasn't made up at all, I suppose, since there was only one passenger in this room?"

Scats bobbed his head up and down in amiable agreement.

"Would you mind opening it now?" Matthew asked.

Honor fixed her eyes on the bunk with a look of misgiving. It had occurred to her, as it had obviously occurred to Matthew, that something might be hidden up there. She tried to dismiss the thought as banally melodramatic, but somehow it refused to be dismissed.

"Sure. No problem," said Scats, reaching up and unfastening the catches that held the underside of the bunk to the ceiling.

Matthew and Honor both watched attentively as the bunk slowly folded down from the wall.

"That's it," said Scats.

There was nothing there but the ladder that passengers used to climb up into the bunk, which was stored on top of it when it wasn't in use. That and, of course, the bedclothes.

"Whew!" said Honor with overstated relief. "Thank God! I was half expecting something gruesome."

Matthew searched through the bedclothes and down the sides of the bunk but found nothing.

"I suppose you've already emptied the waste bin," he asked Scats. "Did you notice anything unusual in it?"

"No, sir. Just the regular stuff. Some used tissues. The wrapping off a candy bar. A few cigarette butts. In fact, there wasn't much there at all."

"And it's been dumped somewhere?"

"Yes, into the dispose-all."

Meanwhile, Honor had been searching behind the cushions of the compartment seats and had turned up a nickel, two pennies, a hairpin, the cap from a ball-point pen, and a white shirt button. None of them looked particularly promising as evidence. The shower cubicle, which they looked into next, was clean and empty. They were about to give up and leave the compartment when Matthew thought to look in the small closet by the door. All it contained was a number of coat-hangers, each of them identical except one. Matthew lifted it out.

"This isn't one of the standard hangers," he said to Scats.

"No, but passengers sometimes bring things aboard from a dry cleaners, things they've picked up on the way to the station, and sometimes they leave the hangers behind."

The object in question was a cheap wire coat-hanger with a paper cover advertising the name of a Chicago dry cleaner on West Madison Street.

"Could you be sure that this wasn't there before this Miss Van Hoven joined the train?" Matthew asked.

"Yessir, I'm sure. I always check every compartment thoroughly before the passengers board."

"It's not much to go on," said Honor.

"No, but it could give us a lead as to who this woman is."

So carrying his unimpressive trophy, Matthew led the way out of the compartment and back towards the stairs.

"I wonder who's in the compartment underneath Room A?" Honor ventured.

Scats, who was close behind them, grunted meaningfully and said: "That's where that prince is."

"Prince?"

"Yes, Miss Moore. The black guy. He's a prince from somewhere in Africa. Seems kinda full of himself."

"He might have heard something during the night. If he did, it would help to confirm that Nash boy's story."

"We might as well be thorough," Matthew said. "Anyone along the lower corridor might have heard or seen something. We should check them all out."

Honor shrugged.

"If you still believe something bad happened to your friend Shaughnessy, I guess we should."

Matthew turned to Scats.

"Who else is on the lower corridor?" he asked.

Scats was ready for that question.

"Well, sir, right here in Room J," he said indicating the first door to their left, "you've got a real famous person — Glamora. Next door to her is Mr. Bracciano. I think he's a prize-fighter. Then in Room H, there's another foreign lady — Miss Hentzen. Dr. Kadourian's in Room G, and the last room is the prince's."

"I keep hearing this name — Glamora. What's her claim to fame?" Matthew asked.

Honor looked at him sceptically.

"You mean you don't know?"

"Should I?"

It was Scats' turn to look at him sceptically.

"You're joshin' me, sir, right? Glamora is — well, she's

like a white Tina Turner — only more so, if you know what I mean."

"No, I don't," said Matthew, "but I get the picture. She's a celebrity."

"Ri-i-ight," said Honor. "And King Kong is a monkey. Glamora, for your information, is the all-time, all-purpose, in-your-face superstar. Your basic singer-dancer-actor-model-fitness guru. And anti-smoking activist. Listen, I've got an idea. It'll save time if we split up. You take Glamora and I'll do the boxer. Then you can do the foreign woman in H, and I'll do Kadourian. After that we can tackle the prince together."

"It sounds like a tidy way of handling it. All right — lead on!"

With an indulgent head-shake, Scats watched them go. In his time, he'd seen a lot of passengers get up to a lot of different things to amuse themselves on a long train journey and if these two wanted to play detective — well, it was harmless compared to what some of the others had done. As for him, he was going back to his *National Enquirer*.

5

Dressed in a skin-tight, one-piece workout leotard in pale-green lycra — from her own collection of Glamora Sportstuff — the celebrated redhead was doing her stretching exercises in Room J. There wasn't a great deal of space to work in, especially for someone of her height, so when Matthew peered tentatively through the glass pane of the door, he was confronted with a startling view of Glamora's trim posterior inches from his face. He cleared his throat and coughed before he knocked.

Glamora straightened up and whirled around almost in one motion. Her face wore a distinctly discouraging expression.

"Ye-e-essss!" she yelled.

"I'm awfully sorry to bother you," Matthew shouted through the door, "but if you could spare a minute, I'd like to ask you a couple of questions."

"No interviews," she shouted back.

"No, no, you don't understand. I'm not a reporter—"

"What are you? A fan?"

"Good heavens, no!" Matthew howled. "I mean ... well, of course ... I don't mean I'm not a fan ... That is—"

Glamora yanked the door open.

"Oh, come in and stop babbling. You're English, aren't you?"

Matthew stepped inside. Tall as he was, he only topped her by — at the most — an inch.

"Yes, I'm English," he said, "though I don't see what being English has to do with babbling."

She took a couple of paces back and looked him up and down.

"You don't, huh?" she said with a satiric twitch of her eyebrows. "Oh, never mind. Sit down. What's your name and what's your game?"

"My name's Prior, Matthew Prior. I'm a writer. No," he added hastily when he saw a scowl beginning to draw her eyebrows together, "I don't write about celebrities. I'm a playwright and I'm on my way to Hollywood to write a screenplay."

" — and it just happened to occur to you that I'd be ideal for the leading role. Listen, I'm a big girl. I stopped listening to lines like that when I was in diapers."

An image of Glamora in a diaper flashed through Matthew's mind and was hastily dismissed again.

"Sorry, no, that wasn't why I wanted to talk to you. The fact is something strange has happened on the train."

Glamora yawned.

"Can't say I'm surprised, given the bunch of weirdos in this car alone."

"Yes ... er ... well, the thing is that this woman I was having dinner with last night left the train unexpectedly in Kansas City."

"She did? What did you do to her?"

Indignation almost choked him.

"Me? Absolutely nothing!"

"There's your answer," said Glamora smugly. "You take a girl to dinner and then you do absolutely nothing. She probably thought she'd find more action in Kansas City."

"She wasn't a girl. She was a middle-aged Irish nanny."

"I've always heard you English guys were hung up on nannies. It's probably got something to do with potty-training."

Matthew sensed that this conversation was going nowhere — or at least it was going a long way in the wrong direction. He sighed and tried again.

"I just wondered if you noticed anything peculiar last night, say between ten o'clock and one-thirty in the morning? Either before we got to Kansas City or while we were standing in the station?"

"Like what?"

"Did you see a woman in a kind of bowl-shaped hat and heavy-rimmed spectacles getting off the train with a woman in a brown dress and a greeny-brown sort of coat?"

"No," Glamora said with a strange smile, "I was kinda distracted round about then."

"Well, did you see anything strange at all between dinner time and the time we left Kansas City."

There was a moment's silence while Glamora considered this with one purple-nailed finger tapping on the window-frame. Then she seemed to come to a decision.

"I did notice something earlier," she said. "Just as I was leaving the dining car, I thought I saw someone at one of the tables ... someone I didn't expect to see. It was strange because I'd seen her only in a photograph, once, more than a year ago — and yet I was almost positive it was her."

"Which table?"

"She was sitting with an oriental-looking guy and another guy with white hair and a black moustache. I'd spoken to the first guy in the lounge in the station."

"An older woman?"

"No, there were two women at the table. She was the younger one. Very dark hair, dark eyes, kinda exotic-looking."

"And who did you think she was?"

Again Glamora hesitated.

"An in-law," she said finally, "from Europe. I'd only seen her in wedding pictures."

"And why did you think your in-law might be on this train?"

"I thought she might be following someone."

"You?"

But Glamora was no longer in a co-operative mood.

"No," she said. "And anyway this has nothing to do with your disappearing Irish nanny. That's it. I don't have anything more to tell you. Vamoose, amigo. Shut the door behind you. I don't like drafts."

Somewhat abruptly, Matthew found himself in the corridor again, not entirely sure of how he got there. It was as if the force of her personality had transported him through the door before he had even had a chance to open it. Shaking his head to clear it, he moved past Room I, where Honor was still questioning the boxer, to the next compartment down the corridor.

6

Aldo Bracciano's ego, still smarting from the indignity of the night before, was slowly beginning to mend under the skilful ministrations of Honor Moore. An experienced interviewer, she knew how to apply just the right amount of flattery to soften a man up without overdoing it to the point where he became suspicious. Besides, the idea that one of the co-hosts of "Hot Flashes" was interested in his bid for the Golden Gloves was distinctly gratifying.

"I'm surprised," Honor was saying, "that you didn't fly out to L.A. I mean, I'd have thought that you wanted to spend as much time as possible with your trainer before the fight. Especially an important fight like this one."

Aldo looked a little shame-faced, lowering his long-lashed eyes and shrugging slightly.

"Trouble is, I get air-sick," he answered. "Most of the

time it's no problem 'cause a lot of my fights have been in the north-eastern states. But if I win this one and get a shot at the championship, I might have to travel outside the U.S. You know, like London, Milan, Manila ... all kindsa places."

"Have you tried any medications?"

"Yeah — Dramamine. Didn't seem to work for me."

"Maybe it's a psychological problem. You should try therapy."

"Sure — and have all the sports pages sayin' I'd gone psycho."

Honor smiled reassuringly.

"Oh, we media people aren't that bad, are we?"

Aldo gave Honor another quick glance.

"You won't say anything on your programme about this airsick thing, will you? That's all I need. It'll make me sound like a big wimp."

"Absolutely not. We'd be interested if you were hiding something major — like having an affair with Ivana Trump — or being involved in a right-wing paramilitary group. But not airsickness. Anyway, to get back to what we were talking about — do you know of any scandals in the boxing world that would make a good feature for the show?"

Aldo wrinkled his brow and scratched his ear.

"Jeez, I don't think so," he muttered, vowing that for sure he wasn't going to tell her about him and Tanya, and certainly not about him and Vito. "After what happened to Mike Tyson, everybody's been making sure that they've cleaned up their act."

"What about steroid abuse?"

"Nah," he said dismissively, "that's the kind of stuff those freaky bodybuilders do."

"Well," said Honor, beginning to make signs of preparing to leave, "if you do think of anything, keep me in mind. We do pay for information — but to someone who's probably going to be winning major endorsement contracts like you, it would probably seem like peanuts."

He grinned.

"Boy, I hope you're right," he said with unconcealed sincerity.

"Oh, there was something else," said Honor, turning back to him just as she reached the door. "Something happened last night that's a bit worrying. I wonder if you noticed anything."

"What kind of thing?"

"It would have been just after the train reached Kansas City. Two women who were booked through to L.A. got off the train and didn't get back on. They were probably together and one of them might have been ill."

Aldo remembered what had happened to him as the train reached Kansas City — suddenly being out in the corridor in his shorts — and he blanched at the memory. He was in such a hurry to get back into his own compartment that he had been in no frame of mind to notice anyone else. All the same, he did recollect something.

"I didn't see nuthin'," he said, "but I was out in the corridor just as we pulled into the station, and I heard footsteps comin' down the stairs."

In fact, it was hearing those footsteps that had propelled him even faster through the compartment door.

"Did they sound like men's or women's?"

"I couldn't tell, but I heard a woman's voice."

"Could you make out what she was saying?"

Aldo hesitated and then nodded.

"Just a few words," he said. "It sounded like: 'Don't make me — somethin' ... somethin'" or "Don't take me — somethin' ... somethin'.' I couldn't get the last words. It was just before I came into this compartment and shut the door, so I didn't hear nuthin' else."

Honor narrowed her eyes in speculation.

"Did the voice have an accent? An Irish accent?"

Aldo shook his head.

"Not Irish. It was more like German ... you know ... real foreign."

So it was the Von Hoven woman or whatever her name was, Honor concluded. Had she been saying: "Don't make me laugh," "Don't take any wooden nickels," or what?

"Did she sound worried or excited?"

Searching his memory for the exact tone in which the words had been uttered, Aldo realized that the woman had sounded just like Vito used to when he was at his most lethal.

"Nah," he said. "She was cool. Cool and mean."

7

Looking through the windows of Room H, Matthew saw that there was no-one home, unless of course, its occupant (a Miss Hentzen, according to Scats) was in the bathroom. He went on to Room G, but the blinds were drawn over the windows of Dr. Kadourian's compartment. Matthew hesitated. Although Honor was supposed to interview the self-help guru, he wanted to get on with the investigation. He was still wondering whether to rouse Kadourian or not when the decision was made for him. The door of the last compartment on the corridor opened and a handsome black man in elaborately embroidered robes came out, looked at Matthew, did a double take, and then held out his hand.

"I thought I recognized you in the dining car last night," he said in an Oxford-accented voice. "You are the playwright, Matthew Prior."

Matthew, flattered despite himself to be recognized by a prince, admitted that he was and at Achmed's invitation followed him into Room F.

"Yes," said the prince when they were seated, "I was at Oxford the year that your first play was performed at the Oxford Playhouse. What was it called? Ah, yes ... *The Sheep By Moonlight*. An under-appreciated play, I thought."

He could say that again, Matthew thought. The critic of the *Oxford Mail* had described it as "an unhappy marriage of historical epic and hysterical slapstick." It had played to thirty percent houses throughout the run and Frank Hauser, the director, had declared it the saddest moment in theatre since the death of Shakespeare.

"You're very kind, Your Royal Highness. I wish more people had agreed with you."

"Ah, well, just remember the words of Descartes when he said: 'I have neither so high an opinion of myself as to be willing to make promise of anything extraordinary, nor feed on imaginings so vain as to fancy that the public must be much interested in my designs.'"

"A very consoling thought, Your Highness."

"We met, you know, quite briefly," Achmed continued, "at an OUDS meeting. You were the guest speaker."

Matthew remembered the meeting. As a Cambridge man himself and a former member of the LMO, one of Cambridge's leading dramatic societies, he had felt that entering the domain of its Oxford equivalent was venturing on enemy territory. However, they had been very civil and some of them even seemed to understand what he had been trying to do in his play. By exerting his memory strenuously, he was also able to remember a more youthful version of the prince somewhere on the periphery of the gathering. They had even been introduced sometime later that evening. Somebody had said simply: "This is 'Ems,'" a nickname that was presumably a corruption of his correct African title, the Emir Achmed of L'mkata. In the democratic fashion of England's older universities, no-one had made a point of informing Matthew that he was being presented to a member of the Zwamalian royal family.

"Yes, we did meet, Your Royal Highness," Matthew agreed.

The prince waved his hand magnanimously.

"Oh, please — the formality is unnecessary. Call me Achmed."

Apparently the nickname Ems was no longer acceptable.

"Thank you," said Matthew, "I'd be honoured. And you must call me Matthew."

"This is a great pleasure for me," the prince continued. "I hadn't expected to meet anyone on this train worth talking to. Instead it is my good fortune to have met two."

"You flatter me, Achmed. And who was the other?"

"An estimable man whose work has had a great influence on me. You have perhaps heard of Dr. Vartan Kadourian?"

Matthew indicated that he had.

"A most impressive mind. Even the President of the United States, you know, has consulted him on occasion. Though not, I think," the prince added with a smile, "about his health reform proposals."

"As a matter of fact," said Matthew, "I was about to consult him myself."

The prince's dark eyes brightened.

"You are interested in the balance of body and mind, Matthew?"

"I suppose I am, but that wasn't in fact what I wanted to consult him about."

The prince raised his eyebrows expectantly.

"I wanted to ask him about a mysterious disappearance. The fact is, Achmed, that a lady I had dinner with last night left the train unexpectedly in Kansas City. I'm worried that she may be in some kind of trouble."

There was a moment's pause as Achmed gazed pensively out of the window. Then he turned his obsidian eyes back to Matthew.

"I remember seeing you with a lady at dinner. Middle-aged, provincial ... at least to look at, but perhaps she has exceptional wit."

"No, not really," Matthew said. "Just a decent, ordinary, well-intentioned Irish nanny. I liked her a lot and I'd hate to think anything unpleasant has happened to her."

"How do you think Dr. Kadourian might help, Matthew?"

"I thought perhaps he might have seen something. I've talked to everyone on the upper level where her compartment is, and now I'm checking the lower level. Perhaps you might have noticed something unusual, Achmed?"

"You say that this lady left the train in Kansas City? In that case, I wouldn't have seen anything. I retired early last night, as soon as I returned from dinner. I parted with Dr. Kadourian at the door of his compartment, came in here, and went directly to bed."

"And directly to sleep?"

Achmed gave Matthew a quizzical look.

"As a matter of fact, I listened to some music on my headphones first," he said. "A very interesting group called Def Leppard. After about twenty minutes, I pulled down all the blinds, took a Valium, and was asleep within five minutes. I didn't wake again until seven-thirty this morning."

"So you couldn't have seen anything," said Matthew despondently.

"Only the pictures that are formed by the action of the dreaming mind."

"And they certainly won't be much help," Matthew responded with a touch of impatience. "By the way, Achmed, if you don't mind my asking, why are you taking this trip?"

The prince seemed to stiffen for a moment, almost as if he were about to resurrect the barriers of royal privilege, then he relaxed again and flashed his bright smile at Matthew.

"I'm going to the International Trade Conference in Los Angeles," he said, "where I hope to renew my acquaintance with the President. We were students at Oxford together."

"Yes, but why by train?"

Before he responded, Achmed lowered his eyes, almost as if abashed or discomfited.

"My astrologer," he mumbled.

"Your astrologer?"

"Well, the court astrologer really. He advised that it was an unpropitious time for air travel, so I sailed to New York, took the Lakeshore Limited to Chicago, and then boarded the Flying Angel."

"It must have taken a while."

"It did. You know, Matthew, sometimes I suspect my uncle, the King, ordered the astrologer to give me that advice, so that I would be away from Zwamali for a long time."

Suddenly it seemed as if Achmed felt he had said too much. He rose abruptly to his feet, held out his hand again to Matthew, and said: "I have enjoyed our conversation, but it is the hour of prayer now and I must say goodbye. We will meet again soon, I hope."

Again Matthew found himself out in the corridor precipitately. He was just about to knock at the door of Room G to see if Kadourian was there when it slid open and revealed the stricken face of Honor Moore, and over her shoulder an equally perturbed Scats Madison.

"Oh, there you are, Matthew," Honor whispered. "You'd better come in here. Kadourian's dead."

Six

Through the Mountains and Into the Desert

1

In the years since his first encounter with murder, Matthew had seen some outlandish death scenes, but he couldn't recall one quite as bizarre as the scene in Dr. Vartan Kadourian's compartment. The doctor had been found crammed into the tiny shower stall, sitting on the closed lid of the toilet with his upper torso leaning against the wall. He was naked except for a black leather posing-pouch decorated with metal studs covering his genitals, and a leather hood with two eye-holes encasing his entire head. The hood had no breathing holes and the mouth-opening was zippered shut. Two metal clamps joined by a chain were attached to his nipples, and there were whip marks and cigarette burns on his back and legs. His chest, back, and arms were covered in elaborate tattoos — the chief motifs of which were dragons and skulls.

On the bunk-bed, which was still made up for the night, a black case lay open revealing an assortment of chains, straps, restraints, flails, and other devices. Scattered about on the floor were a number of pornographic magazines with titles like *Dominatrix* and *Bitches in Leather*.

"I guess it *is* Kadourian?" Honor asked wildly. "I mean — we can't see his face or anything."

It had occurred to Matthew to wonder the same thing. So, although it was axiomatic that a body shouldn't be disturbed, he was prepared — in the absence of any immediate access to official law enforcement — to take matters into his own hands. Carefully, using a towel to keep his own prints off the leather mask, he opened the zipper that ran up from the back of the corpse's neck to the crown of its head, and eased the mask off. The three of them were confronted by a distorted face with a bluish tinge. The blood-suffused eyes stared back at them in frozen outrage.

"It's the doctor, for sure," said Scats.

Honor sank down on the bed and put a hand over her eyes.

"Are you going to be all right?" Matthew asked. "Scats, maybe you could get her a cup of milky tea with lots of sugar in it?"

Scats hurried out and Honor looked up at Matthew.

"I'll be all right. It's just that I've never seen anything quite so horrible before."

It was on the tip of Matthew's tongue to say, "Wait till you've seen a severed head in a coffee sack," but considering that it might make her feel worse, he thought better of it.

"Just sit there and take it easy," he said instead. "You've had a shock and what you need is a good dose of English penicillin."

"English penicillin?"

"Yes — you know Jewish penicillin is chicken soup? Well, English penicillin is a 'nice cuppa,' as they call it in medical circles. In other words, a good hot cup of tea strong enough to stand a spoon up in."

As an attempt at humour it was strained, but it made her laugh faintly, and the colour was beginning to come back into her face. Moments later, Scats was back with the tea he had made at his work station, carrying it with the skill of long experience so that not a drop spilled, even though the train was lurching quite noticeably. Honor drank it in appreciative gulps.

Meanwhile, Matthew had been looking more closely at the body.

"I think it's pretty clear it wasn't suicide," he said. "There are marks on each wrist that suggest that his hands were tied together, either with a strap or more likely handcuffs. Perhaps this pair over here."

He pointed to a set of handcuffs in the black bag on the bed. Honor instinctively shrank away from them.

"He'd have been helpless to prevent anyone from putting enough pressure on the front of the mask to asphyxiate him. You can tell from the bluish tinge on his skin that there was a restriction of the flow of oxygen into his bloodstream."

The death of Kadourian put an entirely different complexion on the disappearance from the train of Teresa Shaughnessy and her mysterious companion. For one thing, it suggested to Honor Moore and Scats Madison the possibility that the women's sudden departure was nothing less than guilty flight. Matthew, on the other hand, was inclined to absolve Teresa of any complicity, arguing that the other woman might have compelled her to leave to confuse the issue and throw any investigation off course.

Obviously, the first thing to do was to report the death

to the authorities — but since the train was travelling through the desert and not scheduled to reach their next stop until late in the evening, this didn't at first seem the easiest thing in the world to do. However, as Scats quickly pointed out, the Flying Angel was a state-of-the-art train. The conductor's work station was equipped with a built-in laptop computer and fax/phone with which he maintained constant contact with the Amtrak signal centre. The question then became which authorities to get in touch with. Should they call back to Kansas City, their last major stop, to Caliente, their next stop, or (since they were now passing through Colorado) to Denver?

"I think I'll go and consult whatsisname," said Matthew after some minutes of inconclusive discussion.

"Who?" Honor asked.

"The CIA man."

"Nash," said Honor.

Scats looked startled. "Mr. Nash's with the CIA?"

Matthew nodded. "His son told us. I don't think he really wanted it known."

"I suppose he should have some idea about who has jurisdiction in a case like this," Honor conceded. "Of course, I could call our office in Chicago. The research library there could tell us."

"Let's try Nash first. And, Scats, you'd better close this compartment up and make sure no-one else knows what's happened for the time being."

"I gotta report this to the conductor right away, Mr. Prior. He's got to be notified of anything like this that happens on the train."

"All right, you go and report and we'll guard the door

till you get back. Oh, and you might ask him to find out if there's a doctor on the train."

As they waited in the corridor, they noticed that the compartment next to Kadourian's was still empty.

"I wonder where Miss Hentzen has got to," said Matthew. "She wasn't in when I passed earlier."

Honor shuddered. "I'm not looking in any more showers," she said. "Your friend Hitchcock has a lot to answer for."

"What do you mean?"

"I mean, suddenly we're in a different movie. We've moved from *The Lady Vanishes* to *Psycho* — and I don't want to end up as Janet Leigh."

2

Through the windows of the dining car, the grasslands of eastern Colorado were beginning to give way to the foothills of the Rocky Mountains. In the distance to the south-west, the great peaks of the Sangre de Cristo Mountains stood out sharply against a brilliantly blue sky.

Anderson Nash and Buzzy were having their usual lunch-time argument about whether Buzzy should order a bacon double-cheese burger with fries or a nice tuna sandwich on wholemeal bread with a green salad on the side. Buzzy as usual won, this time by suggesting that he had heard there was a tuna alert, and that tuna were notoriously full of mercury. Nash countered with botulism in the ground beef but Buzzy trumped him with toxic pesticides on the salad greens. Nash ended up eating a tuna sandwich and salad just to prove his point, at the same time watching enviously as Buzzy feasted on the burger and fries.

Just as Buzzy swallowed his last mouthful, the public address system sputtered on and the voice they had heard giving an occasional commentary on the passing scene made an announcement.

"Attention, folks ... if there's a doctor on the train, would he report immediately to the conductor's station? Repeat: we need a doctor urgently. If there's one out there anywhere, come to the conductor's station right away. Thank you; that's all."

There was an immediate buzz of conversation in the dining car.

"Wow, Dad," said Buzzy, "you think somebody found the body?"

"Don't start that again, Buzzy! It's probably something perfectly ordinary — like a heart attack."

At this point they were joined by Matthew and Honor.

"I'm glad we found you," Honor said after Nash indicated they were welcome to share his table.

"I didn't know we were lost," said Buzzy, wiping some green relish off his chin.

"Don't be smart, Buzzy," his father cautioned. "Still, he's right you know, it'd be hard not to find us. There aren't many places you can disappear to on a train."

Matthew picked up the menu and studied it with great concentration. It seemed to cover the gamut of North American cuisine from California fruit salad to New England clam chowder.

"I think I'll have the bacon double-cheese burger with fries," he said after he had weighed all the possibilities.

Buzzy gave him an approving thumbs up.

"I don't feel like eating at all," Honor murmured. "Not after what happened."

"What happened?" said Nash.

Matthew was studying the dessert list and trying to decide between Mississippi Mud Pie and Pennsylvania Apple Cake. Honor gave him a nudge, and when he didn't respond to that, added a kick.

"What the — ? Ouch, that was my ankle, Miss Moore!"

"Mr. Nash wants to know what happened!" she said unrepentantly.

"What happened? Oh, we found a body."

Buzzy wriggled excitedly. "See, I told you, Dad!"

"But it wasn't in the room where you thought you heard a murder being committed."

A look of disapproval clouded Nash's face.

"I hope this isn't some kind of joke," he said. "I don't think it's healthy to encourage a boy to dwell on these morbid fantasies."

"No, I'm serious. We found a body in Room G."

"Buzzy, go and wash your hands."

"Aw, Dad—"

"—or go into the observation car. I'll come and get you when it's time for dessert."

"But, Dad—"

"Out!"

Dragging his feet resentfully, Buzzy made his way out of the dining car and Nash turned back to Matthew.

"I hope you're not being serious, but even if you are, I don't want Buzzy having nightmares about it."

Somewhat ashamed of his own lack of consideration,

Matthew apologized.

"No, you're quite right," he said. "I should have known better. I have a son myself and I wouldn't have wanted him to hear the details of a murder when he was that age."

This was news to Honor, who fixed him with an accusing stare.

"You never told me you were married."

"Separated."

"Where have I heard that one before?"

"Let's save that for later, shall we?" Nash interrupted. "Right now we're talking about a murder — and, by the way, what makes you think it *is* a murder?"

Painstakingly, Matthew laid out his own observations at the scene of Kadourian's death, and explained their dilemma about reporting the death to the proper authorities.

"OK. It sounds like it could be a homicide case," Nash said after a moment's thought, "but as to who has jurisdiction — that's not such an easy call. He could have died in Missouri, Kansas, or Colorado. We won't be able to say where until the time of death is established, and that'll take a medical examination. But usually, if there's an ambiguity about where the homicide actually occurred, the rule is that it comes under the jurisdiction of the state in which the body was discovered."

"So it's Colorado, then."

"How do you come to be involved in this anyway?" Nash asked, narrowing his eyes. "Aren't you a playwright or something?"

"He's writing a screenplay about a murder on a train," Honor chipped in.

Matthew groaned. That revelation wasn't likely to reinforce Nash's confidence in him. In fact, Matthew could see Nash's face growing grimmer by the second.

"Look, that's just a coincidence," he said hastily. "It's got nothing to do with this."

"I've got a feeling you're both jerking me around," Nash groused, the tips of his ears reddening.

Honor, realizing that she had caused a problem, exerted her not inconsiderable charm to cool Nash off again.

"Oh, please," she said. "We're sorry. Shock does funny things to people, and I guess it's made us both a little wacky. Don't get all down on us. We need your help."

Possibly he was more than usually susceptible to the appeal of an intelligent and attractive woman, having spent so much of his time lately in the company of a ten-year-old boy, who — however lovable — was limited in his interests and conversational scope. In any case, Nash softened again.

"OK," he said. "Look, let me get Buzzy his dessert and get him settled, then I'll come with you and have a look at Room G."

3

This time, when they got to the murder scene, Honor stayed out in the corridor. She had no desire to see Kadourian's body again, so it was left to Matthew to accompany Nash into the compartment.

"Jesus," said Nash. "You weren't kidding. This is some scene all right. The guy must have been a sex freak."

He examined the body closely, checking the wrists for the marks Matthew had mentioned and looking for any other signs of trauma on the body.

"And he was wearing this mask?" he said indicating the limp piece of leather.

Matthew nodded.

"Did you notice this thread caught in the zip that goes across the mouthpiece?"

"I didn't," Matthew said. "I was more interested in seeing who was under the mask than the mask itself. But you're right."

He bent his head towards the mask and peered at the zip. There was a shiny green thread about a quarter of an inch long caught between the zipper's teeth.

"Hmmm. It doesn't look like a colour a man would wear, except possibly in a tie. I wonder..."

Matthew paused for a moment and cast his mind back over the people he had interviewed that morning.

"You know," he said, "Glamora was wearing a sort of bodysuit this morning, and I'm pretty sure it was this colour."

"Glamora in a bodysuit," said Nash, "that could be interesting to check out."

Meanwhile Matthew began going through the compartment, looking for any other signs of a female presence, but turned up nothing more than a hair-pin down the back of the seat, which could have been left in the compartment at any time. In Kadourian's closet, a dark suit was hanging. Matthew went through the pockets, but came upon nothing unusual. The built-in ashtrays in the compartment were also empty. Then he turned to the single seat, which — as in all the other deluxe bedrooms — was next to the window and opposite the long bench seat. That's when he found what appeared to be a significant piece of evidence. His hand touched and drew out from the narrow space between the chair and the wall a small white envelope.

"Found something?" said Nash.

Matthew showed him the envelope, opened it, and extracted three colour photographs.

"Good God," he said. "Look at these!"

Over Matthew's shoulder, Nash saw a photograph of what appeared to be two bodies, one male and one female, lying together on a blood-soaked patch of grass. Incongruously in the background a large white bird with a long-plumed tail seemed to be hurrying away from the scene. The second photograph was a close-up shot of the man — young, swarthy-complexioned and dark-haired, with splashes of blood on his face and shirt. The third was of the girl — also young, but fair-skinned and fair-haired. She would have been pretty but for the mess of blood that must have jetted from the wound in her throat and spattered her cheeks.

There was a long, slow exhalation of breath from Nash as he took in the full horror of the images.

"I guess this could be a motivation for the murder," he said. "A revenge killing."

"You mean if Kadourian murdered these two young people?"

"It's a possibility, isn't it?"

"But who took the photographs? It appears that they were taken before anyone else came on the scene. There's no crowd of horrified onlookers; no police paraphernalia; no roping off of the crime scene. So unless whoever took the photographs was hot on the heels of the killer, the more likely supposition is that the killer took them himself."

"If it was a him! All right then, supposing Kadourian somehow got his hands on the photographs and was blackmailing the killer? He might have been killed to stop the blackmail. "

"I wonder if he was killed before or after the train got to Kansas City," mused Matthew.

"What difference does it make?"

"It might tell me whether Teresa Shaughnessy is still alive or not."

"You think this Von Haven woman might be behind this?"

With unnecessary precision, Matthew stacked the three photographs one on top of the other, carefully aligning the edges.

"Could be," he said, then peering more closely at the top photograph: "That's interesting."

"What is?"

Matthew fanned the pictures out again, and looked at each one in turn.

"These photographs have the date and time printed on them — just like a video camera prints the date and time on a tape when it shoots a scene."

"Sure — there are regular cameras that do that too. I don't see how it helps us in this case. If one of the shots was of Kadourian's corpse, it would help establish the time of his death, but we don't even know who these people are."

"Ye-e-s," murmured Matthew absently, "pity we don't."

The door to the compartment was suddenly pushed open and Scats appeared with two men: one in an Amtrak uniform and the other in the garb of a scoutmaster.

"Mr. Prior, Mr. Nash," he said. "This is Bob

Bonsecours, our conductor ... and this other gentleman is Dr. Holloway."

"Holliday," said the scoutmaster.

He was an earnest, balding man of about thirty-five with a bony nose and a ginger moustache and he carried an official-looking black bag.

"The boys call me 'Doc.' You know! The OK Corral? Wyatt Earp?"

"Right," said Matthew, laughing dimly, "Doc Holliday the gunfighter."

Nash looked at both of them as if they had lost their senses. Meanwhile, Dr. Holliday had pushed further into the compartment and was looking interestedly at Kadourian's body.

"So this is our corpse," he said, cheerfully rubbing his hands. "My, my, quite a specimen!"

"I think it's a case of suffocation," said Matthew. "I'm afraid I removed the mask to identify the victim."

Dr. Holliday looked puzzled for a moment.

"Mask? He was wearing a ... Oh, I see. Part of his fantasy costume. We see a lot of this kind of thing. People who hang themselves to get a sexual kick, but don't manage to release themselves at the last minute."

"Maybe so, doctor," Matthew interposed, "but I don't think this can be self-inflicted. If you'll look at his wrists, I think you'll see some marks that suggest he was handcuffed or bound in some way."

Holliday moved closer to the body and began a slow and very thorough examination, muttering under his breath occasionally and sometimes whistling softly. The others watched in silence till he had finished.

"Definitely asphyxiation," he said when he straightened up. "You can tell from the petechiae and the cyanosis of the skin."

"Petechiae?" Nash asked.

"Little outbreaks of blood — see? Just inside the lips and on the eyelids. And cyanosis is the bluish tinge of the skin — comes from too little oxygen in the blood. The whip and burn marks were made before death, and I agree that the wrists must have been bound. The marks on the wrists don't come from normal after-death lividity. Besides, there are small abrasions in the skin, which suggest that something rough rubbed against it repeatedly. Probably as he was struggling to get free."

"Can you tell anything about the time of death, doctor?" said Matthew.

Holliday rubbed his bony nose thoughtfully.

"That's always a hard one. Judging by the cloudiness of the corneas and the rigidity of the body, I'd guess he's been dead between eight and twelve hours, but it could be as much as eighteen hours. I can get a slightly better fix if I take the body temperature anally."

At this point, Scats hastily excused himself. The doctor, giving him a farewell grin, reached into his bag and took out a rectal thermometer, which he proceeded to use on the corpse. Matthew, Nash, and the conductor averted their eyes.

"It's at 82 degrees," Holliday announced brightly. "That would more or less make the death between 11 and 12 hours ago. But let me stress that's only a ballpark figure. There're so many variables. For instance, the air-conditioning has kept this compartment very cool. That could speed up heat loss in the body."

"But between one and two this morning would be a good guess?" said Nash.

"A good working hypothesis, certainly."

Matthew cleared his throat. "Er — doctor?" he said, "you seem very at home with these procedures?"

Holliday grinned so broadly that his ginger moustache seemed in danger of disappearing up his nose.

"I should be," he chuckled. "I work for the Kansas City medical examiner's office."

If he had said he was Lawrence of Arabia they could hardly have been more astonished.

"You don't know how glad we are you showed up!" said Nash with manifest sincerity.

"I second that," Matthew added. "So if the killing happened between one and two, the train would probably have been in Kansas City or very near it?"

"That's right," said the doctor. "We had some problems waiting for one of the groups of scouts. They got delayed in Jefferson City, but because we were such a large party of passengers, the conductor agreed to hold the train for us. It was around two a.m., I think, when we boarded."

Matthew turned to Nash.

"So does that mean the Kansas City Police would have jurisdiction?"

"Well, with the homicide committed in one state and the body discovered in another, it could be that both states share jurisdiction. But what the hell, I have an old friend on the Kansas City force, so I'll run it by him first."

"Good," said Matthew. "I'm sure the conductor won't object to you using his fax/phone. Right, Mr. Bonsecours?"

The conductor, who had watched the proceedings in Room G with remarkable impassivity, nodded his agreement and began to lead the way out.

"And while you're at it," Matthew added, "maybe you could see if there's any news of vanishing nannies and their companions."

4

As Honor waited in the corridor, she gazed out of the window at the passing landscape. The Flying Angel had been drawing closer to the mountains since they had met Nash in the dining car and now the contrast between the dark green of the tree-clad slopes and the white peaks cleaving the cobalt sky was sharper. These soaring alps made the Adirondacks of Honor's childhood memories seem timid and safe, and the terrain the train was passing through was no less awesome. Suddenly they were crossing a bridge over a dizzying chasm, where — far at the bottom — the silver ribbon of a river glinted. She turned to Scats, who was just coming back along the corridor.

"What river is that?" she asked.

"The Arkansas," he said. "It rises up near Twin Lakes, runs though Colorado, Kansas, Oklahoma, and Arkansas, an' then it joins up with the Mississippi south of Memphis. An' this here bridge we're crossin' now is the highest railway bridge in the whole country."

"You're good," said Honor admiringly.

He acknowledged the compliment with a polite shrug.

"One thing about this job," he said, "you sure see a lot

of geography."

This struck Honor as being an astute formulation and she was about to say so when she was interrupted by a female voice from behind her.

"Excuse me," it said, "may I get past, please?"

Honor turned and saw the young, dark-haired woman she had last noticed in the dining car the night before.

"Sorry, Miss Hentzen," said Scats, as he and Honor stepped out of the way.

"Oh, you're Miss Hentzen," Honor said. "We were looking for you earlier."

The woman gave a puzzled smile.

"You were? I was just in the observation car. I stayed till it started to get mobbed by boy scouts."

It was tempting to tell her that being mobbed by boy scouts might be preferable to sleeping next door to a corpse, but remembering Matthew's injunction that no-one should know yet about Kadourian's death, she restrained herself.

"I'm Honor Moore. I've been helping my friend, Matthew Prior, find out why someone he met on the train got out unexpectedly in Kansas City."

The young woman slid open the door of her compartment.

"I'm Delia," she said. "Would you like to come in and talk?"

The compartment was exactly like all the others, except that there were a number of books strewn about. Most of them seemed to be autobiographies of actresses or collections of plays.

"Do you work in theatre?" asked Honor.

Delia laughed regretfully.

"I was trained as an actress," she said. "But you know what the theatre's like. I've probably spent fewer hours on a stage than I spent training to be on it."

"Where did you train?"

"In England. At LAMDA."

"LAMDA?"

"The London Academy of Music and Dramatic Art."

"You're obviously not English though. I mean ... your accent."

"No, I was born in the Soviet Union — the former Soviet Union. God, you don't know how good it is to be able to call it that! Anyway, I thought you wanted to talk about this woman who got off at Kansas City?"

The hint of irony in this last question did not escape Honor.

"You'll have to excuse me," she said. "I'm a professional TV interviewer and sometimes I forget the camera isn't on. Yes, I did want to talk about her. I wondered if you noticed her at all yesterday?"

"What did she look like?"

"Plain, middle-aged, with thick-rimmed glasses. She had an Irish accent."

Delia bobbed her head affirmatively.

"She sat at a table across the aisle, one row behind mine, at dinner last night, with a tall man—"

"My friend, Matthew. "

"—and she spoke to the other woman at my table — Aubretia, I think her name was — about being a nurse and having experience with pregnancies. Aubretia was expecting a young woman to join her in Kansas City ... a young woman who was, I believe she said, five months pregnant. The woman at the next table said she was really a nanny but had some hospital training and she'd be glad to help if anything went wrong."

"She did?" said Honor. "Well, that makes it even more extraordinary that she left the train. You see, she'd also promised to meet Matthew for breakfast, which is why he started worrying in the first place. But if she also said she'd help if something happened to this young woman—"

"I don't know if I'd call it a firm commitment," Delia said. "I think it was a fairly casual conversation. There was no reason to think that anything would go wrong with the pregnancy."

Honor frowned.

"No, I guess not. You didn't happen to see her leave the train, did you?"

"No, sorry."

"A few people claim to have seen her leave with another woman, who was also in the dining car last night."

Honor described the person who had become known to her and Matthew as "that Van Hoven woman or whatever her name is."

Delia immediately became more animated.

"Yes, I remember her particularly well. The woman in the brown dress who bumped into your friend as she was leaving. She made him spill his coffee. The funny thing about her is I'm sure I recognized her accent. She sounded as if she came originally from the Galinian Republic."

"I guess as an actress you have to be a specialist in accents?"

"It helps. But it wasn't that. You see, I'm a Galinian myself. Or at least I was born there."

"Ah," said Honor. "So did you see this Galinian woman leave the train?"

There was a slight pause and then, hesitantly, Delia spoke.

"No, but I'm almost sure that I saw her again — after dinner — coming out of the back part of the coach. I was just going into my compartment when I saw someone in a brown dress just turning the corner down there where the corridor jogs. Then I was distracted because I saw the black man in robes and that bearded man, Dr. Kadourian, coming from the other direction together. When I looked back again, the woman was nowhere to be seen."

"You know Dr. Kadourian?"

"He introduced himself to me when we got on the train. He's in the next compartment."

"Boy, is he ever!" Honor thought.

"It's strange," Delia went on. "When I met him yesterday, I had a sense that I'd seen him before. In Solonitza."

"Solonitza?"

"It's the capital of the Galinian Republic."

"Then, he's a Galinian too? There seem to be a lot of you on this train. Quite a coincidence!"

"No," said Delia firmly. "Not a Galinian. He doesn't have that kind of accent. I'd say he's from somewhere in the Eastern Mediterranean. And I could swear that when he was in Solonitza he went under another name. Dr. Something, but not Dr. Kadourian."

"How long ago was this?"

"It would have been when I was fourteen — about sixteen years ago. I wish I could remember the name he went under. It was another Armenian name — like Abkarian or

Avedissian. If he is the same man, I mean. I had a little sister, and this man worked at a pediatrics clinic my mother used to take her to. Sometimes I went along with them."

"Is your sister still in Solonitza?"

A dullness seemed to cloud Delia's eyes for a moment.

"No, she died when she was just a baby. Now, since my brother died, I'm the only one left."

"I'm sorry. Did your brother die recently?"

"Just a few months ago. On his honeymoon. He and his wife were both killed."

"An accident?"

Delia's mouth tightened and her face grew paler.

"No," she said. "It was murder."

5

The voice at the other end of the line sounded bored and impatient.

"You want to speak to who?"

"Malahyde," said Nash. "Is he there?"

"Who wants him?"

"I'm an old friend. Tell him Andy Nash from Washington."

"Hold on."

There were some clicks and buzzes and then a rasping voice with a mid-Western accent said: "Andy?"

"Tom. How're you doing?"

"Fine, I guess. Goin' on vacation tomorrow. Nice little fishin' camp in Michigan. How's the family?"

Nash bit back an irritated response. Goddamit,

Malahyde knew he and Rachel were separated.

"I'm just taking Buzzy back to California — to his mother."

"Oh, right. Pity about you two. You were a great couple."

"That wasn't what I called about, Tom."

He outlined what had happened on the train and explained their dilemma. Tom grunted unenthusiastically.

"Great, dump a homicide on me just before I take off on my first real break in eighteen months. So, you say the train has no scheduled stops till it gets to Caliente? Then I say, let the Nevada boys look after it when you get there. Nobody's goin' to be leavin' the train — not at the speed the Angel goes."

Frustration made Nash exhale explosively.

"C'mon, Tom. I need more than that."

"You want to be deputized? OK! I deputize you. It's unusual, I guess, but this is an unusual situation. You can look after things till the train gets to the next stop, can't you?"

"Fine, Tom," said Nash with studied patience, "but in the meantime I need some information. It's possible that the perpetrator is one of two women who left the train in Kansas City. One was an Irish woman in her late thirties, early forties called Shaughnessy — Teresa Shaughnessy. The other one was some kind of European — German, Belgian, Dutch, maybe — with a name like Von Haven. It seems likely that Shaughnessy had been drugged by the other one and was under duress. Can you check for me and see if there were any reports of sightings of either of them? It's possible that they may be staying at a Holiday Inn or a Quality Inn."

"Only for you would I do this," Malahyde grumbled. "Especially the day before my vacation."

After Nash had hung up, he turned to Matthew.

"I don't know how useful that was," he said, "but at least I have a dubious quasi-official status in the case now. And while we're waiting for Tom to call back, maybe we could just draw up some kind of status report — like what do we know about who did what when."

They thanked the conductor and went back to Matthew's compartment to begin putting together some notes. Outside, the steep mountainsides reared up around them as they sped into the Monarch Pass, and suddenly daylight disappeared as the train roared into a tunnel. There was a momentary flicker as the interior lights came on. At the same instant, Honor opened the door and came in.

"Any luck?" she asked.

Both men looked up at her vaguely, their minds still preoccupied with the details of Matthew's interviews with the other passengers.

"A bit," said Matthew. "Nash is sort of semi-authorized to take charge of the investigation — and we're waiting to hear from Kansas City."

Honor sat down, let her head fall against the back of the seat and closed her eyes.

"I finally found Delia Hentzen," she said, "or rather she found me. She said she'd been in the observation lounge until the boys scouts got too much for her."

"Hmmm," said Matthew in a preoccupied manner, "funny we didn't see her when we went through it on our way to the restaurant."

"That's true. Oh, well, maybe she was in the john or something."

"Did she have anything to tell you?"

"She claims she saw the Van Hoven woman lurking in the lower corridor after dinner. Then when Kadourian turned up with the prince, she made herself scarce."

Matthew tapped his teeth with his pencil.

"So she and the prince may have been the last people to see Kadourian alive," he said. "Did she hear anything from Kadourian's compartment later?"

"I didn't ask her. After all, you said not to let anyone know Kadourian's dead. She would have wondered why I was asking."

"True. Oh, well, I don't suppose you'd have got much out of her."

Nash was scribbling in his notebook. Matthew turned back to him to say something when Honor interrupted.

"You don't suppose I'd have got much out of her?" she drawled. "Then suppose again, friend. She also told me that she overheard the Von Hoven woman speak at dinner, and she's pretty sure that she had a Galinian accent."

Matthew's attention shifted abruptly back to Honor.

"Now that *is* interesting," he admitted. "Teresa Shaughnessy was going to California to be the nanny to the children of the former head of the Galinian Republic. It could be that her encounter with the Van Hoven woman in the Metropolitan Lounge in Chicago was no accident."

When he heard this, Nash looked up from his notebook and began to take notice.

"You mean the Van Hoven woman may have been tracking the nanny?"

"Could be. Teresa told me that she didn't care for the woman but that she kept on making friendly overtures, which sounds as if she was determined to stick as closely to

Teresa as possible."

Honor opened her eyes and sat forward.

"There's something else Delia told me," she said. "She said she was pretty sure that she had come across Kadourian before, years ago in a place called Solonitza and guess what? Solonitza is—"

"—the capital of the Galinian Republic," Matthew obligingly contributed.

"Damn you, Prior," Honor yelped. "You know too darned much!"

Nash's interest was now distinctly aroused.

"Three Galinian connections in one coach on one train — that really does sound suspicious. The odds against it being a coincidence must be hefty. And that brings us into my territory. I have what you might call a watching brief on several of those countries that used to be part of the Soviet Union — and the Galinian Republic is one of them."

Matthew raised his eyebrows.

"Another hefty coincidence," he said, "if it is a coincidence."

A strange look — half of annoyance, half of apprehension — passed across Nash's face.

"Just what does that mean?" he asked.

"Just that maybe your innocent trip with your son isn't as innocent as it appears. Maybe your watching brief extended to anyone who might be in contact with the deposed Galinian leader, Golovyov. Oh, and incidentally, are you any relation to Frank Nash?"

Honor's eyes widened in alarm. It seemed for a moment that Nash was getting ready to blow a fuse, but then his body relaxed and he laughed.

"Honor's right," he said. "You do know too darned much. No, I'm not related to any Frank Nash as far as I know, but you're right about my watching brief."

"So tell me which of the ladies you were watching," said Matthew with a rather ungracious grin of triumph. "Teresa or the Van Hoven woman?"

There was a silence while Nash obviously weighed whether to say any more and if so how much.

"First of all, my trip with my son isn't just a cover," he told them. "Buzzy was staying with me in Washington and I had agreed to take him back to California by train. At the last minute we got wind of a possible threat to Golovyov, and that the person concerned was booked on the Flying Angel. I hadn't meant to give Buzzy quite that much of a treat — travelling first class on the Angel, I mean — but the agency wanted me on this train and in this coach, so they arranged it. It seemed perfect. I would give Buzzy his trip through the Rockies and I could keep my eye on this person at the same time."

"So which one of them was it?" Honor asked. "The nanny or Van Hoven?"

"Neither," he said. "That's why I didn't want to get tied up with that at first. I thought it might get in the way of my job."

"Which was to keep an eye on Delia Hentzen," Matthew concluded.

Honor scowled.

"That's not so smart," she said. "Not after I'd already told you she was Galinian."

"You didn't exactly say she was. You said she remembered Kadourian from meeting him in Solonitza."

Then he turned to Nash. "Is she Galinian?"

Nash again seemed hesitant, as if not sure how much information he could safely disclose.

"If we're really going to work together on this, don't you think you should give us more of the picture?" Matthew said.

Nash raised his hands in a gesture of mock surrender.

"OK, OK, I'll come clean. Yes, Delia Hentzen is a Galinian. She comes from a very political family and her father was what Soviet watchers called an apparatchik, in other words a Communist government insider."

"So not a particular friend of Golovyov?" asked Matthew.

"No, and one of the people behind the uprising against the Golovyov regime was Delia's brother, Fedor Hentzen."

"Hmmm," said Honor, "I guess that's the brother she told me about — the one who was killed on his honeymoon."

"She told you that, did she?"

Nash seemed surprised, as if he hadn't expected Honor's interviewing skills to be so effective.

"Well — to continue — the uprising was only temporarily successful. It got rid of Golovyov, but soon another group that was hostile to Hentzen's crowd took over and Fedor Hentzen had to get out of the country fast. His father, who had worked as a young man at the Galinian Embassy in London, and had married an English girl, had useful contacts in England, so that's where his son went. In the meantime, Golovyov had also disappeared and somehow — in all the chaos — he had managed to transfer a big chunk of the Galinian treasury out of the country. As far as we can make out, he did this with the help of one of the new criminal syndicates that sprang up in the former Soviet Union after it began to come apart. But more interestingly from the CIA's point of view, he seems to have a handle on the criminal trade in nuclear materials. That's why the State Department bent over backwards to get him preferred status as a political refugee with insider knowledge of a situation that has serious implications for national security."

"Whew!" said Matthew. "Honor, you said we'd moved from *The Lady Vanishes* to *Psycho*. We're now into late Hitchcock ... something along the lines of *Torn Curtain*."

The train was still racing through the tunnel and the hollow rushing sound that accompanied its passage and the blackness that enveloped it suddenly seemed unearthly, as if the Flying Angel and its passengers had entered a region of unpredictable strangeness. Honor turned away from the window with a sudden shiver.

"Do you think that Delia had something to do with the nanny and the Van Hoven woman leaving the train in Kansas City?" she said anxiously.

Matthew chewed thoughtfully on his lower lip.

"It's a strong possibility," he said. "The other woman is a Galinian — or at least Delia claimed that she spoke with a Galinian accent. Now that may have been a deliberate attempt to mislead us, but supposing she was Galinian, she could easily be Delia's accomplice, getting Teresa Shaughnessy out of the way while Delia replaced her as the Golovyov nanny."

"But Golovyov would be expecting an Irish woman--" Honor objected, then stopped abruptly.

"What's the matter? You look as if you'd been struck dumb."

She made a face at him and then continued: "It just suddenly hit me that Delia told me she was trained as an actress — and she emphasized how important it was for an actress to have an ear for accents. Maybe she can do a really good Irish brogue."

Nash took up the suggestion eagerly.

"You're right. I remember now I read in her dossier that she was trained at the State Theatre School in Solonitza and after the uprising she went with Fedor to London and enrolled at one of the drama schools there."

"LAMDA," said Honor.

"Excuse me?"

"The London Academy of Music and Dramatic Art," Matthew explained. "As a matter of fact, I know someone who gives classes there. I could maybe find out more about Delia from her."

Matthew was referring to the amazing Nell Finnegan, a well-known if eccentric actress with whom he had been having an affair, on and off, for a number of years.

"I'll send her a fax from the conductor's station," he went on. "Now, what else do we need to find out?"

"God, this is a long tunnel," Honor complained as she gazed out of the window again. "It's a good thing I'm not claustrophobic."

There was a rap at the door and Scats slid it open and poked his head in.

"Phone message for you, Mr. Nash," he said. "Hope it isn't urgent. It came through about half an hour ago."

Nash thanked him and followed him out of the compartment.

"I hope nothing's happened to Teresa," said Matthew. "I've got a bad feeling about this whole thing."

Honor patted his hand.

"We should know something soon," she said. "Be patient."

Matthew couldn't get rid of the vision of Teresa being marched off the train with a gun in her back, drugged and disoriented, to be taken off to who knew what God-forsaken motel and quietly and efficiently murdered. Honor tried to make bright conversation, but his responses were perfunctory and eventually they both lapsed into silence waiting for Nash to return. As they waited, the train finally burst out of the tunnel into brilliant sunlight and they found themselves racing through a narrow valley enclosed by massive, snow-capped ridges.

Less than ten minutes later, Nash was back with a bleak look on his face.

"Well?" asked Matthew.

"The darndest thing," Nash answered. "They found the nanny in the ladies' room at the station in Kansas City."

"Dead?" asked Honor in a strangled croak.

"No, she was alive. Alive, but totally out of it. Didn't know who she was or how she got there. She also had a handgun that had recently fired two shots. The Van Hoven woman was the one who was dead. In one of the cubicles."

6

Buzzy had finished his dessert and gone back to the compartment. His dad was still out, running around with the English guy and his girlfriend, getting to do all the exciting stuff, while he was stuck there alone with his camcorder and his comic books. He'd finished reading all of the latter hours ago, so after rustling desultorily through a few of them, he got out his camcorder and began taping the passing landscape. More rocks, more sand, more weird-shaped mounds and knolls. Red dust, blue sky, white clouds. Not a human being in sight; not even an animal. Somehow this gave him such a lonesome feeling that he couldn't stay by himself any more, so he put his camcorder away, and headed out of the compartment and towards the observation car. At least there'd be people there.

There were people, but mostly they were those geeky boy scouts. Even if they hadn't been geeky, the youngest ones were a year older than him. He walked to the centre of the observation car and slumped down on one of the vacant seats. To his right was a group of three scouts. The one nearest him, a dark-skinned boy with dark-brown hair, green eyes, and a friendly smile, looked a bit less geeky than the others. After a few minutes of alternately looking out at the landscape and glancing surreptitiously at each other, the scout spoke to Buzzy.

"Where you from?" he said.

Buzzy looked sharply at him to see if there was some hidden motive behind the question. The boy gazed back frankly and good-naturedly.

"I'm from Costa Mesa. It's in California."

"Oh, so you're on your way home, huh? You been on a trip?"

"Been to Washington to stay with my dad."

The boy looked knowing but sympathetic and suddenly stuck out his hand. Buzzy shook it.

"I'm Ryan," said the boy.

"I'm Buzzy."

"That's a neat name. How did you get it?"

"My initials — B. B. Nash. 'Bee' — 'Buzzy' — get it?"

"Buzzy Nash? It's cool; I like it. I'm Ryan Woolf. That's not so cool. Some kids in school used to call me Virginia because of that movie."

"What movie?"

"Oh, just some dumb movie. I punched a few of them out and they stopped saying it."

Buzzy laughed and the other boy joined in.

"Where are all you guys going?" Buzzy asked.

"There's this big World Scouts Jamboree near Anaheim. I decided to go because it's a chance to see Disneyland."

"You've never been there?" Buzzy was almost incredulous.

"Nah. We live in Hickory Hill, Missouri, and the furthest we've been on vacation is to that Six Flags Over Georgia place."

"Cool. Hey, you want to know something mega-weird?"

"Yeah, what?"

"There's been a murder on this train."

Now it was Ryan who looked incredulous.

"For real?"

Buzzy bobbed his head up and down with so much fervour that it seemed in danger of bobbing right off his shoulders. Ryan moved closer and the two boys entered a conspiratorial huddle while Buzzy outlined the facts of the case as he knew them.

"Wow, maybe we could catch the killer," Ryan suggested in a breathless croak. "Listen, there's a couple more OK guys in my troop. They'd be great for something like this. Mind if I clue them in?"

A little doubtfully, Buzzy agreed. Soon six of them were round a table in the downstairs lounge, drinking sodas and scheming to mount their own investigation into the death of the late Vartan Kadourian. Buzzy, unfortunately, wasn't able to enter into it quite as wholeheartedly as the others because of a disquieting sense that his dad and the English guy would be less than gratified with this unsolicited support, however enthusiastically offered.

7

Half an hour later Anderson Nash, Matthew, and Honor arrived in the lounge-bar for a much-needed drink. All the tables were full, and Nash was surprised to see his son, Buzzy, at one of them with a group of boy scouts, one African-American with amazing green eyes, one Asian, one Hispanic, and two white cornfed country boys. He was even more surprised when after a nudge from Buzzy and a whispered colloquy, the black scout motioned to the others to vacate their seats, which they did quietly and politely, the black boy and Buzzy leading the way. Buzzy nodded self-consciously to his father as they left.

"Now, isn't that nice?" said Honor. "Who says that kids nowadays aren't well-behaved?"

Nash seemed rather less impressed with their demeanour.

"If you ask me, when they behave that way, they're probably up to something. Still, I'm glad Buzzy has found some guys to hang out with."

Matthew went to get drinks from the bar and when he came back, the three of them discussed what Nash had learned from his contact in Kansas City.

"So you were saying," Honor said to Nash, "the Kansas City police have arrested the nanny?"

"They haven't decided on the charge yet. Right now, she's in a psychiatric facility. They've done some initial testing there and it looks like she'd taken a substantial amount of burundanga."

"Burundanga? I'm sure Matthew knows what that is," said Honor acidly.

Matthew beamed at her.

"As a matter of fact, I do. It's derived from a Colombian shrub of the nightshade family called borrachera. It's odourless, colourless, and soluble, and anyone who takes it loses their will and memory for anything from twenty-four hours to three days. It's a form of chemical hypnosis. Colombian crooks mix it with a sedative and then slip it to a victim, who can then be robbed or made to do a number of things they ordinarily wouldn't — like smuggle drugs — and usually they have no memory of anything that happened while they were under its influence."

Honor rolled her eyes till almost nothing showed but the whites.

"Oh, thank you, professor," she breathed. "It's such a privilege to be in your class."

"In that case," said Nash, ignoring this sideshow, "it looks as if the nanny might have killed the woman she left the train with while she was under the influence of this stuff. Incidentally, the name of the dead woman isn't Von Haven, it's Verhaeven — all one word."

The other two at the table made an effort to return to a more serious frame of mind.

"I find it hard to believe that Teresa would have killed anyone — even under the influence of a mind-altering drug," said Matthew.

"I've known more improbable assassins," said Nash. "The woman doctor who killed the Russian TV host, for instance."

"A woman doctor?" said Honor.

"A gynecologist. She shot him in full view of hundreds of people and escaped."

"Isn't that against the Hippocratic oath or something?" Matthew snorted.

"If that kept doctors from killing people, the population of the world would be considerably larger than it is. Some of the most famous murderers have been doctors. Crippen in England, Petiot in France, Bolber in the U.S."

Nash patiently steered the conversation back on course again.

"I guess until we have more information from Kansas City, we probably can't come to any conclusions about Miss Shaughnessy," he said. "What about Miss Hentzen? If she and this Verhaeven person were accomplices in a plot to get Miss Shaughnessy out of the way so that Hentzen could pose as an Irish nanny and get close to Golovyov..."

He trailed off uncertainly.

"...then she might have killed Kadourian because he found something out?"

"God!" said Honor suddenly. "I've just remembered something. When I was speaking to Delia, she said she thought she had met Kadourian years ago in the Galinian Republic — in Solonitza. He looked like a man who worked there in a pediatric clinic, but his name wasn't Kadourian, it was Abkarian or Avedissian. Maybe she went to his compartment last night, to confront him about that and saw those photographs ... the two bodies. And maybe, just maybe, they were the bodies of Delia's brother and his wife."

"There's one way to find out," said Matthew. "Come on, let's go and visit her. She might be the key to the whole mess."

8

Before he went with Nash and Honor to Delia Hentzen's compartment, Matthew stopped off at the conductor's station to send two fax messages: one to Nell Finnegan to ask if she could shed any light on the character of Delia Hentzen, and one to Dorothy Bedlington, a high-ranking officer at Scotland Yard, to beg her to check unofficially on Kadourian, Delia, Teresa, and any woman with the name of Verhaeven who might be known to the police. Many times in the past, he had obtained very useful information from these two sources. He hoped this time would be no exception. Given that Dorothy was currently being rather cool to him because of his inability to decide between her, Nell, and his wife, Henrietta, he was afraid that this might be one time when she wouldn't feel like co-operating. If she had known that he was also allowing himself to be distracted by a blonde American TV personality called Honor, his privileged access to the files of Scotland Yard would have come to a screaming halt.

When they left the conductor's station, he watched the Honor in question walking ahead of him down the corridor and couldn't help noticing that she had the most perfectly shaped legs he had ever seen on a woman, at least what he could see of them from the knees down. Just as this was going through his head, Honor turned and looked at him and, almost as though she had seen his thought projected on his face, responded with a friendly and encouraging smile. He smiled back and a warm feeling of euphoria coursed through him. Maybe all the silly bickering they had been doing was a way of trying to conceal from themselves a mutual interest that might yet lead somewhere.

He followed her down the stairs to the lower level, with Anderson Nash close on his heels. As they approached Delia's door, they saw that Scats Madison was still guarding Kadourian's compartment.

"'Scuse me, folks," he said. "I'm not gonna be able to stand here much longer. I have other stuff I've gotta see to."

"Give us another ten minutes," said Nash, "and I'll figure something out."

Honor knocked on the door of the compartment.

"Delia? It's me. I've got a couple of people with me who would like to ask you a few questions. Is that all right?"

Delia peered out at Matthew and Anderson Nash, then nodded and slid open the door.

"Come in, please," she said. "Excuse all the clutter, but I was looking for an audition piece. You'd think with all these anthologies I'd be able to find something, but so far..."

She made a gesture of dismissal as if to say she would worry about it later, and gathered the books up into a pile at one end of the seat.

"You're going to Los Angeles to audition for something?" Matthew asked, as he and the others sat down.

"Yes, there's a group there that workshops new plays. Very often they get someone with a name to take the lead. You know — movie actors who aren't quite stars but who are on their way up. Anyway, a friend I trained with in London suggested I come out and try for a spot in the company."

"It seems awfully risky," said Honor. "Coming all that way just to audition."

Delia lowered her eyes, looking almost embarrassed.

"I suppose it is. But nothing was happening for me in England, and in Hollywood there's always the hope that someone might see you, and ... well, you know--"

"And offer you a chance to appear in a movie with Mel Gibson," Matthew added. "Excuse me, I'm not making fun. I know the feeling. I'm going to Hollywood, hoping to write the next box-office blockbuster. We both know the odds against us, but if we didn't dream like that, we wouldn't be human."

Delia smiled at him gratefully.

"It sounds so foolish," she said, "but I had to take this chance — or spend the rest of my life doing bit parts in BBC mini-series."

"How long had you been in England, Miss Hentzen?" Nash asked.

She glanced up at him warily.

"About four years," she said. "Two years at theatre school and another two trying to find work."

"Were you on your own in England? I mean, did you have any family there?"

"Not at first, but my brother came to join me about a year ago."

"Your brother Fedor?" asked Nash.

She seemed a little startled that he knew the name.

"That's right, but how did you know ... I mean, I don't remember mentioning his name to anyone."

"I'm with the CIA, Miss Hentzen. I know about your brother's involvement in the anti-Golovyov uprising. I know he took off for England after the regime he was backing failed."

"Yes, it was a very bitter time for him. He was very unhappy at first in London, but then I introduced him to someone I'd been at drama school with, and they fell in love and got married. Fedor was so happy and so much in love with Anna."

For a moment her voice trembled and it appeared that she was on the verge of tears.

"This Anna," Nash went on, "was an American, wasn't she?"

"Yes," said Delia. "I believe she was from Idaho."

"What was her family name?"

"Lundgren. I think her people came originally from Sweden. Her great-grandparents were immigrants, and the family became farmers. Potato farmers."

Nash nodded.

"Do you remember where in Idaho their farm was?"

"As a matter of fact, I do. We were watching an old movie on television one night about the battle of the Little Big Horn, and she laughed and said her county in Idaho was named after General Custer."

"So, somewhere in Custer County, Idaho?"

"That's all I know. I never heard the exact address."

"Does this look like her, Miss Hentzen?" he said, passing her a photograph.

She took one look at it and put a hand over her mouth almost as if she was about to vomit.

"Oh, God!" she gasped. "How horrible! How could you show me this! You're a very cruel man. Oh ... poor Anna!"

She thrust the photograph back at him and turned her face away. Tears were spilling out of her eyes and trickling down her cheeks. Honor gave Nash an indignant look, went over to Delia, and put a consoling arm around her shoulders.

"I suppose we should give you credit for not showing her her brother's photograph too!" she stormed. "Honest to God, the lack of sensitivity of some guys!"

Delia turned back towards Nash, tears still flowing.

"You have a picture of Fedor too? Let me see it."

Nash demurred, half-ashamed.

"I don't think you'd better," he said.

But suddenly Delia was fierce and resolute.

"Give it to me! I want to see my brother's photograph!"

Reluctantly, Nash held it out to her. She almost snatched it from him and then sat looking at the picture of her brother's body in absolute silence for some moments.

"Ah, Fedor," she sighed eventually and then, blinking back the tears and visibly struggling to stay calm, she asked: "Where did you get this?"

Indicating Kadourian's compartment with a motion of his head, he said: "Next door."

"You don't mean Dr. Kadourian had them?"

"They were in his compartment. We don't know if they were his or whether the killer left them there."

Delia now looked completely mystified. The three watching her came to the conclusion that either she was a much more accomplished actress than her career so far would indicate or she genuinely had no idea what had happened in Room G.

"Killer?" she said. "What killer?"

"Dr. Kadourian died last night of suffocation."

She seemed even more bewildered.

"But ... why?" she said. "Why would anyone kill him ... and why would he have these photographs of my brother and his wife, dead?"

She looked from one to another of them as if she expected to see some kind of answer in their faces.

"We don't know," Matthew admitted finally. "It may be he was blackmailing the killer with these pictures, and ended up as the killer's next victim. The other possibility is that the killer believed Kadourian was responsible for the deaths and killed him in revenge."

"But that would mean it was someone who was close to either Fedor or Anna! Oh, no! You think it was me. You think I killed him because of Fedor!"

The two men looked uncomfortable and Honor glared at them.

"Well, I don't think it was you," she declared firmly. "But according to what you told me you were one of the last people to see him after dinner. You saw him with Prince Achmed in the corridor outside his room. You also saw the woman in the brown dress lurking at the other end of the corridor."

"Yes, that's right. Dr. Kadourian and the prince seemed to be very friendly. They were laughing and talking about California."

"Did you see them go into their compartments?"

"No. After I looked down the corridor the other way and saw that the woman in the brown dress wasn't there any more, I went straight into my compartment and shut the door. They were still out in the corridor then."

Honor gave a nod of satisfaction.

"So the prince could have gone into Kadourian's apartment," she said to Nash and Matthew.

"Did you hear anything through the wall?" Matthew asked. "Any conversation or any other sounds?"

Delia thought for a moment and then said: "About half an hour later, I heard a couple of bumps. Almost like someone knocking on the wall next door. But I listened for a while and there weren't any more, so I forgot about it. I mean, if anyone had really been in trouble and trying to attract someone's attention, I thought they would push the bell for the attendant, not thump on the wall."

"It would be difficult to ring for the attendant if your hands were handcuffed behind your back," said Nash.

Again, there was no reaction from Delia that would suggest that she had any idea what Nash was talking about. She merely looked puzzled.

"Were they?" she said.

"There were marks on his wrists that pointed to that, certainly," said Matthew.

She looked at her own wrists and then looked up again at Matthew. At the same time a subtle change in her posture suggested a shift towards defensiveness.

"It would take someone quite strong to overpower a man of Dr. Kadourian's size," she argued. "How could I have put handcuffs on him?"

The look of discomfort on Nash's face grew more pronounced.

"The way I see it," he said, "the handcuffs were put on him as part of some sadomasochistic game. There were burns and whip marks on his body too."

This time Delia's incredulity seemed so genuine that even Nash couldn't believe she was faking.

"And you think that I could ... that I was ... you can't really believe that!"

"We have to consider every possibility," mumbled Nash.

She drew herself up and gave him a withering glance.

"I think that's one you can safely discount," she said. "And now, if you don't mind, I'd like to be left alone."

Matthew rose and led the way to the door.

"I apologize, Miss Hentzen, if we've been in any way offensive, but I'm sure you understand that until we have more information, everyone in this coach is equally under suspicion. And I must ask you one more question — do you happen to have a green dress or a blouse or a scarf, possibly in some silky material?"

"Like this," Nash said showing the thread they had found caught in Kadourian's mask.

She glanced at it perfunctorily and shook her head.

"I have nothing in that colour."

"Have you noticed anyone wearing something in this colour?"

"I haven't."

It was clear they would get nothing more out of her at this point, so they muttered hasty good-byes and left.

"Obviously the next person to question is the prince," said Matthew. "He saw Kadourian before he went into the compartment last night and his room is like Delia Hentzen's — right next door to where the killing took place. He may have heard something."

Nash coughed nervously.

"It's going to be tricky. God knows what with diplomatic immunity and protocol and Muslim sensitivities about being accused of every damn terrorist act in the U.S., I'd rather not have to take on Achmed myself."

"Don't worry," said Matthew. "Achmed and I get on like a mosque on fire. Follow me."

9

If Matthew had hoped that his friendly encounter with the prince earlier would translate into an easy interview about Kadourian's death, he was disappointed. The prince was clearly displeased about having his privacy invaded by three almost total strangers. After offering some conventional regrets about Kadourian's death, he merely repeated to Matthew his earlier statement that he had listened to some music, gone to bed, taken a Valium, and fallen asleep almost immediately.

Less than five minutes after they had entered the prince's compartment, they were in the corridor again. Scats was still guarding the door to Kadourian's compartment, but with an ever-growing look of desperation.

"I've gotta go," he said to them as they reappeared. "There's stuff I'm supposed to do."

"OK," said Nash. "We'll figure something out. Thanks for standing by."

Scats hurried off towards the staircase.

"I'm not sure what our next move is anyway," Nash sighed.

Matthew leaned against the window, bracing himself as the train racketed along the track. He could see a vast panorama of jagged peaks lining the horizon while in the foreground a broken terrain of brown rock and scrubland signalled the desert that lay ahead.

"Whip-marks and burns," Honor said suddenly. "Does that suggest anything to you?"

"Apart from the Marquis de Sade, not much," said Matthew.

"One of Glamora's most successful albums was called "Whipsongs and Painchants" — or something like that. And she's always been famous for that dominatrix look."

"Yes," Matthew answered, still gazing at the landscape, "and she also has a rather fetching outfit in green lycra which might possibly match that thread we found."

"I guess we've got our next move then," Nash broke in,

and turning to Honor added, "if you wouldn't mind standing in for Scats while we talk to her."

Surprisingly, Honor made no objection. In fact, Matthew thought he detected a note of relief in her voice when she agreed. It then occurred to him that perhaps Glamora was the mysterious object of Honor's own investigation — the story that was supposed to "blow her audience through the walls."

It took them a moment or two to rouse Glamora, who had dozed off over a copy of *Express*, the Amtrak magazine. She opened one eye and closed it again. Then, with an expression of weary resignation, she beckoned them in. Matthew noted that she was still wearing the green lycra bodysuit.

"Two of you this time," she commented. "Must be getting serious. OK, so sit down and spill it. Find your Irish nanny yet?"

"In a way. This, by the way, is Anderson Nash."

She acknowledged him with a derisive salute.

"When we talked earlier," Matthew said, "you mentioned that you thought you recognized somebody in the dining car ... someone you felt might be an in-law. Was she married to your brother?"

"I don't have a brother."

"So you do have a sister?"

The suddenly flaring nostrils and blazing eyes clearly signalled that Glamora was getting fired up to blow her top.

"No, I don't have a sister! I used to have a sister! She's dead. Now get the fuck out of my compartment! I've had it up to here with you!"

She had risen to her feet as she spoke and now stood eye to eye with him. Matthew didn't flinch, though it took considerable effort on his part to hang on to his composure.

"I'll go in a minute," he said, "but first I want you to look at this picture."

He nodded to Nash, who produced the envelope and took out the photograph of Anna Lundgren. Matthew passed it to Glamora.

"Have you ever seen it before?" he asked.

Glamora's reaction to the picture of the dead Anna Lundgren was quite unlike Delia Hentzen's. She examined it with great care and concentration. Though her eyes were like chips of flint and her mouth was bitter, she did not fall apart as Delia had. It was almost as if the scene was much less horrifying than the one she had carried in her mind.

"Where did you get this?" she demanded, when after a long silence she lifted her eyes from the photograph.

"From Dr. Kadourian's compartment," said Matthew in as neutral a tone as he could manage.

She frowned as if completely mystified.

"Kadourian's compartment? Why would he have it?"

Anderson Nash took the photograph out of her hand.

"We thought you might be able to tell us that."

She shook her head impatiently.

"Well, I can't. Why don't you ask him?"

"Because he's dead, Miss Lundgren," Nash said.

There was no doubt that his answer shocked her.

"Dead?" she said. "Kadourian?"

"Dead, crammed into the shower-stall, almost naked, with signs that some kind of sadomasochistic activity had been going on before he died. Perhaps he was a fan of your 'Whipsongs and Painchants' album."

Glamora looked at Nash as if he had just crawled out from under a particularly slimy stone.

"You sound like one of those guys in Congress that blame Hollywood movies for the decline of America," she exploded. "What the hell do you mean tying my album to what happened to Kadourian?"

"Somebody must have been with him ... somebody he would have wanted to have this kind of sex with ... somebody attractive and aggressive ... somebody who would have been strong enough to overpower him and smother him."

"And I'm elected! Didn't it occur to you, wiseass, that it could have been a man? Maybe Kadourian was into gay S and M."

Nash shrugged.

"He could have been, I suppose. But according to the porn magazines we found in his compartment, it seems unlikely. Magazines like *Dominatrix* and *Bitches in Leather*."

Something about what Nash said made Glamora laugh and collapse back into her seat.

"Funnily enough," she said, "I don't really qualify in either category. So, though I'm sorry as hell to ruin your theory, I wasn't in Kadourian's compartment last night playing bitch goddess to his slaveboy. I'd had my fun and games for the evening."

Matthew coughed.

"Might we ask who with?" he said.

She turned her steely gaze on him and tried to shrivel him with her eyes.

"You know, you've got a nerve, Prior. First you lose your nanny and then this New Age bozo gets iced, and you come round here flappin' your lip at me. Well, as it happens, I was spending an interesting evening with a boxer — a guy called Bracciano — and if I have any more harassment from either of you dickheads, I'll see that he hears about it. You'd both look better with a few less teeth."

"Very likely," said Matthew, "but we're not absolutely sure what time Kadourian was killed, so Mr. Bracciano may not be all that helpful. Now, if you don't mind, I'd like you to look at this thread we found in his compartment."

Nash produced the thread and Glamora peered at it.

"So I've looked at it. So what?"

"We thought it might possibly have come from that rather fetching bodysuit you're wearing," said Matthew.

Glamora grabbed one of the shoulder-straps of the suit, pulled it out and let it snap back.

"See that? Lycra stretches. Does that thread?"

Nash tugged at the thread. It was clear it had no give.

"And the colour! Have you guys no colour sense? This suit is emerald green. That thread is more of a grass colour. And it's a coarse thread. Like you would find in an upholstery fabric. Jeez, what am I doing, standing here giving you lessons in textiles! Will you both just buzz off?"

Nash tucked the thread away and took a deep, controlled breath.

"I've got to tell you, Miss ... er ... Lundgren, that you'll have a lot more questions to answer when the state police take over the case. I'd advise you to be more co-operative with them."

"Oh, you would, would you?" Glamora began, a dangerous glimmer appearing in her eyes.

Matthew interrupted her hastily.

"Look, we're going. Really. I'd just like to ask one more thing. Did you and Anna have any brothers or sisters?"

His persistence in the face of her wrath obviously amused Glamora.

"You're a tough nut," she said. "No, the Lundgrens just

had two kids. Anna and me. Now, for God's sake, will you beat it and let me rest."

With some ill grace on Nash's part, the two men finally left the compartment.

"Damn," said Nash, "that's one hard-nosed bitch. Do you believe she was with this boxer?"

Honor overheard this from where she was still standing guard at Kadourian's door.

"She was, at least until the train got to Kansas City. I heard them talking together earlier through the door of her compartment. And when I talked to Aldo, he said he was out in the corridor just as the train reached the station."

"She probably threw him out," said Nash bitterly.

"He did seem a little uncomfortable talking about it," Honor admitted.

Matthew grinned.

"She seems to think he's her personal hit-man, ready to commit mayhem at a moment's notice. In any case, if she threw him out as the train reached Kansas City, she doesn't have much of an alibi."

"Nor does he," said Nash. "Nor, as far as I can make out, does anyone on this corridor."

Honor chewed her lip thoughtfully.

"Could it have been someone from another part of the train?" she said. "I guess those two security types would have noticed if anyone who didn't belong in this coach tried to get in from the observation car or the bar. I certainly got a pretty thorough once-over from the one who was guarding the door from the bar — and Buzzy seems to have been screened by the one upstairs in the observation lounge."

"The prince's guys," said Nash. "We'll have to check them out. And then there are the people on our level. The thing is, they're all two to a compartment. Presumably they'll be able to alibi each other, but we'll have to verify that. Then there are the people from the back part of the coach…"

"But Scats was on duty all night. He would have seen or heard anyone moving about from one part of the coach to another, wouldn't he?"

"Perhaps," said Matthew, "but don't forget — in Kansas City he got off the train to help Aubretia and her pregnant friend get aboard. Come to that, when I woke up in the middle of the night, I saw him standing on the platform. Depending on how long he was off the train, there would have been some opportunity for someone to sneak from the back of the coach and get into Room G."

"So what next?" Honor asked.

With weary deliberation, Nash laid out the necessary steps to follow: "First question the prince's security guards; then interview Bracciano and the people on the upper level again; I'll get a background report on the Lundgren family from the Idaho boys; I'll also get the Chicago police to look into Kadourian's associates, particularly any connection he has with the S and M scene there."

"While you're talking to Chicago," said Matthew, "better check with that dry-cleaner — the one whose hanger we found in the Verhaeven woman's room. They might know something about her if she's a regular customer — even if it's only her address or telephone number."

Nash took out his notebook and scribbled a note in it.

"And who's going to guard this door?" Honor added. "You don't suppose that I'm going to stand around here like an idiot all day, I hope."

"I think I'll be able to get one of the prince's guys to do that," said Nash. "If anyone is going to try to get in there, I'd rather have a guy with a gun standing in the way than Miss Moore. No offence, but you wouldn't be much of a deterrent to a really determined killer."

Honor gave him a forgiving smile.

"That's OK, Nash. I'll take it as a compliment. And since I won't be guarding the door, Matthew, I'll be free to help you."

"Oh, joy," said Matthew, echoing a previous taunt of hers, but it was clear to Honor that he didn't find the prospect completely unappealing.

Seven
Mirages in the Sand

1

"I think we must be in Utah now," said Sven Sanchez as he stared out of the window at the expanse of rock and sand stretching all the way to the horizon with its distant panorama of sculpted mountains and mesas, peaks, and pinnacles, desolate as the half-buried ruins of an ancient civilization.

Eddie Tsubouchi glanced up from his copy of Eisner's *Comics and Sequential Art* and saw the spectacular red sandstone formations Sven was busy sketching.

"Yup, you're right," he said. "If I remember my high-school geography, we're passing through Utah's canyonlands. Those tall spindly things over there are the Needles. Awesome what a few million years of wind and rain can do."

Sven grunted, keeping his concentration on the process of capturing the landscape on his pad.

"You're gonna use this as background for a Warrior Lords adventure, right? It'll be the planet Zanthos, the renegade world of the Medusa Galaxy. I can just see Lord Mardak zooming down in his terracruiser to foil some piece of dirty work instigated by the Faceless Foe."

Again the only response was a grunt. It was obvious that Sven wasn't in the mood for any friendly verbal skirmishing. Eddie shrugged and went back to his reading, and for a while the only sounds in the compartment were the whisper of Sven's pencil on the leaves of his pad and the rustle of a page being turned in Eddie's book. At last, Eddie couldn't resist breaking the silence.

"Now, me," he said, gesturing to the landscape outside the window, "I can see wilder landscapes than this in my mind. You know I've always thought that was the problem with the guys that did the cover illustrations for the old *Amazing Stories* and *Astounding Science Fiction* pulps. They were too much like a slightly more exotic version of earth. Just like the space ships were really intergalactic Cadillacs!"

Sven put his pencil down and looked across at Eddie.

"So you're saying my drawings are too pedestrian."

Eddie was taken aback at the seriousness of Sven's tone.

"Whoa," he said. "Don't go putting words in my mouth. Listen, I think you're a terrific draftsman. Your drawings are strong and dramatic. I just think it wouldn't hurt to let your subconscious take over a bit more."

There was another, briefer silence while Sven seemed to be digesting this comment, then he closed his sketch pad carefully and put it on the seat beside him.

"I've been thinking about what you said in the hotel," he said. "Maybe I do need to take a fresh look at things. I don't know that there's much I can do to rejuvenate the Warrior Lords, but I might be able to do better with a new project, something more in tune with the times. After all, before we know it we'll be in the twenty-first century. I guess my universe is an old-fashioned one where people get into spaceships and travel billions of miles from galaxy to galaxy.

They may travel faster than the speed of light but otherwise they obey all the rules of scientific reality. There're different concepts of space now — cyberspace, virtual reality, wormholes in the time-space continuum that can lead to new dimensions. Yeah, Eddie, when you get right down to it, the Warrior Lords are just old-fashioned cowboys locked into a worn-out vision of the cosmos."

It was the longest speech Eddie had ever heard Sven give and though there was despondency behind it, there was also a new conviction.

"You know what I said, man," he answered. "I'd love to help. In fact, I'd love to work with you. Think of it — class and *chutzpah* working together. We'd be unbeatable."

What Sven's response might have been at that point was fated to remain a mystery, because just then there was a knock at the door of their compartment.

"Sorry to bother you again," said Matthew Prior, after he had entered at Sven's invitation, "but there's been another — er — incident."

"Another disappearing nanny?" Eddie joked.

"Rather more serious than that, I'm afraid. Did either of you notice a dark-haired bearded man in the dining car last night?"

Eddie nodded vigorously.

"Vartan Kadourian — the Mind/Body Man. One of the New Age gurus. He was at a table with that black guy."

"Prince Achmed."

"Oh, sorry — that black prince, then."

"Did you see him at any time after dinner?"

Sven answered for them this time.

"Yes, about half an hour after dinner. We were in the

bar. In fact I did a drawing of him."

Picking up his sketch pad, Sven flipped through the pages until he found the one he was looking for, then passed the pad across to Matthew. Again Matthew was impressed by the economy and boldness of line that Sven had employed to produce a striking likeness of Kadourian. He was leaning back in his seat, his eyes fixed in what seemed like alarm on a woman sitting opposite him. The drawing of the woman was equally arresting. She was leaning forward towards Kadourian and there was an accusing expression on her face. One hand was raised, the index finger pointing directly at her table companion, while the other hand held a highball glass, the contents of which seemed in danger of slopping onto the tablecloth. Altogether it was a remarkably vivid sketch of Aubretia Adams.

"The woman with him: isn't she the one who wanted to know if Teresa Shaughnessy was a nurse? The one who sat with you at dinner yesterday evening?" Matthew said, almost sure that he was right, but wanting Sven to confirm it.

"Right," said Sven. "That's Aubretia. By that time she was getting pretty high, but I think that may be a fairly constant state with her."

"She also looks furious about something."

Eddie gave a reminiscent chuckle.

"You bet," he said. "The old babe was going apeshit. She kept calling him Dr. Avedissian, and he kept telling her his name was Kadourian."

"Avedissian? Hmmm ... did you hear anything that would tell you what she was so angry about?"

Eddie shook his head.

"No, the only time they got really loud was over the

name. The rest of the time they kept their voices down."

"Did she calm down eventually?"

"Kind of. After a couple of minutes, she seemed to get really confused and she got up and stumbled off. I guess she went to bed."

"Do you know what time that was?" Matthew asked.

"I guess around eleven-fifteen."

"And what time did Kadourian leave?"

"Just before we did — around eleven-thirty."

Matthew pondered for a moment.

"I don't think your friend Aubretia would have gone to bed at eleven-fifteen, not when she was expecting someone to join her in Kansas City," he declared finally. "I was asleep when the train got there. You were obviously up, because you did those sketches of Teresa and her companion getting off the train. Do you remember what time the train actually arrived in Kansas City?"

"It was due in at quarter to one," said Sven, "but that delay in Chicago put us behind schedule. We made up some time, but it was still late getting in. I'd guess it was about quarter after one, and then we were stuck waiting for those boy scouts until after two."

Eddie snickered.

"Trust meticulous old Sven to keep an eye on the time. Why is it so important, anyway?"

"Because we're trying to establish a timetable of events. It's necessary in a murder case."

"Murder case?"

"Yes. Dr. Kadourian was murdered last night."

Both Sven and Eddie seemed stunned by the news.

"Kadourian!" said Eddie. "You're kidding!"

Matthew shook his head.

"No, I'm quite serious. Incidentally, were either of you out of each other's sight at any time between say eleven-thirty and two a.m.?"

"We don't watch each other go to the bathroom," said Eddie," but other than that, no."

"I did go out to stretch my legs in the corridor," Sven said.

"OK, I guess technically you were out of sight, but I could certainly hear you clumping up and down. And you weren't gone long enough to commit a murder."

They both looked worried but not, in Matthew's estimation, guilty.

"So you can give each other an alibi?" he said. "Well, I can't say either of you were high on the list of suspects. But till we know more, everyone in this coach will have to get used to the idea that they're under suspicion. Meanwhile, if you think of anything else that might help, let me or Anderson Nash in Room D know right away."

Silently, the two men nodded and Matthew left them, murmuring the name "Avedissian" to himself and looking distinctly less composed than when he arrived.

2

Seconds later, when Matthew knocked on Nash's door and entered his compartment, he found Nash in conference with Dr. Holliday.

"Anything new?" he asked.

"New but not good," said Nash. "Doc was just in touch

with the psychiatric hospital and it looks like your Irish friend has slipped into a coma. So we won't be getting any information out of her for a while."

"Damn!" said Matthew. "She was such a nice ordinary woman; why did this have to happen to her?"

"Nice ordinary folks often end up as victims. Usually because they aren't expecting other folks to be lawbreakers. But we still don't know which of those categories this Shaughnessy belongs to."

"I'd stake my next Hollywood contract on her innocence," Matthew said. "My guess is that the Verhaeven woman pulled a gun on her and that they struggled and Teresa got the gun away from her just as it went off. What kind of gun was it, by the way?"

Nash paused and then, with apparent reluctance, replied.

"That's one thing that might support your theory. The gun is one that's commonly known as a Firebird. It's actually a Hungarian-manufactured nine-millimetre semi-automatic, the Parabellum 'Togakypt.' The Baader-Meinhof gang in Germany used them."

"Hungarian-manufactured? Aren't Hungary and the Galinian Republic near neighbours?"

"Very near. And I'm sure Firebirds are common anywhere in the Balkans. But there must be thousands of them in use all over Europe ... so that doesn't get us very far."

Matthew turned to Doc Holliday.

"Any news from the medical examiner's office about the dead woman?"

"Not yet. They haven't completed the autopsy. There should be some information in a couple of hours."

"So much for the Kansas City end, then," said Matthew. "Any information from Chicago about Kadourian?"

Nash hauled out his notebook and flipped it open.

"Kadourian?" he said. "Well, he was a highly regarded civic figure, contributor to the right political funds, regular donator to high-profile charities, on the board of a couple of art museums, unmarried, escorter of wealthy divorcees to expensive restaurants, and a member of the 'O' Club, a meeting place for well-to-do sadists and masochists. He was a switch-hitter in that area apparently. Sometimes he was the dominator and sometimes the dominated."

"The 'O' Club?" said Matthew. "At least that confirms that the scene in Room G wasn't staged to throw us off the track. How long had Kadourian been established in Chicago and where was he before that?"

"He arrived on the Chicago scene about ten years ago, via New Zealand and Switzerland. Nobody knows much about his career before that, except that he claimed to have a degree from the University of Smyrna."

"I wonder if the reason nobody knows about his earlier career is because he wasn't known as Kadourian then. Two people have mistaken him for a Dr. Avedissian. Can you run that past your sources and see if it leads anywhere?"

Nash scribbled in his notebook, and then turned back to an earlier page.

"Here's another bit of news from Chicago," he said. "You remember that dry cleaner you asked me to contact? Well, the manager there remembered Miss Verhaeven quite well. Had an address and a telephone number for her, so the Chicago boys are checking that out now. But one other thing:

she said one of her employees found a letter in a jacket that had been left for cleaning by Verhaeven. The letter had been written to her address in Chicago but the name on the front was Varya Krasna. So either she had a visitor staying with her, or she was travelling under an assumed name."

"And it certainly isn't a Dutch name," said Matthew. "In fact it sounds like a Russian name to me. Or perhaps a Galinian one. Delia did say she thought the woman had a Galinian accent."

Nash seemed to have drifted into a state of abstraction and was staring intently at the entry in his notebook.

"You know that name seems to trigger something," he mused. "I've a feeling the woman who shot the Russian TV guy was called Krasna. I'd better run that by our Virginia office."

Dr. Holliday interrupted them with a diffident cough.

"I think I'm a bit redundant here, right now. Besides, I should go and see what my boys are up to. I'm not the only scoutmaster on the trip, but sometimes it takes all of us all our time to make sure they don't revert to total savagery."

The other two men apologized for detaining him unnecessarily and asked him to be sure to let them know the minute he had any report on the autopsy. After he left, they lapsed into silence for a moment, sitting on opposite sides of the window and watching the fantastic formations of red sandstone, some grouped like giants at a titanic cocktail party, some spread out like massive misshapen palaces abandoned by their mad inhabitants, as the Flying Angel whirled past.

"I'm going to demand a refund," said Matthew. "I've missed at least half the scenery on this scenic trip, running around looking for missing nannies and murderous dominatrixes."

"One consolation: It'll be out of our hands in Caliente when the Nevada guys take over."

"When do we get there?"

Nash looked pointlessly at his watch.

"I guess about nine o'clock tonight."

"Well, that gives us a few hours to solve the case," said Matthew. "I always work better with a deadline. What's our next move?"

3

In Room I, Honor was conducting a second interview with Aldo Bracciano. The nervous young boxer kept pushing the hair away from his eyes and fiddling with the signet ring on his left hand as he answered her questions.

"Yeah, like I said before I was out of her room and into the corridor just when we were gettin' to Kansas City. So — yeah — it was about one-fifteen, something like that."

"And you went to her compartment straight after dinner?"

"Yeah. Around ten-thirty."

"And you were with her all through dinner? She didn't leave at any point?"

"No. Like I told you, I was with her from about seven-thirty all the way through to when — er — when the train got to Kansas City."

Honor wondered why he blushed when he said this.

"Did you happen to hear her or see her leave her compartment later on?"

"No, but I had the blinds down and I was listening to the sports news with my stereo headphones on. I wouldn't have seen or heard anything. Then I went to sleep."

"Were you still awake when the train left Kansas City?"

"Yeah, I felt the train start to move, that's when I took off my headphones and turned the light out."

Bracing herself for the next question and putting on her most reassuring smile, Honor slid just a little closer to Aldo along the train seat.

"Now, I hope that you won't feel that I'm being too personal, but it's very important that you answer this next question frankly. You see, the situation has gotten much more serious ... not only do we have a person who may have been abducted from the train, but we also have two people dead: the woman who left the train with the Irish nanny, and Dr. Kadourian. So please tell me — did you and Glamora make love in her compartment?"

Aldo was clearly both scandalized and mortified. He almost writhed in his seat with embarrassment.

"Jeez, lady," he faltered, "that's a very personal question. I mean, things like that — they're, like, private between two people. You know what I'm saying?"

Honor slid just a little closer and smiled even more reassuringly.

"I know what you're saying — and I respect you for it. It shows you have the right instincts. But this is a homicide case. Eventually you're going to have to tell somebody — and they might not be quite as understanding. So what happened? I promise I'll treat anything you tell me with the greatest discretion."

"I just don't see what it has to do with this other stuff."

"Trust me, there could be an important connection."

"Oh, jeez, OK," he moaned finally. "We did kinda neck a bit, but there was nothing else — honest. I never really touched her."

"You necked without touching her?" said Honor incredulously. "How does that work?"

Aldo looked even more miserable.

"She made me let her tie my hands behind my back," he muttered.

Honor's smile remained unwaveringly reassuring.

"Really," she said. "And what was the idea of that?"

"It was supposed to get me to relax," said the agonized boxer.

"To relax. I see. And did it?"

"Like hell it did! She was driving me nuts with her fingernails and her hands."

"And how long did this go on?"

"Jeez, I don't know. Maybe an hour."

"And what? You finally had enough? Or she got bored?"

Aldo squirmed and ducked his head.

"She threw me out. Didn't even give me a chance to put my pants on. I was out in the corridor when the train came into Kansas City in just my shorts. Jeez, I tell you, it was one of the worst moments of my life."

Honor could see how that would very probably have been the case.

"But what made her throw you out?"

"She wanted me to do something for her and I kinda balked."

"What kind of something?"

Again Aldo looked sulky and uncomfortable. He squirmed about in his seat and chewed at his nails.

"She wanted me to be — like — a bodyguard. Either there was some joker on board who she thought was after her for some reason, or there was somebody she wanted roughed up as a payback ... I don't know. But I'm no torpedo. I'm not some guy you can hire to give the business to whoever you have a beef with. I'm a professional fighter!"

It was clear that his *amour propre* had been hurt by Glamora's attempt to use him, and Honor felt an impulse to pat him reassuringly as if he were a pouting schoolboy. However, she overcame the impulse.

"So you left her room at about one-fifteen," she said. "And you didn't see her or hear her at any time later in the night. Did you leave your room at any time after the train left Kansas City?"

He shook his head silently.

"So you wouldn't have seen anyone going or coming from Dr. Kadourian's room?"

"Nope. Listen, this is all about the murder investigation, right? I mean you've got this TV show and all; you wouldn't bullshit me just to get a story about me and Glamora?"

And what a story! Honor thought. It would certainly be as good as the one about the Senator and the Lithuanian lap-dancer. But even though her scruples in these matters were usually decidedly elastic, something about Aldo made her want to be humane and honourable.

"Aldo, don't worry. I won't put anything about you on "Hot Flashes" that you don't personally agree to."

He grabbed her hand and shook it.

"That's a deal then. And thanks. You're a pal."

Honor left Room I, wondering whether this new for-bearance on her part had anything to do with Matthew. Was she losing her edge because of one idiotic Englishman? Well, if she lost it, it probably wouldn't be permanent; after all, nothing else was.

4

The prince had been surpris-ingly co-operative about lending his security men to the investigation. Not only did he direct Jackson to stand guard at Kadourian's door, but he sent Harrison and Morrison to question the passengers in the rear of the coach, while Jones stayed with the prince in Room F. The reason he had chosen Jones to stay with him was that he was marginally more com-panionable than the other three. It was actually possible to hold a conversation with him, providing one stayed away from more arcane topics — like the philosophy of Descartes. In fact, he could be quite voluble on the subject of, say, American football, or the works of Tom Clancy, or even the relative merits of David Letterman and Jay Leno as late-night TV hosts.

On this occasion, however, they were talking about none of those things. This time, the topic was murder.

"In your country," the prince was saying, "murder seems to have become part of the entertainment industry. Your most successful films seem to consist largely of people being riddled with bullets, or blown up, or thrown off tall buildings. The biggest television event has been a celebrity murder trial. And I believe there is some support among the public for televised executions. Can you explain this, please?"

Jones considered this question for some moments, his brow furrowed, his ovoid head tilted to one side, his lower lip thrust out judiciously.

"How I look at it, Your Royal Highness," he said eventually, "is that our society likes to think of itself as still a frontier culture — you know — where right is right, justice is swift, and every guy who is really a guy carries a gun. Of course, ninety per cent of them are sitting on their butts in an office, or sitting on their butts in front of a TV set. They're scared of losing their jobs, scared their kids are turning into druggies or fags, worried that the women in their lives are having their minds taken over by feminists, or that the men in their lives have other women in their lives. I hate to say it, but I think a lot of them are only a few heartbeats away from going beserk on the streets with a Uzi. So Bruce Willis with an assault weapon is a kind of safety valve. He's their proxy, kind of, if you know what I mean."

"Fascinating," said the prince. "But you — and Jackson and Morrison and Harrison — really live the lives they dream about. You carry guns. You live, as they say, on the edge. You are, I imagine, sometimes called upon to face death. You must be happy to be so much a paradigm of your culture."

"A which?"

"An exemplar, a role model if you like."

The corners of Jones's mouth turned down in a grimace of repudiation.

"Nah, Your Royal Highness," he sighed, "it's like any job. The longer you do it the more fucking tedious it gets — if you'll excuse my language."

Prince Achmed arched his eyebrows.

"So why continue?" he asked.

"What else would I do?" Jones answered, "I'm not qualified for anything else."

The conversation was beginning to depress the prince, so he was relieved when he heard a tentative tap at the door. Jones put his hand inside his coat and grasped the butt of his Browning M1935.

"Yes, you may come in," the prince called.

His eyes were fixed at the level where he would expect to see the face of an adult, but to his surprise, when the door opened he had to lower them a good eighteen inches. When he did, he saw a young boy of African descent in a scout's uniform and another of Anglo-Saxon heritage in a Dodgers T-shirt and baggy shorts.

In a dissonant and imperfect unison, they chorused: "We're investigating a murder."

5

In a relatively short time, the interrogation of the passengers in the rear section of the coach was completed and yielded nothing in the way of new information. Similarly, a further interview with Aubretia and her young friend, Natalie, produced no results — Aubretia clearly had been too fuddled by alcohol to remember much of the previous night, and Natalie had gone straight to bed when she boarded, being tired and pregnant, and had seen and heard nothing out of the ordinary.

It was late in the afternoon before Matthew had any replies to his fax messages. He was sitting with Honor in his compartment, when Bob Bonsecours came by to deliver them to him. The first was from Nell Finnegan. It read:

Not again, darling. Really, you should stay home if your presence is going to be a cue for murder. What do I know about Delia Hentzen? Well, an attractive girl, looks good under stage-lighting, moves well, a competent performer, good at supporting roles where she doesn't have to carry a large part of the play. A bit reserved. Not many friends at LAMDA. Best friend Anna Lundgren, pretty blonde American, with real potential as a lead player. Anna hooked Delia's sexy brother, Fedor. I was at the wedding. Very small affair. Bride upset that her brother couldn't be there, but apparently he was on tour. I think he's some kind of singer. And you know the rest: bride and groom murdered on honeymoon. Devastated everybody at the school. Delia was in shock for a long time. Probably what prompted her to leave England. That's all, I think, darling. Look forward to seeing you later in the summer. Kisses and things, Nell.

The other fax was from Dorothy Bedlington:

Matthew, Nothing much to report. Nothing known of any woman called Verhaeven. Shaughnessy has no criminal record, no known association with any political or quasi-political action group in Ireland. Her work history in child-care seems legitimate. Hentzen is known to British intelligence services, daughter of a Communist official, brother of Fedor Hentzen, leader of radical youth group in Galinian Republic. No known direct involvement in any political action group, may possibly be pursuing personal vendetta against former president Golovyov. Kadourian's history prior to U.S. is as psychotherapist in New Zealand, as staff psychologist at the Eisenbach Institute in Switzerland, which was closed down by Swiss authorities in 1986. Prior to that no record. No-one by name of Kadourian has degree from medical school of University of Smyrna at any time when he could have graduated. Hope you will have sorted out your feelings by time you get back. My patience is running out. Dorothy.

Matthew read the two documents with furious concentration and in total silence until he came to the end of Dorothy's, at which point he muttered, "Damn!"

"Anything wrong, Matthew?" Honor asked.

"What? Er — no, not really."

"Can I see the faxes?"

Hastily, he folded them up and tucked them into his inside pocket.

"Privileged communication," he said. "I can tell you the relevant information, though. Anna Lundgren had a brother, and Kadourian's real name wasn't Kadourian."

Honor gave every appearance of being dissatisfied. She

narrowed her eyes and tightened her mouth.

"I don't see why you won't show me the faxes," she complained. "Don't you trust me?"

"It's official policy. I'm prohibited from showing confidential reports from Scotland Yard to members of the journalistic profession."

"What about the one from your friend at that British drama school?"

"It's — er — it's a question of personal privacy. He's having some marital problems and I don't think he'd want me revealing them to strangers."

"He? I thought it was a woman: Nell something or other?"

Matthew laughed nervously.

"No, no. Not Nell — Neil!"

"Neil?" she repeated sceptically.

Fortunately for Matthew's equilibrium, Nash knocked and entered the compartment at that moment.

"Just had some news from Idaho," he said. "The Lundgrens are still farming in Custer County, and they only ever had two children: one girl called Anna, and one boy called Victor. Anna was married to Fedor Hentzen, and died with him on the Isola Bella on Lake Maggiore. Victor is still alive."

Before Matthew could speak, Honor leapt in triumphantly.

"And is on this train," she crowed, "passing as a woman called Glamora. I knew it! It's my big story. It's going to—"

"I know," said Matthew acidly. "It's going to blow your audience right through the walls."

6

Aubretia Adams was worried. Not that this was an unusual state of mind for her. Her haphazard life had created many occasions for worry. In her flounderings to escape them, she had more often than not multiplied them. This time she was faced with a worry that made any previous one seem like a day at the beach. Kadourian was dead.

Those two guys — the English type and the one from Washington — had dropped that news on her when she was feeling particularly fragile, thanks to a heavy intake of bourbon the night before. But the real concern was that the binge had brought on one of her major blackouts. She couldn't remember one solitary goddam thing after she had stumbled back to her compartment with Natalie.

Speaking of whom — at least she still had a grip on her whoses and whoms — speaking of whom, what a stimulating companion she was! She did nothing but lie there, bitching about her back and her legs, reading *Cosmopolitan*, having Scats bring her snacks from the dining room because she felt too bushed to move. And as for conversation! Well, it was like talking to a fire hydrant.

"Was I noisy last night, Natalie?" "No, Auntie Aubretia, you were fine." "Did you hear me get up?" "No, Auntie Aubretia, I was fast asleep." Blah, blah, blah.

Every man, woman, and child on the train could have been massacred overnight, and she wouldn't have noticed. Look at her now — with her eyes riveted on some twittering article about seven signs to look for in a troubled marriage.

That'll be a big help to her. A troubled marriage would be a one hundred per cent improvement on her present situation. Still, she was going to be the baby's mother — *her* baby's mother — and for that reason alone, Aubretia was willing to put up with her. At least until she got out of the delivery room.

If only Natalie hadn't been such a sound sleeper. Then she might be able to swear that Aubretia hadn't left the compartment during the night in a drunken daze and gone to ... and gone to ... Oh, the uncertainty was driving her nuts! She remembered the bar. She remembered shouting at him while he stonily repeated: "My name is Kadourian." Then nothing but blackness and fog till she was out on the platform, waiting for Natalie to show up.

All she was really sure of was that she had wanted to kill him. She had felt it in her mind, in her body, in her hands. God knows, he deserved to die. And that woman too, the one he was so chummy with. Never got a really good look at her face ... but she was as deep in it as he was. Two heartless bastards together.

Suddenly she was weeping again. Not wanting Natalie to see this and offer useless sympathy, she pulled open the door and blundered out into the corridor. The only answer was the bar. Maybe a few more drinks would take her back to that safe darkness where nothing mattered.

7

"So Honor's convinced that Glamora is the guilty party," said Matthew, when all three of them had reassembled in the bar after Nash had sent his fax inquiring about Varya Krasna.

"Well, take the fact that Kadourian's wrists were tied behind his back. That's exactly what she — er — he — did to Aldo."

Honor was leaning forward, waving a pencil for emphasis. Matthew took it from her and scribbled something in his notebook. She grabbed it back.

"And then there's the relationship with Anna Lundgren and Fedor Hentzen."

"Glamora never met Hentzen," said Nash.

"It doesn't matter. He was her brother-in-law. Kadourian was responsible for his death and Anna's. It's obviously a revenge killing. Glamora's certainly big enough and tough enough to handle someone of Kadourian's size."

"But why should Kadourian kill Fedor and his wife?" Matthew objected. "There's no evidence that he had any connection with either of them — and certainly no indication of any motive."

Honor frowned and twisted a strand of her hair around one finger.

"According to Delia, he used to live in the Galinian Republic. Someone he knew there could have paid him to do it."

Nash objected this time.

"Kadourian doesn't have the profile of a hired killer. Besides, when those murders happened, he was already well established — probably well enough known even in Europe through his books and video-tapes to make it hard for him to be anywhere near the scene of a murder without somebody noticing. The best hired killers are chameleons. They blend in and take on different personas. Kadourian was a very distinctive-looking guy."

"Well, then," Honor persisted, "he didn't do it. Somebody planted those pictures in his room to fool Glamora into thinking he did it."

"That seems more likely," said Matthew, "but how would Glamora have found out he had them. I'm sure he didn't just go up to her and say, 'Like to see some pictures?'"

"And she'd — he'd — have no reason to go poking about in Kadourian's room," Nash added.

Honor was nothing if not persistent.

"All right, how about this? Glamora gets invited into Kadourian's room, because — with his S and M inclinations — he's been turned on by her album and video. He initiates a session — shows her his collection of chains and handcuffs and whatever — and ends up with the hood on and his wrists fastened behind his back. She gives him a few belts, burns him with a cigarette, and then maybe lets him lie there for a bit, tied up and virtually gagged and blindfolded by the hood, to build up his anticipation for the next round of punishment. To fill in the time, she starts snooping about and comes across the photographs. She assumes he's the killer, loses her marbles, and suffocates him."

The two men looked impressed.

"It certainly seems to hang together," said Nash. "What do you think, Matthew?"

Matthew winked at Honor.

"I always knew you were a smart girl," he said maddeningly. "Just two points: where did the green thread come from, and why the cigarette burns?"

"That's right. The green thread certainly wasn't from

Glamora's bodysuit," Nash agreed. "But I don't understand your question about the burns."

"You don't? Well, you and I both saw that Kadourian's body had cigarette burns on it. I searched his room. There were no cigarettes, no lighter, no matches. Glamora is a famous anti-smoking crusader, and there was certainly no sign of cigarettes or matches in the ashtrays in her compartment."

Before Nash could answer, Scats approached their table.

"Bob sent me with this fax for you, Mr. Nash," he said, flourishing the document in his large brown hand.

"That was quick," Matthew commented.

"Sure," Nash grinned. "The agency is on its toes these days after all the bad press it's had. They're scared to let any lead slip by."

Nash thanked Scats. As soon as he had gone, he read the fax over to himself and then read it aloud to Matthew and Honor.

"Confirmed Varya Krasna suspected assassin of Moscow TV host, Kukolnik. Subsequently linked to leading Russian criminal gang, operating internationally. Formerly gynecologist with Children of the Revolution Pediatric Clinic in Solonitza, Galinia. Worked in partnership with pediatric health specialist, Harout Avedissian. Employment of both terminated due to inquiry into blood transfusion experiments on newborns that resulted in AIDS deaths of several infants. Inquiry initiated in response to complaints to WHO by prospective adoptive parent from U.S."

When Nash stopped reading, Matthew whistled.

"Well, that provides a couple of new motives for murder," he said. "Somebody could have killed Verhaeven — if she really was Krasna — either in revenge for Kukolnik's death, or in revenge for the baby deaths in Solonitza."

Honor began waving her pencil at him again.

"And since Kadourian's been killed too," she said, "it seems likely that — if he really was Avedissian — the two deaths are linked and the motive behind both of them is the same."

"So all we need to do now to prove your case," Nash summed up, "is find out (a) if Verhaeven was Krasna, and (b) if Kadourian was Avedissian."

"And (c)," Honor broke in, "who the prospective adoptive parent from the U.S. was."

A voice from behind them said: "That would have been me."

8

With a double bourbon already working its internal solace and another one on the table in front of her, Aubretia Adams told Matthew, Honor, and Nash her story.

"I had a son," she said. "His name was Christopher, and my husband and I loved him very much. When he was seven he caught meningitis from some other kid in his school in Westchester. I don't think I've ever seen a human being in so much pain. My husband, James, was rich and paid for the best treatment available, but our little boy died. After we had got over most of the misery, we tried again. And again and again. Nothing seemed to work. Finally we decided to adopt.

I had a fierce belief that after we adopted I would conceive again. Well, it had happened to other people, so why not me? Eventually, after they'd investigated our background, checked out our home, studied us from stem to gudgeon, they gave us their approval and within a year or so we adopted a boy. He was three years old and looked a lot like Christopher at that age. We called him David. But having him didn't work any miracle as far as my fertility went. I still didn't conceive. David was with us for four years — and then one day when he was out on his bicycle, he was hit by a delivery van and killed instantly. He was almost exactly the same age as Christopher was when he died."

Aubretia paused and took a long gulp of bourbon. The three listeners waited in silent dismay.

"That was when I really started to hit the sauce. And, boy, let me tell you — I took to the booze like a New York cop takes to doughnuts. Well, that didn't do my marriage any good. The more besotted I got the more disapproving James became. And you've never seen disapproval until you've seen a New England Adams demonstrating it. Anyway, it ended in divorce. I moved away from Westchester, got an apartment in Manhattan, and proceeded to live the life of a bourbon-swilling divorcee. But I couldn't get rid of the obsession of needing a child, needing someone I'd be important to, someone I could — what's the word? — nurture, I guess. Of course, the adoption agencies don't look with too much favour on booze-swilling divorcees, so my prospects weren't exactly dazzling. Anyway, one night at a party I met someone who knew someone who said that adoption rules in the Galinian Republic were quite lax and, provided I could get a visa to visit the country, there were orphans there for the picking."

It was obvious to her listeners that, though Aubretia had — up to this point — maintained her composure remarkably well, the recollection of these events was beginning to affect her. Her voice wavered and her eyes were growing damp. However, she brushed aside the suggestion that she should take a break, and after another liberal dose of bourbon, she continued.

"Well, it wasn't easy to get a visa but after a long wait I got one. I flew to Solonitza and started inquiries. I was passed from official to official till I finally met up with Dr. Harout Avedissian, who was a consulting physician at the Proskovya Orphanage in Solonitza. He took me personally to the ward where they kept the newborns, mostly children of single mothers who hadn't survived childbirth. I walked through that ward and saw child after child, lying in shabby cots, obviously getting only the most basic care. And then I saw one — blue-eyed and fair-skinned — who I knew immediately was the child I wanted. Of course, there was a lot of red tape. I couldn't just pick him up and walk out of the orphanage with him, though that's what I desperately wanted to do. So I went back to the hotel and waited. And I waited. After about four days, a messenger came from the orphanage. It wasn't Avedissian, or one of the nurses, or even one of the clerks, it was literally the odd-job man — the one that ran errands for them. I went down to the lobby to meet him, and of course I couldn't understand a word he said. An assistant-manager at the reception desk translated for me. The message was that the baby had died of some kind of infection. I went into a rage. The staff of the hotel had to restrain me and eventually a doctor came to my room and gave me a sedative. I stayed on another week, hoping to find out more, and I did hear gossip — rumours of some blood transfusion experiments at the orphanage and the Children of the Revolution Pediatric Clinic, where Avedissian and his girlfriend, Dr. Varya Krasna, worked. Blood experiments that had transmitted a mystery virus to a few babies, who had then died suddenly. It was a very destructive virus, but it seems they wouldn't have died so quickly from the infection alone. Rumour said that the doctors had panicked when they realized what they'd done and to try to cover up had given the babies something to end their lives, something that would make it look as if they'd died of natural causes. Unfortunately for them, somebody got suspicious, autopsies were done — and the truth came out. Or it came out within the hospital. The authorities didn't want it to go any further. It would all have been forgotten, I'm sure, if it hadn't been for me and a sympathetic foreign correspondent and the World Health Organization. But in the end it didn't do much good. Avedissian and Krasna were fired, but it didn't improve the lives of the orphans, and the reports about the virus were buried, which is criminal in itself, because now there are strong suspicions that it might have been an early manifestation of the AIDS virus."

Aubretia searched in her bag and pulled out a handkerchief, and dabbed at her eyes. She then blew her nose.

"That's terrible," Honor said, reaching across the table and patting her hand. "But you didn't give up, did you? On adoption I mean. I guess you plan to adopt your friend Natalie's baby?"

Aubretia tucked her handkerchief away again and smiled moistly at her.

"I suppose that was obvious. It's her parents who are

really my friends — or maybe acquaintances is the better word. I met them on a trip to Europe. Natalie came over here on a student visa, and had an affair with this boy on campus. When he got her pregnant she was afraid to tell her folks back in Europe. They're kind of stuffy old-fashioned bourgeois. She had heard about me from her parents and she had my address. I guess she felt I'd be more broad-minded. Anyway, she got in touch, and we worked out a deal. Not a strictly legal one, but we think it's going to work. She's already had the ultrasound thing, so we know it's going to be a boy."

"I hope things work out for you this time," said Matthew gravely. "But, tell me about this Dr. Avedissian. Do you believe that he and Dr. Kadourian were the same person?"

Aubretia put her glass down so hard that Honor feared she might have cracked it.

"I know they were. He may not have remembered me. I've changed a good bit in fourteen years, but he hadn't. I couldn't mistake those eyes or that voice. He was Avedissian."

There was an awkward silence. Nash fumbled with the pages of his notebook, Matthew glanced uneasily at his watch, and Honor fixed her eyes on the passing landscape.

"If you're sure about that," Nash said eventually, "maybe you've got some idea about who killed him."

"Oh, I have," said Aubretia. "I'm very much afraid it must have been me."

Eight
Showdown in Caliente

1

"Hey, that prince guy was cool."

Buzzy Nash and Ryan Woolf were on their way up the stairs to the second level, having canvassed the lower level with mixed success.

"Yeah, he was OK till you said your dad thought he looked like Eddie Murphy," answered Ryan. "He got kind of burned about that."

"He liked you, though," Buzzy said. "He said you were an uncut gem or something. And who was this Deck Art guy he kept going on about?"

"Beats me. So who do we talk to next?"

"The guys in Room E — right here."

They had reached the top of the stairs and turned left down the corridor where Buzzy's compartment was. The first door to their left was open and they saw an older man with olive skin, white hair, and a black moustache and a younger man with a ponytail who was clearly Oriental, sitting at opposite sides of the small fold-out table by the window, playing a card game.

"Hey, guys, what can we do for you?" Eddie Tsubouchi called out.

"Hi, I'm Buzzy Nash from next door and this is my partner, Ryan Woolf. We're investigating a murder."

Sven turned his head towards them and raised his eyebrows.

"Isn't that a bit superfluous?" he said. "Half the people in the coach already seem to be doing that."

Buzzy was unfazed by this.

"Yeah, I know," he said. "My dad's one of them."

"What's really needed on this case," said Eddie mischievously, "is the Warrior Lords."

Ryan's mouth fell open in disbelief.

"You guys read comic books?" he gasped.

"We guys make comic books. Meet Sven Sanchez, creator of the *Warrior Lords* — and Eddie Tsubouchi, the brains behind *Spirit Shifter*."

Both the boys were noticeably impressed. Though they found the Warrior Lords a little old-fashioned now, there was still a lingering respect for them as archaic figures in the boys' mutual mythology — and Spirit Shifter was cool but a bit weirder than they were ready for yet.

"I drew a comic book once," said Buzzy. "My dad thought it was kinda neat for a first go."

Sven gathered up the cards and stacked them into a deck.

"What was your comic about? Did it have a superhero?" he asked with genuine interest.

"Yeah, it's about Scopeman, Seer of the Universe. He can see what's happening on distant planets, and he can look into the future and the past. The only thing that can cloud his vision is the Black Mist."

Ryan was also looking interested, and impressed.

"You made that up yourself?"

"Sure," said Buzzy.

"Tell me about the Black Mist," Sven prompted.

"Well, it's, like, this mysterious force that comes from somewhere in interplanetary space. It might even be an intelligent being. Nobody knows for sure. Or it might be controlled by beings from another galaxy. Anyway, it stops Scopeman from seeing ... and then he has to rely on Drog — who's half-dog half-dragon — to guide him."

Sven put the cards aside and turned his full attention on Buzzy.

"You know, Eddie," he said. "There might be something here."

"Yeah," said Eddie, "I like the combination of space, the occult and sword-and-sorcery fantasy. It's got possibilities."

"Can I see some of you guys' drawings?" Buzzy asked.

Sven reached behind him and pulled out his sketch pad.

"Here," he said, "help yourself."

Buzzy leafed through the pad, stopping every now and then to study one particular drawing with greater concentration. Ryan peered over his shoulder.

"These are all regular people," said Ryan with some disappointment. "I mean, there's no comic book characters here."

"That's because I base all my drawings on regular people," said Sven. "There's so much variety in human faces, and I often find particular ones that suggest possible new characters for my series."

"Hey, I know this one," said Buzzy suddenly, tapping one finger on the page in front of him.

"Which one?"

Buzzy held the pad out to Sven.

"This is the deaf lady I thought was a spy," he said.

Sven took the pad and studied the picture.

"That's the woman who got off in Kansas City with the Irish nanny."

"You've got her wrong, though."

Sven was mildly affronted by this. He brought the pad closer and examined the figure again.

"What do you mean?"

"You've got her moving wrong."

Eddie laughed uncharitably.

"Boy, did you ever put your foot in it. Sven prides himself on his skill at capturing bodies in motion."

Sven frowned and held the drawing out to Buzzy again.

"Here, show me where it's wrong," he challenged him.

"Give me a second," Buzzy said, "and I can really show you."

Buzzy ran out of the compartment and came back in a matter of seconds with his camcorder.

"Here," he said. "This has an LED screen."

He turned on the power, switched to playback, rewound the tape to the section he wanted, and then showed it to Sven. The time — 01:16 — and the date appeared on the bottom of the screen as the scene began, then disappeared again as it continued. What Sven saw was the platform of Kansas City station and then two women appearing on the right of the screen and moving towards the left. One had a basin-shaped hat and large glasses and the lower part of her face was concealed by a scarf. The other was unmistakably the woman whom Buzzy had referred to as "the deaf lady." She was walking very closely behind the other, almost treading on her heels, and she had a tapestry bag slung over her left shoulder and a brown suitcase in her right hand. Her left hand was invisible, hidden between her body and the body of the other woman.

"See," said Buzzy. "She leans forward a bit when she walks. You've got her too straight."

"You're right," said Sven, fascinated.

The scene he was watching ended as the women passed through the door into the station building. There was a moment of blackness and then another scene began — again with the time and date flashing on at the bottom of the screen.

"I see," he said. "Each time you start recording, it registers exactly when you did it."

"Right," said Buzzy.

"Interesting! I could use one of these. Especially to capture backgrounds."

Eddie snorted in incredulity.

"What's wrong with a still camera for that?" he argued.

"It doesn't catch the effect of the changing light on the background. Hey, wait a minute. What's this?"

Buzzy leaned forward to see which scene Sven was watching. It showed Aubretia and Scats on the platform at 01:43, and approaching them was Aubretia's pregnant friend. Aubretia moved forward to meet her.

"I think we'd better find your dad, Buzzy, and that English guy and his girlfriend," said Sven. "This is going to be very interesting to them."

2

The Flying Angel raced on through the desert as the blazing blue sky softened and deepened towards dusk. The sinking sun touched the peaks of the westerly mountains with fire, and the clouds above them were streaked with brushstrokes of blood and emerald and saffron. In an hour or so, darkness would have fallen and the train would be at rest in its next port of call, Caliente, Nevada.

Neither Honor nor Matthew had time to pay more than the most fleeting attention to the sunset. They were accompanying Aubretia to her compartment, and wondering how to deal with the information she had given them.

"You're saying that you don't remember anything that happened after Natalie arrived on the platform?" Matthew asked.

Aubretia shook her head impatiently.

"No, I told you: I don't remember. But God knows I wanted to kill him. I hated him enough to do it. I can't help feeling I must have done it."

"Do you smoke?" said Matthew.

Aubretia seemed startled by this question.

"No. But I used to smoke like Bette Davis," she said, when she realized he was serious. "That whole thing about lighting cigarettes, drawing the smoke down into your lungs, and waving the cigarette about as you talked at cocktail parties. I was deeply into it, but a close friend developed emphysema and died, and I quit cold turkey. And why am I jabbering on like this about smoking?"

"Just something I needed to know," Matthew replied. "Ah, here we are. After you, ladies."

He slid open the door of Room C, and Honor and Aubretia preceded him inside. Natalie Lindenhoff was still lying on the long bench seat, but she had given up on *Cosmopolitan* and was now listening to something on her Walkman through headphones. Matthew judged from the way she was beating time that it was something musical and probably something with a backbeat. Some of her hair had come loose from her ponytail and was straggling over her forehead. She waved a limp hand at them as they entered.

"Sorry to disturb you again. I hope you're feeling better," Matthew said.

Natalie lifted the ear-pieces of her headphones away from her ears.

"Sorry, I didn't hear you."

"It's all right. I was just saying I hoped you felt better."

Natalie grimaced.

"It'll be four more months before I feel better," she said.

Again he was struck by the curious quality of her voice. Almost a cross between Meryl Streep in *Sophie's Choice* and Marlon Brando in *The Godfather*. Not a particularly attractive sound.

"Were you disturbed at all last night?"

"Disturbed?" she said. "What do you mean?"

"Did you hear Aubretia leave the compartment — or come back in?"

She looked at him half-sullenly.

"Auntie Aubretia? No, I didn't hear anything. I was fast asleep. I mean, I'd been waiting over an hour in the station for the train to come in, and I was tired. You've no idea how tired you get lugging a baby around inside you all the time."

Matthew had wandered over to the window as she spoke and now was bending forward looking with interest at something to the side of the small folding table.

"I've heard that it's not a good idea for pregnant women to smoke," he said holding up a cigarette stub that he had picked out of the built-in ashtray.

"I don't," she snapped. "It must have been whoever had the compartment before us."

Honor noticed that as Matthew turned away from Natalie, he surreptitiously pocketed the cigarette stub.

"Scats must have been slapdash," Aubretia said, and then added with a small sigh, to Matthew: "You don't seem to be getting anywhere. Natalie heard nothing."

"And Scats and the prince's guards apparently saw nothing. So it seems unlikely that you were doing any somnambulistic stunts after you and Natalie had gone to bed."

Natalie laid aside her headphones and glanced peevishly at Matthew.

"What's all this about anyway?" she demanded. "Has it to do with your missing friend again?"

"No. It's nothing to worry about," Honor said briskly. "Aubretia lost something and she thought she might have been sleepwalking last night and dropped it somewhere."

"What kind of thing?"

"Oh, nothing important," Aubretia said. "Just an inexpensive ring. It was rather pretty and it had some sentimental value, but I'll get over it."

Matthew smiled at Aubretia, and she wrinkled her nose at him in reply.

"All right, Aubretia," he said. "If we can be of any further help, let us know."

When he and Honor were out in the corridor again, he whistled admiringly.

"My, aren't we quick-witted."

"Don't be patronizing," Honor admonished. "You have to be quick-witted in my job. Anyway, I didn't think an expectant mother ought to be burdened with all this stuff about Kadourian."

"Quite right, too," said Matthew.

They walked on down the corridor towards the stairs.

"And what's all this business with cigarettes? Next you'll be telling me you've written a monograph on thirty-nine different kinds of tobacco."

"If you're referring to Sherlock Holmes, it was a hundred and forty forms of cigar, cigarette, and pipe tobacco. And if you're so quick-witted, I shouldn't have to remind you about the cigarette burns on Kadourian's body."

Just as they came abreast of the last compartment before the stairs, the door opened and Sven Sanchez popped his head out.

"Oh, good," he said. "I was just coming to find you. Can you come in here a minute? I've got something to show you."

3

Aldo Bracciano sat slumped in his compartment, looking as if someone had just slammed into him with a tractor-trailer. First, Glamora had come to his compartment rather than demanding he come to hers.

Second, she had apologized for her behaviour the previous evening, and had explained that Jackson, one of Prince Achmed's body guards, had once busted her when he was a cop in Idaho and she was afraid that he might be about to use this against her — which was why she had asked Aldo to help her. Third, she had told him something that he had never expected to hear from any woman, let alone one as stunning as Glamora. His mind tried numbly to deal with it as she went on talking.

"I guess I knew it had to happen sooner or later," she was saying. "I was even prepared for it to happen. But things don't always work out the way you expect them to."

Aldo made a strangled sound.

"Oh, I know it must be a shock to you, slugger — and I guess it's going to be a shock to most of my fans. Still, I'd rather come out with it myself than have it dragged out into the open by a lot of sleazy tabloids."

She caressed his cheek consolingly and he watched her as someone might watch a tarantula slowly crawling nearer.

"Anyway, it's time for the truth, and if I play it smart, I could be bigger than ever. Especially in the nineties — when a drag queen like Ru-Paul can be the spokesperson for a line of cosmetics. And he's at least as tall as I am — probably taller. So I've talked to that blonde from "Hot Flashes" and I'm giving her the exclusive. She was on my trail anyway, and so was Jackson. I'll come out on national television in front of millions of viewers. If nothing else, it'll one-up Madonna."

At last, the choking noises Aldo had been making resolved themselves into intelligible speech.

"You're a guy!" he moaned.

Glamora looked at him pityingly.

"Surprise! Surprise!" she trilled. "Oh, come on, hot stuff, it's not that bad. No-one's going to point a finger at you. We never actually did any naughties. So don't get your hetero drawers in a tangle about it. After this trip's over, we go our separate ways, and I promise I'll never rat on you, slugger. You can go back to being an A-Number One, macho, stud jock."

She turned away from him and gazed out at the smoldering sky, though for some reason the view seemed a little blurred as if seen through a rain-spattered window.

"Damn! Have you got a tissue or something?"

Dumbly he handed her his handkerchief, and watched as she dabbed cautiously at her eyes, trying not to smear her eyeliner.

"Aw, Vikki," he grieved. "Jeez, don't cry. You've got my mind all fucked up. I don't know which side is up anymore."

His mind flashed to Tanya and to Vito and then somehow the two of them melted together and became Glamora. He stood up and put his arm around her shoulder.

"This is fuckin' crazy," he said. "But you know what? I think I love you."

She turned away from the window towards Aldo, and in less than a heartbeat, they were in each others' arms ... as the Flying Angel rushed on into the approaching night.

4

The observation lounge was full of boy scouts as usual, but there was a difference in the atmosphere. Instead of passing the time in a variety of desultory activities, they had formed small groups, each of which was composed of six or seven boys talking together in lowered voices and occasionally looking over their shoulders. It appeared that some giant conspiracy was afoot. Occasionally, Ryan and Buzzy would make a circuit, dropping in on each group in turn and whispering urgently to them.

When Doc Holliday came through, the whole scene underwent a phenomenal transformation. Suddenly the boys were yawning, punching each others' upper arms, whistling through their teeth, shuffling cards, and doing the hundred and one other inconsequential things that boys do when they're cooped up together on a long journey. If Doc was aware of any undercurrents, he didn't show it.

He continued on into the restaurant, which for some reason was anything but full. Delia Hentzen was at a table on her own. Jackson and Jones were eating together at another table. A few people from coaches further up the train were studying menus or beginning their first courses. At the end furthest from the observation lounge, three scout masters were sitting together and as Doc approached, they beckoned to him to join them.

"Anything new on the murder?" one of them asked.

"Not so far as I know," he said, scanning the list of entrees. "I guess the Nevada cops will be waiting to board in Caliente. I just hope it doesn't delay us too much more. You know how the boys get on a long trip like this."

"Sure do," said another. "I'll never forget that trip to Oregon. Talk about reverting to barbarism! It was like *Lord of the Flies*."

"I have a funny feeling they're up to something now," said Doc. "It might be a good idea to keep a close eye on them — at least till we get to Caliente."

The other three nodded. All of them were used to deal-ing with the unpredictable impulses of adolescents, but they didn't underestimate the hazards of the task.

Pete the waiter approached their table with his usual friendly grin.

"What can I get you, folks?"

They were busy ordering when Bob Bonsecours came hurrying in from the forepart of the train.

"Message for you, doctor, from Kansas City," he said, handing over a fax sheet.

Doc Holliday studied it carefully, folded it and put it in his shirt pocket.

"You'd better hold that order a while," he told Pete. "I've got to find Mr. Nash."

He made his way back through the restaurant, into the observation lounge, where the boys were still behaving with suspicious normality, and on into the rear coach. There was no-one in Matthew's compartment and no-one in Nash's, two doors away. He glanced into the end compartment and there they all were. Matthew, Honor, Nash, two kids — one of whom was the Woolf kid from the Hickory Hill troop — and two guys he hadn't met. They all seemed pretty excited about something.

"Take a look at this, Doc," said Nash when he entered. "This is my boy, Buzzy, and he took this video while we were stuck in Kansas City."

Dr. Holliday nodded at Buzzy, who handed him the videocamera. It was one of those fancy new ones with the LED screen so you could view your video immediately after you'd taken it. He pressed the start button and watched as the scenes fitfully unreeled. First, there was the almost empty platform, a lighted stage in the surrounding darkness waiting for its first actor. At the bottom of the screen the time and date were recorded. It was 01:16 that morning. Next came the attendant, Scats, helping two women to descend from the train. One was muffled up in a scarf and had on an old-fashioned hat like an upside-down bowl with a brim, and big owl-like glasses; the other was hatless, her brown hair disordered. They wore coats of a similar greeny-grey colour, and both carried brown suitcases, though the hatless woman also had a tapestry bag slung over her shoulder. Once they had disappeared, the platform was empty except for Scats.

The screen went black and when it lightened again it showed the time as 01:31, and again an empty platform except for a solitary porter pushing a large trolley, stacked with wooden crates. Again the screen went black, then lit up registering a time of 01:43 and revealing Scats and a thin, middle-aged woman with a yellow scarf around her head standing waiting by the door to the coach. Almost immediately a figure appeared from the inside of the station building and walked towards them. It was a youngish woman with her tawny hair pulled back in a tight ponytail and a face that had a kind of basic prettiness diminished by a too-lavish use of makeup and by what his physician's eye diagnosed as pregnancy bloat. She wore a loose cotton top, white with cornflowers embroidered around the neck, and a calf-length loose skirt in blue denim. The way she walked suggested weariness but also the stress of carrying some extra poundage she was unused to, or it may have been the weight of her two bags: the blue nylon suitcase in her right hand and the tapestry bag in her left. As she lurched forward, the woman in the yellow head-scarf rushed out to meet her, her arms held wide. She stumbled and almost lost her balance. The girl instinctively dropped her bags and ran forward to prevent her from falling, but the woman steadied herself and the protective clutch turned into a hug of greeting. Scats went over to the bags and picked them up before helping both women onto the train.

The next scene, which was imprinted with the time 01:51, began again with an almost empty platform, except for Scats, who was standing near the door of the coach, waving a greeting to another attendant who had exited the train a little further up. They sauntered towards each other as the other attendant lit a cigarette and they stood talking on the platform. At the same time, in the parking lot beside the station building, a teenage boy could be seen, up against the wire fence, looking towards the train.

After that there was a scene that started at 02:02 and lasted for about eight minutes. It showed a large group of boy scouts straggling across the platform towards their coach. Scats was still on the platform, though the other attendant had disappeared.

The last scene, marked 02:12, showed the empty platform slowly drifting to the left as the train began to pull out of the station.

"So, Doc, do you make anything of that?" Nash asked.

"I'm not sure," he said. "What am I supposed to be looking for?"

"Anything that strikes you as out of the ordinary," said Matthew.

Doc Holliday pressed the rewind button on the camcorder till it reached the beginning of the sequence.

"Maybe if I start again from the beginning," he said. "Now here, for instance — the two women getting out of the train — I presume they are the two who ended up at opposite ends of a gun in Kansas City. But which is which?"

Matthew pointed out on the screen which of the figures was Teresa and which was the Verhaeven woman. The doctor played the scene involving them two or three times.

"Odd," he said, then wound the tape on till he came to the scene in which Scats and Aubretia welcomed Natalie Lindenhoff. He also played that scene over a couple of times, and then paused it and pointed to Natalie: "This woman joining the train in Kansas City is pregnant, right?"

"That's Aubretia's friend, yes. An unmarried mother-to-be," said Matthew, "who's going to give birth in a California nursing home, courtesy of Aubretia."

"What month of her pregnancy is she in?"

"The fifth month," said Honor. "And it's really telling on her: back pains, fatigue, you know how it is."

"I do, indeed. Obstetrics and gynaecology isn't my specialty, but I've had enough female relatives go through childbirth to be pretty familiar with the territory. Now this friend of your friend Aubretia's walks like she's pregnant, though I'm a bit surprised to see her moving so agilely when Aubretia tripped. On the other hand, the woman who got off the train with your friend Teresa doesn't move like she's pregnant at all."

Nash and Honor looked puzzled. Sven and Buzzy looked as if they were readjusting something in their minds.

"Move like she's pregnant?" Nash barked. "Why the hell should she? That was this Verhaeven woman. The one who got shot."

"Because the autopsy report just came through, and

the woman Teresa seems to have shot was five months pregnant."

Holliday produced the fax and handed it over to Nash. Matthew read it over Nash's shoulder. The woman in Kansas City, who had been identified as Katharine Verhaeven, had died as the result of two bullets from a nine-millimetre semi-automatic, fired at close range. The second bullet had also killed the unborn child she was carrying. It was as if a mosaic had tumbled apart and reassembled itself in a new pattern.

Sven said: "I think Buzzy deserves a lot of the credit for this. He got me thinking about bodies in motion. And the more I studied that tape the more I was certain that the woman who left the train with the Irish nanny was the same woman who got back on the train as Aubretia's friend. As Buzzy noticed, the first woman moved with a distinct forward inclination of the body. When I saw that against the second woman's style of walking, I realized they both did the same thing."

"You're right," said Doc Holliday. "A pregnant woman will tend to walk upright or with a slight backward lean. Tilting forward would be distinctly uncomfortable for both her and the baby."

"In other words," said Matthew, "you're saying the dead woman in Kansas City is Natalie Lindenhoff, and the woman in Aubretia's compartment is the Verhaeven woman — or rather, Varya Krasna."

"That's certainly the way it looks," Nash agreed. "And that raises some very interesting questions."

5

The boy scouts in the observation lounge were positively pulsating with excitement. It was about half an hour to Caliente and Buzzy and Ryan had spread the word — the murderer had been found and they were to stay on the alert and take up positions to counteract any escape attempt. Not that escape would be easy, given that the Nevada police would be waiting on the platform when the train drew into Caliente.

"She won't outwit Scopeman," said Buzzy menacingly. "He can see three moves ahead of her."

Ryan cheered, half-derisively: "Right on, Scopeman! Nobody's gonna beat the Seer of the Universe!"

"Except when his eyes are clouded by the Black Mist," Buzzy reminded him. It was always good to have an out if things didn't work according to plan.

Meanwhile, in Matthew's compartment, an argument was proceeding about how to protect Aubretia when the moment came to move in on Varya Krasna, an argument that was complicated by the fact that Nash insisted they needed more concrete evidence of guilt.

"Supposing you're right," he said to Matthew, "and she did switch identities with Natalie Lindenhoff. That doesn't prove she killed her. She could have made the switch after Teresa killed her. It was an opportunity for Varya to get back on the train without anyone realizing it, and in such a disguise that it didn't look strange if she stayed in her room and spent most of her time with her face turned to the wall, reading a magazine. How many people would have taken enough notice of her in her Verhaeven role to be able to see any resemblance between the woman who got off the train in Kansas City and the one who got on half an hour later? The only people who spent much time with her as Verhaeven were Teresa Shaughnessy, me, and Buzzy. With Shaughnessy detained in Kansas City on suspicion of murder, she had only me and Buzzy to worry about, and it was very unlikely that in the ordinary run of things either of us would have gone into that compartment."

Matthew snorted disbelievingly.

"But why in the world would Teresa want to kill Natalie Lindenhoff, of all people?"

"I don't know!" growled Nash. "She was full of this Burundanga stuff, wasn't she? People have been known to do crazy things when they're on that."

"But usually at the direction of others. No, I say, if Teresa shot this poor girl, she did it under Krasna's direction. She was the perfect patsy, and for Krasna, the fact that the corpse in Kansas City was apparently hers would make it all the easier for her to carry out her plan to assassinate Golovyov. None of his henchmen would be expecting another assassin to show up disguised as a pregnant woman."

Honor couldn't restrain herself from interrupting at this point.

"But I thought the scheme was for her to get Teresa out of the way so she could turn up disguised as Teresa."

Matthew nodded.

"I think that originally was the scheme. I think in fact she intended to get rid of Teresa before she got on the train. Something Teresa told me made me think there'd been some fast switching of bags going on. You remember they were both carrying brown suitcases that looked very much alike. Well, Teresa told me that when she first met this Krasna person, the woman had bumped into her in line at the Metropolitan Lounge. It would have been easy to distract someone like that, and switch bags at the same time. So Teresa would have turned up dead somewhere in the station with the Verhaeven identification on her person, and Krasna would have simply got on the train as Teresa, and then there would have been no need for this little drama in Kansas City."

Nash frowned. It was clear that something was still bothering him.

"We've got to have more than a theory based on a videotape and some drawings," he said. "And there's also Kadourian's death. How do you figure that fits in?"

"Very neatly, I'd say," Matthew answered. "Kadourian and Krasna were colleagues in Solonitza. Aubretia also referred to Krasna as Kadourian's 'girlfriend.' Presuming she was, and that his sexual tastes were the same then, she was probably his partner in sadomasochistic sex. What would have been easier than for her to persuade her old flame to indulge in a session for old time's sake? Then when she had him helpless, kill him."

"Kill him why?"

"Because he was a danger to her plans. He was the only one on the train who knew who she really was and she didn't want the name Krasna associated either with her Verhaeven identity or her Lindenhoff impersonation."

Nash was doggedly unconvinced.

"You're saying she was good enough at disguising herself to fool everyone but Kadourian?"

"Hell, Nash, as a CIA officer, you must have heard of 'maskirovka.' It was a term used by the KGB. They had a number of spies who were especially good at assuming different identities, different appearances, and they referred to them as using good 'maskirovka' or deceptive camouflage. Krasna is obviously in that class. For her Lindenhoff impersonation, she brushed her hair straight back in a ponytail, put on heavy makeup, padded her waist, and put pads in her cheeks to give her that look of pregnancy bloat. The pads in her cheeks also had the effect of muffling her voice. No wonder I thought she sounded a bit like Marlon Brando in *The Godfather*. Maybe Kadourian wouldn't have recognized her as the dowdy Miss Verhaeven, particularly if she was careful to keep out of his way, but she couldn't be sure he wouldn't notice the younger-looking, more sexually attractive Lindenhoff, even if apparently swollen with pregnancy. I suspect in fact that he was looking out of his window when she boarded the train at 1:43 and that they saw each other. She would have had enough time before the train left at 2:12 to do what was necessary. Twenty-four minutes to dump Aubretia in her befogged state in Room C, make her way down to Room G, persuade Kadourian to indulge in a little sexual entertainment, smother him, and get back to Room C before Scats got back aboard."

"It's tight," objected Nash. "Are you saying she got off the train with Teresa Shaughnessy at 1:16, killed Natalie Lindenhoff, planted the gun on Teresa, changed her clothes and her make-up, and reappeared on the platform at 1:43, got on the train again, killed Kadourian and was back in her compartment before 2:12?"

Matthew was unshaken.

"That's exactly what I'm saying. We're talking about a period of fifty-six minutes. An efficient, cool-headed operative like Varya Krasna could probably commit a couple of murders in that time *and* do the *Times* crossword puzzle."

Honor couldn't resist putting a spoke in Matthew's wheels.

"But how could she have known she'd run into Natalie Lindenhoff?"

"She didn't. I think what happened was she got off the train with Teresa, intending to dispose of her and switch identities with her. Of course, she'd have to dispose of me too, or discredit me in some way, since I had spent enough time with Teresa to be able to recognize an impersonator. That's why she drugged my coffee as well as Teresa's. That drug, by the way, I believe wasn't burundanga. It was a strong sedative. I think she administered the burundanga to Teresa in Room A later. In fact about the time Buzzy heard those noises. When she got Teresa off the train and into the ladies' room at the station, this pregnant young woman, looking very much like the one in the photograph Aubretia dropped in the restaurant, was there tidying up before getting on the train. It probably didn't take long to establish that the young woman was, in fact, Natalie Lindenhoff, and immediately Krasna saw an opportunity to take on an identity that would be easier for her to sustain than that of an Irish nanny, and at the same time get Teresa out of the way, at least until she'd killed Golovyov."

"Hmmm," said Honor sceptically. "Talking of photographs, how do you explain the ones found in Kadourian's compartment?"

"The photographs of Anna and Fedor? Well, I think they fell out of the tapestry bag. You remember the videotape: it shows Krasna getting off the train with a tapestry bag — the one I remember seeing her with in the dining car. Then it shows Natalie getting on the train with an identical bag. Judging by the colours in the weave, it's the most likely source for that thread we found caught in Kadourian's mask. So, assuming she took the bag with her to Kadourian's compartment, the pictures could have fallen out during her struggle with Kadourian, or when she took her cigarettes out to play her little torture game with him."

Nash shook his head obstinately.

"Matthew, it makes a nice story, but there's still no proof. There's no way the Nevada guys are going to buy it without something more concrete."

"There's only one answer to that," said Matthew. "The tapestry bag. I'm positive the one the fake Verhaeven carried off the train is the same one that the fake Lindenhoff carried on. You've been deputized; you have got the authority to search Aubretia's compartment."

With a certain amount of reluctance Nash seemed about to agree when Honor interrupted.

"You'll be putting Aubretia in danger," she said. "If Krasna suspects you're on to her, she might do anything."

"Then we'll have to think of a way of getting into the compartment without arousing her suspicion," said Matthew.

Nash gave a humourless laugh.

"Good luck on that," he said.

6

"Our next stop is Caliente," the conductor's voice said over the public address system. "Caliente — our next stop — in approximately fifteen minutes."

There was a sudden buzz of excited conversation among the boy scouts in the observation lounge, which just as suddenly died down when they saw two of Prince Achmed's security men advancing towards the rear coach, grim-faced and with their right hands resting on their shoulder holsters inside their jackets. The boys watched until they had passed through and then the buzz broke out again louder than before.

The two men, Harrison and Morrison, entered the rear corridor, where they were met by Anderson Nash, who after muttering some rapid instructions to them led them to the door of Room C. Nash rapped sharply on the door and called out: "Mrs. Adams, this is Anderson Nash." The door opened a few inches and Aubretia's startled face appeared in the gap.

"Aubretia Adams," said Nash with cold formality, "I am placing you under arrest for the murder of Vartan Kadourian. You have the right to remain silent..."

As Nash proceeded with the rest of the warning, Aubretia gave a choked cry and swayed forward. Immediately Harrison and Morrison grabbed her by the arms and drew her out into the corridor. Behind her, the supposed Natalie Lindenhoff struggled up into a sitting position and exclaimed indignantly: "What's going on here? You leave my Auntie Aubretia alone!" Ignoring this, the two security men continued to propel Aubretia along the corridor towards the observation car. Simultaneously, Matthew and Honor appeared from the door of Room B, as if in response to the commotion.

Natalie pushed herself to her feet and lurched towards the door of Room C. It was obvious from her expression that she was torn between playing out her role as concerned friend and staying within the security of the compartment.

"What're you doing with her?" she demanded in her curiously muffled and oddly accented voice.

"She's being arrested for murder," Nash said impatiently. "I'd advise you to stay where you are."

"God!" scolded Honor. "You guys have no sensitivity at all. I think Aubretia needs some support right now. It's Natalie's right to be with her! Come on, Natalie, we'll go and see that they treat her properly."

"Well, I--" Natalie began hesitantly.

"Oh, go ahead!" Nash barked. "I don't want anyone complaining about police brutality."

Still half-undecided, the other woman allowed herself to be urged out of the compartment and towards the observation car by Honor. Immediately she was out of sight, Matthew and Nash entered and began to search. They had no difficulty finding the tapestry bag. It was stowed in the bottom of the clothes closet by the door.

"Let's see that thread, Nash," Matthew said.

Nash took the thread they had found caught in the zipper of Kadourian's leather hood out of his pocket and held it against the fabric of the tapestry bag. The colour certainly matched the shade of green that was woven into the pattern, and the texture seemed the same.

"Not conclusive," Nash muttered, "but I guess I'd have to say it's significant."

They managed to get the bag open and upended its contents onto the seat. Among a tangle of pantyhose, cosmetics, and other feminine accoutrements, they found some interesting items: a bill from a luggage shop in Chicago's Union Station dated the day the Flying Angel had departed for California and marked "tapestry hold-all: $49.95"; a Polaroid camera — and two photographs: one of a youngish woman lying on the floor half in and half out of a toilet stall with bullet wounds in her head and abdomen, and another of

Vartan Kadourian, hooded, handcuffed, and sitting propped up in the shower stall of Room G; lastly, a carton of Marlboros from which a couple of packs had been extracted. Matthew compared the butt he had collected from the ashtray in Room C with the tips of one of the Marlboros. They were identical.

"She obviously liked to keep a record of her work," said Nash, holding up the photographs.

"It's not the same camera that took the other shots," said Matthew. "There's no date and time printed on either picture."

"I don't think that's going to be a problem," Nash predicted. "We know the first murder happened after 1:16 when Teresa left the train with Krasna and the other could only have happened between 1:43 and 2:12. It's the only time the murderer wouldn't have been spotted by Scats."

Between them, they returned the bag's contents and replaced it in the closet. Already they could sense that the rhythm of the Angel's wheels was slackening as the braking system came into play and the speed began to decrease. Outside in the darkness, isolated buildings with their windows lit against the evening began to appear, only to slip backwards out of sight in the wake of their passage.

"OK," said Nash. "I guess it's time for the showdown. With those two security guys there, Miss Adams should be safe, and we need to secure Krasna to hand her over to the boys in Caliente."

"Showdown at Caliente," Matthew said. "Now we're in another movie ... from Hitchcock to John Ford. I must say I've never known life to imitate art as much as it does in the U.S.A."

Nash's only reply was a dismissive grunt. Suitably chastened, Matthew followed him out of the compartment and on towards the observation lounge.

The scouts had all mysteriously dispersed and the only people there apart from Aubretia, Harrison, and Morrison were Honor and Natalie. Aubretia looked like a marionette whose strings had been cut, as she stood slumped between the two security men. Honor and Natalie were between her and the door through which Nash and Matthew entered, Honor murmuring soothingly to Aubretia and Natalie looking distinctly uneasy.

"All right, folks," said Nash in his flat official voice, "we'll be arriving at the next station any minute. I want to apologize, Miss Adams, for putting you through this. As for Natalie Lindenhoff, a.k.a. Kathryn Verhaeven, a.k.a. Varya Krasna, I'm placing you under arrest for the murders of Natalie Lindenhoff and Vartan Kadourian. If it was in my power I'd like to charge you with the murder of Miss Lindenhoff's unborn child and the children in Solonitza you and Kadourian experimented on."

Varya Krasna stood frozen as she heard Nash recite the charges. Only her eyes moved, darting from side to side as if in search of some unimpeded path to freedom. Aubretia, however, listened with growing horror, and when she realized that this woman who had masqueraded as her friend was in fact responsible not just once but twice for denying her the opportunity to become the mother she had always wanted to be, she gave a great roar of rage and lunged for Varya's throat. Her action threw Morrison off balance, distracted Harrison, and gave Varya the opportunity she was looking for. She wrested Morrison's gun away from him, grabbed Aubretia in a choke hold, and placed the gun against Aubretia's temple. It happened so quickly that Harrison and

Nash scarcely had time to draw their own guns. By the time they did, the advantage had already passed to Varya.

"Drop your guns and back off," she demanded. "If I see anyone making any move at all, any move I don't like, I'll blow this bitch's drunken head off."

There was no question in any of their minds that a ruthless killer like Varya Krasna would be quite capable of carrying out this threat with as little compunction as she would feel about stepping on an ant. They dropped their guns and backed off. Matthew was furious with himself for not having foreseen how the unmasking of the so-called Natalie Lindenhoff would affect Aubretia. He should have remembered what she told him about how the news of the baby's death in Solonitza had affected her. But he could see no way of stopping Varya.

As they stood there at an impasse, the train slowly ground to a halt with a shriek of brakes alongside the main platform at Caliente Station. Matthew peered along the brightly lit platform, hoping to see a large contingent of uniformed police, but he could see only two men in Stetsons and short-sleeved shirts who looked as if they might be Nevada law officers. When the train had come to a full halt, they could hear doors opening further up the train as passengers began to exit. Varya backed towards the door to the rear coach and through it into the upper corridor.

"Anyone who tries to follow me will be writing this old fool's death warrant," she yelled back at the group in the observation lounge.

As soon as they heard the two sets of footsteps retreating towards the central staircase, they unfroze.

"Go the other way — through the restaurant," said Nash. "Let's see if we can head her off somehow."

All five of them raced headlong out of the observation lounge and between the rows of tables as the waiters dodged out of the way. They ran on down the central corridor of the next car to the staircase halfway along and clattered down the stairs to the exit. There they saw an extraordinary sight. Stretched across the entire width of the platform was a line of boy scouts, effectively blocking the way to the exit. Doc Holliday and the other two scoutmasters were frantically ordering them to get out of the way, but the scouts seemed to have developed a collective deafness. They began to move forward in unison. Varya was waving her gun at them and screaming at them to keep away.

There was a second doorway on the platform. Varya began to move backwards towards it. The line of scouts began to yell at her to let her captive go and give herself up. Under cover of the noise and while she was focussed on the scouts, two short figures darted from behind the bulk of a baggage cart to her rear and positioned themselves behind her on all fours, in the classic school-yard position used to trip the unwary. Varya was too preoccupied to notice, but Aubretia did. While Varya was still waving her gun at the scouts, Aubretia threw her body against Varya's. Varya tottered back, toppled over the human hurdle behind her, taking Aubretia down with her, and the gun went flying out of her hands. Swift as a cat, Ryan Woolf pounced on the gun and held it, two handed, arms extended, feet apart, in the stance of the guys on his favourite cop show, pointed directly at Varya. Buzzy Nash, standing proudly by his friend, yelled: "Dad, we've got her!"

Nine

At Long Last L.A.

Pristinely gleaming and with massive composure, the Flying Angel glided into the rail terminal in downtown Los Angeles at seven minutes to eight the following morning. It seemed that the rigours of mountain and desert, the conflicts of passenger with passenger, the dawning of love, the revival of hope, the shadow of death, the exuberance of a hundred and fifty boy scouts, had done nothing to alter her flawless veneer by so much as a hairline scratch.

Redcaps came forward with trolleys as the passengers began to descend, friends and relatives waved and shouted, newspapermen and photographers swarmed all over the platform, television news teams with video cameras became entangled in each others' cables, and the usual assortment of plain gawkers filled up any unoccupied space. Matthew and Honor came down the steps just behind Delia Hentzen, and as they did so they saw Glamora and Aldo Bracciano standing there, deep in conversation.

"I really should introduce you," said Matthew impishly. "Excuse me, Glamora ... er ... Miss Lundgren!"

Glamora turned and fixed him with her jade-coloured eyes.

"Are you babbling again?" she said with a slight quirking of the corner of her mouth.

"I'm English, if that's what you mean," said Matthew. "Anyway, I'd like to introduce you to your in-law, Delia Hentzen."

Delia held out her hand, but instead of taking it Glamora swept her up in a great hug that lifted Delia almost off her feet.

"Hi, hon," she said. "I'm Victor Lundgren. And this is my significant other, Aldo."

Aldo shambled forward, blushing and looking sheepish, but he didn't deny Glamora's characterization of him. He too embraced Delia and kissed her on the cheek.

"Why don't we three share a cab?" said Glamora after the salutations were over. "Me and Aldo are going to be staying at the Beverley Hills Hotel. Why don't you let us treat you to a room there till you find somewhere to settle down?"

Waving goodbye to Matthew and Honor, the three left together, chattering like old friends.

"Well, there's one for the tabloids," said Honor.

At that moment, Nash and Buzzy appeared. Buzzy panned across the scene with his camcorder. Behind them were Sven Sanchez and Eddie Tsubouchi.

"You know, young feller," said Sven to Buzzy, "we're going to have to sign a proper contract with you. You'll have a byline in every issue of our new comic book — 'from an original idea by B.B. Nash.' How about that?"

"Cool," said Buzzy. "Can I watch you draw it sometime?"

"Sure can," said Sven. "You can watch both of us. Eddie and me are going into partnership."

Anderson Nash shook hands with them, as did Matthew and Honor, and then watched them go towards the barrier.

"Nice guys," he said, and then with a slightly rueful sigh, "Well, I'd better get this boy back to his mother. What d'you say, Buzz?"

Buzz looked up at his father and said: "It's been really cool, Dad. Let's do it again sometime."

Another voice broke in on them suddenly.

"Buzzy!"

It was Ryan Woolf, looking dazed with excitement, followed by Prince Achmed in his regal robes, and the four security men, Harrison, Morrison, Jackson, and Jones.

"Guess what, Buzzy," said Ryan. "The prince guy wants me and my folks to go visit him at his palace in Zwa-some-where-or-other."

The prince fondly patted Ryan's frizzy head.

"As Descartes said," he announced to no-one in particular, "'the intelligent nature is distinct from the corporeal' and I think that I have never seen that demonstrated so clearly as in this young unassuming African-American. Definitely an uncut gem. Make sure that Harrison has your address, young man, and I shall see you in my home country. Oh — and don't forget to bring me the latest Def Leppard CD."

The prince swept away with the other three security-men as Harrison fumbled with his notebook and took down the necessary information from Ryan. Matthew wondered whether it would be much of a treat to be the guest of Prince Achmed, but perhaps if Ryan took him a few Scopeman comics it would take his royal mind off Descartes' *Discourse on Method* for a day or two.

Matthew and Honor said goodbye to Buzzy and his father just as the reporters descended on Nash to get his version of the Flying Angel murders.

"It's a real Hollywood ending," said Matthew. "Everything resolved in the most satisfactory way. I gather from the last report Doc Holliday got from Kansas City, Teresa is out of danger and won't suffer any permanent harm from her experience."

"It's kind of ironic, too, don't you think?" said Honor, "Golovyov was assassinated before the train even got to Caliente. What was the name of the guy who did it?"

"Marminski. One of the least efficient of the Russian mafiya's hired killers. He must have been having one of his rare lucky days. Except for the fact that he got caught."

"You know, there's one thing that wasn't neatly resolved," Honor said.

"Oh, what?"

"Over there," Honor answered, motioning with her head to a figure standing negotiating with a redcap a few yards away.

"You're right. Aubretia. No, she didn't get much out of this except the satisfaction of seeing Varya arrested. No nice little bundle to hold in her arms. But you know, maybe that's not such a bad thing. Can you imagine what a child would go through being brought up by Aubretia? It would be like having a parent who was a cross between Auntie Mame and Elwood P. Dowd."

"I don't know what you're talking about," Honor said frostily. "Anyway, I'm going over to talk to her."

Matthew signalled to a redcap, and managed to get his

and Honor's luggage stowed on a trolley. He was just about to join her when somebody crossed the platform right in front of him. It was a portly gentleman, bald-headed and with a pendulous lower lip, dressed in a dark-blue, well-cut, double-breasted English suit. As he passed, he gave Matthew a curiously shrewd glance and then proceeded augustly on his way. Matthew did a double take and then shook his head.

"It can't be," he said to himself. "He died in 1980."

And then, whistling a few bars of the theme from the Alfred Hitchcock TV series, he went to join the ladies.